SUBDUCTION

©2019 by Larry LaVoie

This book is a work of fiction. All persons, places and events are purely fictional and a product of the author's imagination.

Acknowledgements

I want to thank my wife Anna, who is the first to review my work. Her insight and story-content help are greatly appreciated. I would also like to thank my editor Sharon Shafa for her encouragement, professional eye for detail, constructive review, and editorial critique.

SUBDUCTION

A SCOTT TANNER THRILLER

Prologue

June 20, 1945

The War in Europe is over, and it is only a matter of time before the war in the Pacific will end. All of America is watching anxiously as the allies turn their attention to Japan. Plans for a massive ground invasion are in the final stages.

A few days earlier Osaka Japan had been heavily bombed and Japanese Admiral Ota Minoru had surrendered to Allied Forces, causing him to commit ritual suicide for his failure to defend his homeland. In Central China, Japan is in general retreat.

Even with the prospect of certain victory, the largest offensive battle ever planned is looked on in fear that it could be the bloodiest battle ever fought. Japan was poised to defend its homeland with the life of every man, woman, and child. Total annihilation of Japan is the only way a land battle can be won. The people of Japan were religiously devoted to their emperor and would willing give their life to defend him. The allies are faced with the grim reality they could lose millions of soldiers in a fierce land battle. They had not yet seen Truman's secret weapon.

July 1, 1945 The Pacific Ocean, fifty-seven miles off the Oregon Coast

Captain William R. Shunt, skipper of the Merchant ship *Carissa*, flying the American flag, walked briskly along the gunwale of his ship on his way to the bridge. The fog was dense, making it impossible to see the bow of the ship from his midship position. It was eerily quiet, the fog seemingly dampening all sound, still he should have heard the constant drum of the engines as the ship glided silently in a southerly direction. According to his watch, sunrise had arrived an hour earlier, but it was nowhere to be seen through the dank, gray muck.

Twelve hours earlier Shunt had piloted his ship from Portland, where he had taken on a cargo of aviation fuel in fifty-gallon drums to be delivered to the Navy base at Eureka, California. The fuel was stacked along the center of the ship, three drums high, and secured with heavy cables stretched to their limit. There were 1800 drums in all, a sizeable load for his ship that usually carried milled lumber from northwest ports.

It had been a slow trip from the docks in Portland, down the Willamette

River to the Columbia, and over the treacherous bar into the Pacific Ocean. The Columbia Bar had claimed many ships throughout recorded history and he dreaded that part of the voyage even with Coast Guard escort. They had prepared the ship on short notice and in the middle of the night, and he had lost much needed sleep. But this trip had gone unusually smooth and he had managed to get four hours of sack-time once they reached open water.

Four hours earlier, he had turned the helm over to First Mate Eddie Jones. It had been a crystal-clear night with millions of stars lighting the way as the moon had yet to rise.

Now, as he gripped the dew laden railing, *how quickly the weather can change in the Pacific Northwest*, he thought. But the fog on this voyage could be a blessing. Throughout the war he had managed to avoid all enemy contact, and there was anticipation the War in the Pacific would soon end. The fog would shield his ship from the eyes of enemy submarines that might be lurking about.

Early in the War the Japanese had been patrolling these waters on a regular basis, and had sunk a number of merchant ships, but with the war in the Pacific turning against Japan, no submarines had been reported in several months. Still, with an abundance of caution, he hoped the course he had charted would give any enemy patrolling the waters a wide berth. He hoped the biggest threat he faced at the moment was the fog and the remote chance he may collide with another ship. They were running silent, without the use of the fog horn, as was wartime protocol in these waters, and that always made him nervous. This late in the War he was sure it was just a precaution and no longer necessary, but he was a man who played by the book. Still, he couldn't hear the engines. That was highly unusual. He had to get to the bridge and find out what the hell was going on.

"Why are the engines cut?" Shunt asked, as he entered the wheelhouse.

Eddie Jones was looking into the fog through a pair of 50mm binoculars. "Protocol, Skipper," Jones responded, keeping the glasses pressed tightly to his eyes. "One of the men on watch spotted what he thought was a submarine."

"Why didn't you wake me?" Shunt demanded.

"It just happened, not five minutes ago. To tell the truth, I don't think it was a credible sighting. I haven't seen a damn thing." He lowered the binoculars and let them hang from the leather strap. "He said it was a German sub." He laughed. "There aren't any German subs operating in the Pacific. Last I heard

Germany surrendered back in May."

"But you're certain he saw a submarine?" Shunt asked. Shunt believed he had survived the war because of his abundance of caution. Any sighting of a submarine must be taken seriously. At least Jones had cut the engines.

"Honest, Skipper, I don't believe there was anything there. I've got three others on watch and not one of them saw anything. I think Pappy was drinking again."

"Did you smell his breath?"

"I couldn't smell anything, but a German submarine? Come on, Skipper, you think it's credible? I sent him below, but thought it would be prudent to cut the engines just in case. I knew you wouldn't want to take any chances."

Shunt was pissed. Something didn't add up and he was going to get to the bottom of it. "Stay at the helm, I'm going to have a word with Pappy."

Shunt found Pappy, a rotund man in his fifties, nursing a cup of coffee in the mess. Shunt grabbed a cup and sat down across from him.

"How are you feeling, Pappy?" Shunt asked. He could see Pappy was shaking. Pappy had a history of hitting the bottle and he couldn't tell if the shaking was from the DTs or nervousness.

"I know what I saw, Skipper. That

weren't no Jap submarine. I seen one of them before and this weren't nothin' like it."

"Have you been drinking?"

"No! I haven't touched a drop. Honest, Skipper. You got to believe me."

"Tell me what you saw," Shunt said. At the moment, he was inclined to believe Pappy. He sounded sincere and his speech wasn't slurred.

Pappy looked at him with wide eyes. He spoke in a raspy whisper. "It was gray as a ghost and had black zig-zag marking along its length. The tower was huge with large numbers painted in black. There was a red swastika in front of the number U-2500."

"And it was just sitting dead in the water?"

"Dead as a ghost, I swear. I never seen anything like it before."

"How far away was it?"

"That's just it. We nearly run over it. It was no more than ten yards off our portside bow."

Shunt rubbed his short beard while he considered whether Pappy was telling the truth. "Look me in the eye and tell me you haven't been drinking again."

"Just one sip. I swear. I ain't drunk. I know what I seen." Shunt had known Pappy for over five years. His eyes were clear. He had no reason to think he'd made up the story. In fact, he thought the guy was not capable of coming up with such a prodigious story.

"All right, Pappy. Return to your watch. I believe you saw something and we need to get to the bottom of it."

Five minutes later, Shunt was back in the wheelhouse. "All engines, full ahead."

"Skipper?" Jones asked.

"You said, you didn't believe him. I sent a message to the Coast Guard. They can sort it out. We've lost too much time already."

"Sir, what if he was right?"

"If they would have spotted us, we would have been torpedoed by now. If there is a German submarine operating in our waters, I don't want to stick around until they discover we're here."

"Captain aren't you concerned the engines on could give them a bearing. We could make ourselves a target."

"We've been dead in the water for half an hour. Start the engines full ahead. We've had enough excitement for the day."

"Aye, aye, sir," Jones said, "full ahead."

Shunt, still nervous, figured the cover of the fog may have saved them. He wasn't going to stick around and give them another chance. "I hope you're right, Jones, a German submarine in the Pacific is absurd."

Jones made certain they were on the proper heading and picked up his tin cup. "You care for coffee, Skipper?" he asked, grabbing a thermos. He took a drink of his coffee which had turned cold, and made a face. He set the cup down, refilled his cup, poured one for the skipper, and handed it to him.

Shunt took a sip of the brew. "Heads up, the fog is beginning to lift."

As *Carissa* emerged from the fog, Jones got a glimpse of the submarine. "Skipper, it's right in front of us!"

Shunt never saw the submarine nor heard the explosion that quickly followed.

July 1, 1945. Yaquina Bay Coast Guard Station, Newport, Oregon

A few minutes earlier, Radioman Tony Rocco had taken the message from *Carissa*. He decoded it and handed it to duty officer LT J G Osterman. Osterman read the message, shook his head and chuckled. There had been numerous sightings of submarines off the Oregon Coast early in the war, but no credible ones for over a year. The gigantic *Gray*

Whales, in migration, had sometimes been mistaken for submarines, especially in times of low visibility, but a Nazi U-boat, that was a new one. He wasn't going to interrupt Commander Goodman's weekend for a highly questionable sighting of a German submarine. He made an entry in the log and forgot about it.

Two weeks earlier

June 20, 1945 Osaka Harbor, Japan

Kimmo Takakura, the Japanese commander of U-2500 had held a desk job with the Japanese Underwater Navy until two weeks earlier when he had been quickly assigned to the newly delivered German U-boat, U-2500. His orders were to get it ready to sail immediately. The order came from a high-ranking officer and as soon as the U-boat was stocked, a dozen officers, all above Takakura's rank, boarded. He'd never before seen so many high-ranking officers in such close proximity. When he had embarked, a Japanese seaman dressed in black was hanging by a harness with a bucket and a brush getting ready to paint over the German markings, but one of his superiors scolded the man and told him to get down immediately. There was no time for that. Under the orders he'd been given, they were to leave the harbor in complete secrecy. There were no written orders and they were under a strict communications blackout. He didn't know the destination even two weeks into the voyage, just a course to stay on until the senior officer gave him further instructions.

Commander Takakura, standing in the tower with the hatch open, took in a much-needed breath of fresh air. It had been a grueling trip with many high-ranking officials looking over his shoulder. He tossed his cigarette the moment he heard the approaching ship. It emerged like a ghost from the fog. He could easily read the name *Carissa* painted in huge letters on the bow. He spotted a man screaming in a language he had not heard before, but assumed it was a version of English. The ship churned by not ten meters from him. The size of the ship caused the submarine to rock hard in its wake. He immediately went below and sounded the dive alarm. There was no doubt they had been seen. He was now faced with a dilemma. The orders were to proceed, avoiding all contact with the enemy, but now they had been spotted. He woke the senior officer and soon ten of the top military leaders were engaged in a frantic conversation of what to do. The conclusion was they needed to be certain the ship they had spotted would not report their position. They must sink the ship immediately or their plan to establish *New Japan* would be in jeopardy.

Chapter 1

June 13, Present Day

Pacific Ocean, Fifty-seven miles due west of Cape Perpetua off the Oregon Coast

Scott Tanner brought the deep-water submersible to the surface and remotely steered it into the open bay on the lower deck of the treasure recovery vessel *Hunter*, the ship he and his partner had commissioned for underwater exploration and treasure hunting. This ship was a larger and more modern version of Scott Tanner's original ship which bore the same name. He had wanted to call it *Hunter II*, but David and he were in disagreement. David had insisted on *STE*, the initials of Stafford-Tanner Enterprise. To settle the disagreement, they both agreed on the name remaining the same, saving reams of office paper and a lot of website reconstruction.

On some occasions, testing equipment and treasure hunting could be accomplished at the same time, but today was different. This was a boondoggle as far as David was concerned. As Stafford-Tanner Enterprises grew, David

Stafford, the technical whiz kid and
inventor of underwater devices, had
soured on Tanner's treasure hunting as
a business, but Scott Tanner was the
perfect guy for testing his many
underwater devices and Scott insisted on
keeping his side of the business alive.
There was no new equipment being tested
and no treasure. Scott was miles out in
the ocean searching for a shipwreck that
couldn't even be salvaged for the price
of scrap iron.

For David to be aboard *Hunter* was
unusual. With all that was going on at
the company headquarters, he should have
been in San Diego, but the circumstances
were unusual and David had flown his
helicopter out to *Hunter* to talk Scott
into going back to San Diego with him.

Scott believed he had found the
location of *Carissa*, a ship that had
been lost in the final days of World War
II. He came across the unusual
disappearance of *Carissa* while
researching a Japanese submarine that
had been reported sunk by a Navy PBY,
the flying boats sometimes referred to
as Sub Destroyers. He believed the
submarine was intact when it went down
and could possibly be recovered and used
as a display in a marine museum
dedicated to the War in the Pacific. The
sub had proved to be elusive and his
search was drawing to a close. In a
last-ditch effort, he decided to revisit
some of the stranger submarine sightings

he'd come across in his research. One, in particular, had baffled him and he'd been looking for more information on it for several years. *Carissa* had gone missing in the last days of the war and the last message received from the ship was at the crux of the mystery. It involved a submarine, a German U-boat to be more precise.

Scott had stumbled across the message from *Carissa* in an archived WWII Coast Guard log book. *Carissa* was privately owned and had been leased to the Merchant Marines. It was a cargo ship, but on this trip, it was transporting 90,000 gallons of highly flammable aviation fuel. The deck was stacked with 1800 barrels and on its way from Portland, Oregon to Eureka, California, a voyage that should have taken less than a week.

There had been a multitude of sightings of Japanese submarines in the early years of the War, and there had been a significant number of Merchant ships lost to those submarines, but this was the only time a Nazi submarine had been reported in the Pacific. The statement from the Captain of *Carissa* was quite specific, identifying the submarine as U-2500 which it said was clearly visible on the conning tower. Even though the weather was extremely foggy, the specifics of the message made the report credible to Scott. The "U" designation distinguished it from a

Japanese submarine which had an "I" designation before their number. Other than the number, the message hadn't made much sense. Scott had gone over it a dozen times trying to figure it out. Finally, he had set the message aside, but stumbled across it a year later. His curiosity got the better of him again and he decided to look into the fate of *Carissa*. He started to realize that there were many things strange about the *Carissa*.

The biography of the skipper, William R. Shunt who had sent the message about the U-boat sighting gave Scott an insight into the type of person he was. He didn't fit the profile of anyone who would make an inaccurate report, and with over a hundred voyages under his stewardship, he had avoided being sunk up to the time of his message. He had an exact position of the sighting, and that, in his mind, was worth a few days of side-scan sonar mapping in the area to see if he could find evidence of a wreck.

His partner, David, was not happy about the search and called it a boondoggle.

His research had identified Captain Shunt as a maverick who had served in the Navy for four years before being court-martialed for conduct unbecoming to an officer after starting a bar fight that destroyed a tavern in

Portland in the early days of the War. But seasoned officers with actual experience were in high demand and Shunt was allowed to redeem himself by transferring to the Merchant Marines who were in need of experienced officers, thus he avoided six-months in the brig. There was nothing in his record after being assigned to command Merchant Marine vessels to back the story of him being a maverick and his record of safe trips out to sea, made it unlikely Captain Shunt was a risktaker.

The sighting of the U-boat was the last message from *Carissa* and the actual events of her disappearance were lost to history. Because of the depth of the water along the Cascadia Subduction Zone, a search for *Carissa* had never happened until now. Eventually the record of *Carissa* was buried in the archives like so many other Merchant ships lost in the war.

The message *Carissa* had sent to Yaquina Bay Station was quite clear and specific: it gave the coordinates of the sighting and the submarine identification. The swastika was an unmistakable sign that it was German. If he took the message at face value there was only one interpretation. *Carissa* had run across a Nazi U-boat and had been sunk. If Scott was right, *Carissa* would be found within a five-mile radius of the reported coordinates. Scott thought he had the information he needed to solve the mystery but what he had just discovered was more exciting and brought more questions than answers.

Within a five-mile radius of the coordinates in the message he had discovered what he believed was *Carissa* and a submarine in the same debris field. They were sitting on a mile-deep plateau, and spread out in a string three-miles long. *How the hell did the submarine sink at the same time as the* Carissa? It still wasn't clear whether the submarine was German, but Scott didn't believe in coincidences. If a German submarine had been sighted and a submarine was on the bottom with the ship, what other conclusion could be reached?

Scott was barely able to contain his excitement. He loved a mystery and his efforts had paid off. Now, all he had to do was gather enough evidence to determine if there was anything other than historical value to his find. Scott's curiosity was enough for him to continue the search, but David Stafford was a lot more reserved. He had new equipment waiting to be tested and he wanted Scott in California.

Scott found David in the mess leaning over his computer. "I expected you to be breaking out the champagne, but you're sipping on a latte reading the latest news. I thought you'd be thrilled. Do you realize the significance? This ship was at the exact spot reported in the message and a submarine is in the same debris field." He was still so excited he couldn't contain it.

David gave Scott a blank look. "You do realize this boondoggle you've been on has cost the company millions and there isn't even a treasure involved?"

"I thought you were on board. You're always telling me the hunt is half the fun. Besides, this find is going to have historical significance. Think about it; no one believed the Nazi's were anywhere in the Pacific in World War II. This find will change the history books!"

David took a swig from his latte and stood up. He was nearly a foot shorter than Scott and looked completely out of place on the ship. In truth, he was completely comfortable in the surroundings, as long as the waters were calm. With his dark rimmed glasses, David looked like a diminutive accountant who might be more comfortable tucked away in the back room of a bank, but in fact he was a genius with too many inventions to mention. David had been wealthy from birth and as an only child, the recipient of the family fortune when his parents died at an early age. Unlike some rich kids, David didn't squander his wealth, but increased it substantially after patenting his first robotic submersible vessel he called *Rover*.

"It's okay," David said in a sarcastic tone. "You do the historical research and I'll keep the company solvent with my inventions. Testing my new submersible robot can wait until your curiosity is appeased."

It was unlike David to use his fortunes as a lever to get his way and Scott didn't like it. "Wait just a minute! You agreed when we became partners, I could do underwater recovery efforts as long as I kept up with the testing of your inventions."

"For treasure recovery, not for historical research. Go get a bottle of champagne and we'll drink to your find, but we need to get back to San Diego for the other part of your job. We're running short on time before a penalty clause kicks in. We need to put the new submersible through its qualifying paces."

"I didn't know it was ready for testing. That's why you showed up here unannounced? The Nazi sub has been down there for nearly eighty years. I can go back with you right now if you need me." Scott poured himself a cup of coffee and took a sip. "I thought you'd be as excited as I am that a Nazi U-boat may have been operating along the West Coast of the United States."

"I am, it's just this latest submersible—it's been driving me crazy. We've never been this close to missing a deadline. The software took twice as long as expected to perfect and we have to get the hard testing done. If there are problems, we face some stiff financial penalties from Uncle Sam."

"I know it's not the money you're worried about," Scott said. "Let me guess, this is the phase of the project where you start second guessing yourself. You do this every time and it always turns out fine. You're going to die of a heart attack if you don't stop taking on every challenge thrown in your direction. Give me another day and I'll go back with you."

David sighed. "Break out the champagne glasses, then. Let's drink to your find and we'll figure something out."

That evening, on the deck of *Hunter*, Scott and David stood at the starboard railing watching the setting sun. The sky was pink, with angel hair clouds for as far as they could see. With their light jackets, sunglasses and baseball-style caps, the two could have easily been mistaken for tourists on a cruise, and at that moment they felt the same. It was a part of the job Scott would never tire of.

"I envy you," David said, nostalgically. "You're doing everything you want. Chasing your dreams and ending your days like this."

"You can do anything you want. Why are you so hard on yourself?" Scott asked. But Scott already knew the answer. David wouldn't admit it, but he was hellbent on proving he could make it on his own. Of course, he had already done that a dozen times over, it was part of his DNA. From Scott's point of view, failure was never an option, but it was inevitable, if you pushed yourself far enough. How else would you know your limit?

"Beautiful night for a cruise," David said.

Hunter was anything but a cruise ship. The helicopter David had piloted to *Hunter* rested on a helipad on the aft deck and the ship's rigging made it apparent it was equipped for serious salvage operations not for cruising.

Despite their differences, David and Scott were a well-matched team. By the time they'd finished the bottle of Dom Perignon, Scott had convinced David to take a needed break and stay on board for a few more days while he made another dive with the underwater imaging equipment. David could be useful. The ocean depth was marginal for the equipment Scott was using and he had been experiencing small technical problems. He knew David would know what was happening.

After raiding the liquor cabinet in the War Room, Scott convinced David to bring the new submersible up to Oregon and test it in their current location above the wreckage. They were in deep water and the new underwater robot needed water in excess of a mile depth for testing.

Scott raised a Scotch on the rocks and clicked it with David's glass of Merlot. "I can't imagine *Rover* needs a new version. The one I'm using isn't perfect, but it fills the bill. Congrats on the new one anyway."

"Once you test *Fat Boy*, you're going to want to replace the one you're using. It's old. I gave it to you for Christmas last year, remember?" David was starting to slur his words. "I'm going to steal a line from one of the former presidents, 'Read my lips', no matter how much you beg, you're not getting *Fat Boy* for Christmas this year. At twenty million dollars a copy, Uncle Sam is the only one that can afford it."

"*Fat Boy*," Scott said. "Interesting choice of a name for something that isn't designed to blow up." Scott loved it when David talked with a few glasses of wine in him. Now, getting *Fat Boy*, or a version of it, was a challenge. "I told you *Rover* is working perfectly fine. Keep *Fat Boy*, I'll make do with what I've got."

David looked at him and grinned.

"You say that now. You haven't seen what it can do, yet."

Three hours later Scott had turned in and David was in his cabin going over the video *Rover* had taken on its most recent dive. He wanted to see for himself what Scott was so excited about. As he watched, the picture started breaking up and became fuzzy. It bothered him. He knew *Rover* was operating at near maximum depth for its hull design. When it came to digital electronics, he was a stickler for perfection, but in spite of the video quality, the submarine hull was unmistakable. He was looking for anything that could identify it as a Nazi U-boat like Scott had claimed. But there was something other than the torn wreckage of the submarine that caught his attention. He was certain Scott had missed it. If they were going to solve the mystery of a sunken ship and a submarine in the same debris field, they needed to do it as quickly as possible.

Chapter 2

June 14, Newport, Oregon

Danna Collier showed an article in the *Newport Times* to her brother Paul. The article told of a Merchant ship that had been lost at sea in 1942.

"That was a long time ago," Paul said. "Why are you so interested in it?"

"The *Carissa*, the ship our great-grandfather was on, was lost at sea in 1945. I was in the county office the other day and a local treasure hunter was filing search papers for diving on a wreck he found in the same area."

"Cool," Paul said. "I still don't get it. Was it loaded with treasure?"

"It's history; our history," Danna said.

"History," Paul said. He rolled his eyes. "Boring."

"Well, I for one, am interested in what happened. If they prove it was torpedoed, like the ship in this article, maybe we can profit from it. It says in this article, one of the family members has retained a lawyer to plead their case that Japan is responsible for the death of her grandfather because the ship was torpedoed before Japan and the

United States were officially at war."

Paul's eyes snapped from his smart phone to his sister. "You mean before they bombed Pearl Harbor?"

"Maybe we can sell a story. If Japan torpedoed great-grandfather's ship, we could sue Japan for damages. We are decedents and entitled to something. This is news."

"Cool," Paul said. "What do we have to do?"

"Leave it to me. You know that old trunk Grandma left with Mom?"

"The one in the attic that Mom threatened us with our lives if we ever went anywhere near it? No, never heard of it."

"Can you bring it over to my apartment tonight? I'm thinking I can arrange an interview with the local paper, maybe even put together an article or a book deal. You know I've spent a lot of hours out in those waters doing geological research. Headline: Local family mourns after discovery of seventy-five-year-old shipwreck."

"I hate to burst your bubble, but no one will want to read about a ship that was sunk seventy-five years ago."

"Get me the trunk. If there's enough background information in there, it's worth a try."

"Why do you need more money? You

have a good job."

"Don't you want the finer things in life. A new car, a house on the beach, a boat."

"I never thought about it."

"You never did have any ambition."

"If I get you the trunk, what's in it for me?"

"How about twenty-dollars?"

"That trunk is the size of a small house. It's got to weigh two hundred pounds. I can't do it alone. It's not like I ask Mom and she's going to give it to me."

"Get the trunk, or you get nothing," Danna said. "Okay, I'll split any money I make with you."

"Why don't you just ask Mom for the trunk?"

"I would, but you know how she is; family secrets or skeletons in the closet. She won't let me near it and won't tell me why."

"If she won't let you have it, how am I supposed to get it?"

"Steal it. She never goes up in the attic. I'll get the information I need and you can put it back before she finds out. She'll never be the wiser."

Paul thought about it. "It's worth two-hundred dollars."

"I said I'd split the profit if I sell a story."

"Two-hundred up front, or no deal; and I want a percent of the profit."

"All right, but you don't get paid until I get the trunk."

Paul pursed his lips and frowned. "A hundred now and a hundred on delivery. I'm going to have to pay someone to help me. They aren't going to wait until you sell a story."

"Deal," Danna said, reaching out her hand.

They shook hands and she handed her brother a hundred-dollar bill.

He snapped it and smiled.

"Don't spend it on drugs."

Chapter 3

June 15, Pacific Marine Science Center, Newport, Oregon

"Patricia Westland," Patricia said, to the receptionist. "Here to see Dr. Trask."

"Jason or Gil?" the woman at the desk asked.

Patricia Westland-Tanner was using her maiden and also pen name which she used for her novels. She narrowed her eyes in thought and frowned. "I'm not sure. I'm here to interview a scientist concerning earthquakes large enough to cause a tsunami."

"Oh, you're the writer Gil told me about. When my mother heard you were going to be here, she asked if you would sign her book." She handed it to Patricia.

"I'd be happy too. What's her name?" Patricia said, removing a pen from her purse. After signing, Patricia handed the book back to the receptionist. "Tell your mother she can do me a favor and post a review on my Facebook page."

"I'll be sure and do that," the receptionist said. "You want to see Dr. Gil Trask. He and his father are waiting in the conference room. Follow me." The receptionist escorted Patricia to the room and announced on entering, "The famous writer, Patricia Westland, has arrived."

Patricia put her hand to her mouth to stifle a giggle. She entered and held out her hand to the elder of the two men. "I'm Patricia Westland. I believe we spoke on the phone."

The younger man spoke up. "That would be me. I'm Gil Trask. I hope you don't mind, I asked my father to join us. He's the USGS geologist in charge of Cascades Volcano Observatory in Vancouver, Washington. He can give you a little better insight on the movement of the tectonic plates that are the culprits responsible for the Cascadia Subduction Zone."

"I may not have prepared well enough for two scientists," Patricia said. She looked over both men and felt a little nervous. "I hope you don't think my questions are too basic."

Gil and Jason stretched out their hands and shook, each introducing themselves.

"A father and son team," Patricia said. "Two for the price of one. A bargain at half the price." She looked at them and smiled nervously. "You're not going to charge me for this, are you?" *Stupid*, she thought. *These are serious people.*

Patricia was already forming a plot in her head that included two scientists as romantic interests. These were two very handsome men, not the academic types she had first envisioned.

"We aren't charging," Jason Trask said, "but I'm sure we'd be worth twice the price, if we were. When my wife heard Patricia Westland was going to interview Gil for a novel, my wife volunteered me to come by and help. She says she has read all of your books."

"All three of them, I'm flattered," Patricia said, smiling. He was a ruggedly handsome man, late fifties, or maybe early sixties. Age had treated him well.

Jason Trask continued, "So often novelists get their facts wrong and disaster novels tend to exaggerate the events to the point they lack verisimilitude."

"They *are* novels, after all," Patricia said, defensively. "That might be the whole point."

"Forgive my father," Gil said. "He tends to be a stickler for detail. Maybe you can tell us a little more about the novel and we'll see if we can help."

Gil had dark hair nearly shoulder length and a clean-shaven face. His eyes were as blue as the sky on a clear day.

He had the bronze skin of someone who spent a lot of time outdoors. Other than his age and his father's neatly trimmed beard, Gil was an exact copy.

"Maybe we could start with you Dr. Trask," Patricia said, looking at Gil.

"Please, just call me Gil. With two Dr. Trasks in the room it could get confusing."

"We tend to be casual in the field," Gil's father said. "Jason will be fine. I only use *doctor* if I'm trying to secure a dinner reservation in a five-star restaurant."

"He's kidding," Gil said. "Actually, our degrees are in different disciplines. My father is a volcanologist and I specialize in Geological Oceanography."

"And, since we're being informal, you can call me Patricia. I'm so glad we got that out of the way."

"Tell us about your book," Gil said.

"I'm still trying to form a plot, but I think I want to use the Oregon Coast as a backdrop for a romance between a marine geologist and a local artist." She scrunched up her face. "That's really all I have right now."

"You mentioned a tsunami over the phone," Gil said.

"Yes, Gil," Patricia said, "I

assume you are the one who deals with tsunamis. Tell me what do you do?"

"It's mostly boring work," Gil said. "I study fossils buried in the seabed and try to determine geological events that have happened in the past. By knowing the type of fossils and where they are located, I can predict past events that may have had an influence on the geological makeup of the region. An example would be researching freshwater fossils buried under the ocean, or ancient forests that once grew where there is only salt water today. We can radiocarbon date the trees and count the rings to help piece together a puzzle of events that can tell us what happened, and when."

"And we need to know this, why?" Patricia asked.

"Events of the past are the best indicators of what will happen in the future. It's only a matter of time before they happen again."

"My work is more exciting," Jason said, giving his son a broad grin. "Sometimes the geological makeup of an area causes more than one event. Take the movement of the Juan de Fuca plate under the North American continent, for example. The subduction of Juan De Fuca not only causes massive earthquakes, but also volcanic eruptions such as the eruption of Mount St. Helens in 1980. The entire Cascade Range owes its existence to the subduction."

"I'm not sure I followed that," Patricia said. "What is Juan de Fuca?"

Gil laughed. "It's the tectonic plate that's pushing its way under the continent. It will most likely be responsible for the next tsunami."

"The events are interrelated," Jason said, "but don't always occur at the same time. For instance, there was no tsunami when St. Helens erupted back in 1980, nor was there a subduction earthquake. Nevertheless, the movement of Juan de Fuca under the North American plate causes earthquakes and volcanic eruptions from time to time." He narrowed his brow. "We're still struggling to predict where and when."

Patricia appeared lost in the technical jargon. "So, in a nutshell, Gil deals with geology below the ocean and you deal with geology above the water line?"

"That's a little simplistic," Jason said.

"Close enough," Gil cut in. "Let's sit and you can tell us how a tsunami would fit into your story."

Patricia took a chair across from them at the table. "I'm a little embarrassed." She cringed apologetically. "You see, I write romance novels. They aren't really technical, but I thought by placing my next book on the Oregon Coast and since we hear so much about the chance of a tsunami, I might put a scientist in it as the romantic interest, and a tsunami to give it some suspense."

"A romance," Jason said. "That explains why my wife reads your stuff. Carlene told me she liked your books, but didn't mention the genre. I'm probably the last person you want to interview for a romance. She says I'm about as romantic as a pet rock. That's a joke between us geologists, but you get the point."

"That's not true," Gil said. "Dad and Mom have a great love story. They met in the middle of the geologic disaster in Yellowstone."

"Really?"

"It was nothing," Jason said. He gave a look to Gil that said, "don't go there".

"Nothing!" Gil continued. "They fell in love in Yellowstone and barely escaped with their lives when it erupted. Mom used to tell me the story all the time." He looked over at his father and grinned. "It scared the hell out of me."

"You were in Yellowstone before the big eruption?" Patricia's interest peaked.

"You're here to talk about a tsunami," Jason said, diverting the conversation away from the disaster he and Carlene had survived. "Take a look at this chart." He stood and went over to a chart on the wall. "These tectonic plates are colliding and have been for millennia." He pointed to a line that paralleled Washington and Oregon along the coastline. "This is the Subduction Zone that causes the earthquakes, that in turn, produce tsunamis. The collision of the two plates are what caused the formation of the Cascade Mountain Range that stretches through Washington and Oregon. Mount St. Helens is an active volcano because of the friction formed by the Juan de Fuca Plate moving under North America. I mentioned that earlier."

Gil got up and joined his father. "Cascadia Subduction Zone stretches some six hundred miles along the entire length of Washington and Oregon. Down to about nineteen miles the plates are locked together and rarely move, but below that depth they are moving constantly, causing the Cascade Volcanic Arc. In the meantime, the solidified rock above nineteen miles is being compressed to its limit. Every once in a while, the pressure builds to the breaking point; the upper ground shifts, producing a significant event. A subduction earthquake."

"Causing a tsunami?" Patricia

asked.

"Actually," Gil said, "Tsunami isn't an accurate term. It's Japanese meaning harbor wave. We once called them tidal waves which isn't accurate either. The term we use now is, seismic sea wave."

Patricia looked confused. "This is the first I've heard that term. How will my readers understand what I'm writing about? All the signs I see along the highway say tsunami."

"Use tsunami," Jason said. "I doubt a romance novel will be judged too harshly on the technical details."

Patricia swallowed hard. It sounded like Jason didn't think she took her work seriously. "Gil, what happens to cause such a devastating," she hesitated for a moment, "seismic sea wave?"

"It has to do with the ocean floor," Gil said. "About sixty miles off our coast, where subduction is taking place, the depth of the ocean changes abruptly from relatively shallow water along the beaches to extreme depths of several thousand feet. When there is a subduction event, the ocean floor moves, rapidly displacing a great deal of water. Sometimes the shift is accompanied by huge underwater landslides. It's similar to dropping a rock into a pond. The ripples go out in all directions, but as they approach land they are compressed, and not having anywhere else to go but up, they form a wave. In the case of a subduction earthquake, the wave can be several miles long and moving at jetliner speed. It can cross the ocean and show up in Japan five hours later, but we don't have that long. The subduction zone is so close to our coastline, we have only a few minutes before it reaches land. Unlike a normal wave, a seismic wave has enough water and energy behind it to travel a mile or more inland. It will destroy everything in its path."

"That's terrifying," Patricia said. "And this can really happen along our coastline?"

"Every three to four-hundred years," Gil said. "The last major tsunami struck the Oregon coastline on January 26, 1700 at about 9 p.m."

Patricia laughed. "Seventeen-hundred; Nine p.m.? You're joking with me. How would we know when it happened that long ago? If I remember my Oregon history, Lewis and Clark didn't arrive on the West Coast until 1800."

"He's not kidding," Jason said. "And to be exact, Lewis and Clark arrived on November 15, 1805, well after the seismic event."

Gil added, "We know precisely when the tsunami occurred because a layer of freshwater fossils was discovered below sea level and from the depth of the find we can tell how long ago it was. We added that data to the growth rings from a forest of dead cedar trees we were able to date to late 1699. That led us to Japan, where we matched our data with written records from Japan. They experienced the same wave several hours later and recorded the exact time it hit. There are also accounts from the Native Americans living in the area. They made it part of Indian lore. Several Indian villages were destroyed along the Washington and Oregon coastline. The Indian story has a moral, don't build your house near the ocean. More recently we've been able to calculate the strength of the 1700 subduction earthquake at around nine on the Richter scale. The evidence shows the subduction quake extended along the entire length of the Cascadia Subduction Zone."

"I had no idea," Patricia said. "This is much more complex than I imagined. Do we know if there will be another seismic event?"

"You mean when?" Gil asked. "One will definitely happen again. We can't tell you when."

"My husband and I live on the ocean. Should we be worried?"

Gil raised his eyebrows and looked at his father. Patricia catching the glance asked, "Why are all the warning signs being placed along the highway?"

"The best thing to do is be ready."

"You can tell precisely when it happened three-hundred years ago, but you can't predict when it will happen next time. What else do I need to know?" Patricia looked at Gil and his father. Both men were very attractive and would make great characters in a story. All she needed to do was give them some personality. They took their work way too seriously. Still, they were interesting and were like walking tsunami and earthquake encyclopedias.

There was a knock on the door and Danna Collier stuck her head in. "Excuse the interruption, but I heard Patricia Westland was here."

"This is Dr. Danna Collier, one of our scientists," Gil said.

Danna took the introduction as permission to join them, and walked inside. "I heard your husband found a sunken ship from World War Two," Danna said. "There was speculation it was the Merchant ship *Carissa*. My great-grandfather was on that ship."

"He found a ship, but he doesn't share a lot about his work with me. I think he prefers to keep the news quiet until he secures all the permits required to search."

"I'm sorry," Danna lied. "I thought it was public information."

"If you don't mind my asking," Patricia said, "where did you hear about it?"

Danna shrugged. "Maybe it was someone in the county office. I didn't think much about it until I read the article in this morning's paper about another ship sunk by a Japanese submarine during the war."

"I didn't read the article. I'll be sure and pick up a paper. Did they mention the submarine?" Patricia asked.

"Pardon?" Danna tried to contain her enthusiasm. She may have just hit the motherlode.

"I guess it's okay since the news is already out there," Patricia said. "There are two wrecks; a ship and a submarine. He hasn't been able to identify either of them."

"Well, I wish him luck," Danna said. "I apologize for the interruption. It's been nice meeting you."

"You, too," Patricia said, watching her leave. She wondered if she should have said as much as she did about Scott's work. She'd have to remember to tell Scott the news of his discovery was out there.

An hour later, Patricia left the Pacific Marine Science Center. She was troubled from the interview. She had gone there expecting to have a casual conversation about a tsunami and the type of suspense it would bring to her story and instead had been inundated with graphic, even terrifying facts that she couldn't ignore. Her first thought was to call Scott and tell him she no longer wanted to live on the ocean, but after sitting in her car with her satellite phone in hand, she decided against it. Scott had built the rustic looking log home on the beach because it was a place he had loved since his youth. She didn't want to crush his dream of living with a view of the water. The water was his life. He loved the ocean.

But with the thought of a major earthquake and a tsunami, she wondered if she'd ever be able to sleep in comfort again. Gil Trask, in particular, hadn't minced any words. He had told her that it wasn't a matter of *if,* but *when.* The best they could do was prepare to evacuate at a moment's notice and have a good evacuation route in the plan. She pulled out of the parking area fully intent on putting a plan together and bringing up her concerns when Scott returned.

Inside the conference room Gil and his father caught up on small talk and decided to continue the conversation over lunch at a brewery and restaurant a few blocks away, fronting Yaquina Bay.

"She was a seriously stunning woman," Gil said to his father, lifting a pint of *Dead Man Ale*. They clicked mugs and took drinks of the frosty brew.

"She is a beauty," Jason agreed, "but don't be getting any ideas, she's married to a former Navy SEAL. Westland is her maiden name. I'd be surprised if you haven't heard of her husband, Scott Tanner?"

"You really did your homework," Gil said. "What I was expecting, well, it wasn't her. I'm not sure: I wonder if she has a sister." He took another swig of his drink. Suddenly it clicked. "Really, the same Scott Tanner who runs the treasure hunting business?"

"That's him."

"I'm surprised she wasn't more knowledgeable about tsunamis." Gil said.

Jason took a long drink and wiped the foam from his mustache with a napkin. "You may have been a little hard on her. There's no guarantee a subduction earthquake will occur in either of our lifetimes."

"And no guarantee it won't happen while were eating lunch," Gil countered. "She needs to be prepared. Most people don't take the risk seriously enough. We're way overdue."

Jason smiled. He remembered when he

was fresh out of school. He thought he had all the answers, but soon found out making predictions was how most geologists working around volcanoes had gotten into trouble, sometimes ruining their careers. He had made a number of bad calls in his career and had learned to buffer his enthusiasm with facts and statistics, and enough *ifs* and *mays* to avoid being locked into certainty. Mother Nature didn't give up her secrets easily and past performance, like the stock market, was not always a reliable indicator of the future. Volcanoes, over time, did die, even after extremely active pasts. He knew it wasn't the same with earth movement. Tectonic plates had moved for millions of years, probably billions, colliding and drifting, constantly changing the map of the globe. There was ample evidence of continental drift and a million or a billion years from now the continents would be in different places and shapes. Everything changed constantly. That was a fact of nature. But any attempt to predict how and when something would happen was destined to be wrong.

"I can't believe, you of all people, would be down-playing the inevitability of a large subduction earthquake," Gil said.

Jason, not wanting to get in an argument with his son conceded. "You're right. No matter how remote, it's better to err on the side of caution. At least there are mechanisms in place that can warn the public in the rare event it does happen."

"And that's why I chose to live in the hills far beyond any danger from a seismic wave event," Gil said smiling. "I like to practice what I preach."

"I don't know where your mom and I went wrong. We were probably too protective. You have no sense of adventure." Jason smiled. He noted where they were sitting, at sea level on a wharf on Yaquina Bay. The place his son worked was at the same low elevation and nearly as close to the water. "You better pray when a tsunami comes, you'll not be at work."

"Touché! You managed to get in the last word on the subject."

* * *

11:03 p.m. June 15, Newport, Oregon

Danna pulled her Volvo sedan into the parking spot marked Apt. 14. She got out of her car and walked up the dimly-lit stairway leading to her apartment on the second floor. In front of her door was the large trunk and her brother, sound asleep, with his back propped against it. She kicked her brother gently. "Paul, wake up."

Paul looked up at her. He looked stoned.

"You used the money to buy pot, didn't you?"

"You got your trunk. You owe me another hundred."

"Help me get it inside. Have you got a place to stay tonight?"

"Yeah: well maybe I could crash on your couch?" Paul rolled to his knees and got up. He grabbed one of the leather handles on the trunk and with Danna pushing as hard as she could, dragged the trunk into the living room. Danna closed the door and turned on the lights. "Anybody see you?"

Paul looked at her and grinned. "A couple of bums with a giant trunk struggling to get it up the stairs; only half the people who live here."

"But no police?"

"What, do you think I'm stupid?"

Danna passed on a response. "Did you get the key?" She was tired and wanted to see if there was anything of value in the trunk.

Paul reached in his pocket and pulled out a brass key that had an aged greenish-black patina. "Give me the money and you get the key." He reached out with the key in his fingers and she snatched it from him.

"Let's see what Mom was hiding. Maybe there is treasure inside." Danna gave him a sideways glance and smiled as she put the key in the lock.

"Mom's going to kick your ass when she finds out about this."

"My ass. You're the one who stole it." She struggled to turn the key. It didn't budge.

"You're not doing it right," Paul said.

"Okay, smartass, you try it. I think you brought the wrong key."

Paul jiggled the key a few times and twisted. They heard the latch click and he looked up at his sister and grinned. "I learned a few tricks in Juvie."

"Open it," Danna said, anxiously. "I want to see what all the fuss was about."

Paul struggled with the heavy lid and Danna helped him. Together they rolled the lid back on corroded hinges.

"It stinks," Paul said, backing away.

"Probably a dead body," Danna said, joking.

"It wouldn't surprise me," Paul said, holding his nose.

Danna lifted a yellowed cotton sheet covering the contents. It smelled heavily of mildew. She tossed it aside.

"Nothing but books and papers," Paul said, standing over her shoulder.

"Damn, I was hoping it was full of gold coins," Danna said.

"Really?"

Danna gave him a look. Paul caught it and said, "I have a hard time knowing when you're serious and when you're joking."

"If you'd lay off the weed, you might catch on a little faster."

"Sure, beat on the guy whose already down."

Danna reached in the trunk and pulled out a stack of papers. There were old newspapers and hand-written letters in faded ink. She handed them to her brother. "Make yourself useful and put these on the table."

Danna lifted out a picture album with an ornate black and red enameled cover. She opened it and leafed through a few pages of brown faded photos.

"Who are they?" Paul asked.

"That's what we're here to find out. Put this with the rest of it."

"I'm going outside for a smoke," Paul said.

"Lay off that shit," Danna said. "I mean it. It fries your brain."

"It ain't done it yet. When I get back you better have my money."

"Fine," Danna called after him. "Rent on my couch is a hundred a night."

Danna started searching through the documents, but many of them were written in German. She recognized the language, but couldn't speak or read it. She glanced over at her brother as he reentered her apartment, but was so enthralled with what she could piece together, she didn't even notice as he stretched out on her couch and immediately fell asleep. Two hours later she fell asleep at the table.

The next morning, she awoke with a start. She had been dreaming and the last document she had been reading was staring her in the face. It had a

swastika in the upper left-hand corner.
She had determined her great-
grandfather was a Nazi. His name was
Wolfgang Warner Schmitt.

Chapter 4

June 16, Aboard *Hunter*, 6:30 a.m.

Across the table in the War Room, David spun his laptop around so Scott could see it. "When you were reviewing *Rover* images, did you notice this?"

Scott looked at the short video taken the day before. "Something stirred up the sediment. Probably a fish. It makes it difficult to see anything clearly."

"I checked the USGS site for earthquakes off the coast. There was a minor quake and we caught it on camera."

Scott, unimpressed with David's seismic discovery asked, "What about the wreck. You saw the ship and the submarine? Can you think of a reason they would be part of the same debris field? I mean, other than it is *Carissa* and the German sub it reported seeing."

"I can't even think of a reason we should be researching them. As far as I can see, neither was transporting treasure, and from this video, neither can be positively identified. It would be a lot more exciting if we were talking about a Spanish galleon filled with gold bullion."

"You got spoiled when I discovered

Isabella. Not all finds are going to be that lucrative. Some have more historical value. Not everything can be measured in money." Scott thought for a moment. "Don't be so certain there isn't anything of value, though." Scott took a sip of his coffee. "There are still those who believe Hitler escaped near the end of the war and ended up in Argentina or Ecuador. What if this is an attempt to hide some of his spoils of war?"

"And Elvis is sitting in a bar in Cleveland," David said, sarcastically. "Hitler committed suicide in his bunker. It's pretty well documented. Besides, Germany wasn't in the Pacific no matter what you think. The South American countries you mentioned are all on the Atlantic side of South America. It would take some serious effort to get German subs to the Pacific Northwest. More likely it is another Japanese submarine. Why can't you go with the more logical possibility?"

"Because the evidence points me in the direction I'm headed. There was a German submarine found scuttled off Argentina some years back so we know the Germans made it that far. Hitler and Japan were allies. Recently, a lot of Nazi documents have been discovered in South America. Who cares what ocean borders the countries?"

"I do," David waved his hands in

defeat, "but I suppose you're going someplace with this."

"If this is a Nazi sub, it may have been ferrying the spoils of war out of Germany. There are tons of captured treasure from World War Two that have never been recovered."

"True, but, come on, not in the Pacific. I can't think of a single reason for a German sub to be in the Pacific. If I were a betting man, I'd stake a good sum you're disappointed when you have all the facts. You'll see I'm right."

"Suppose there is gold?"

"You think we'll find gold aboard the sub?"

Scott lifted his eyebrows. "Why not?" Now he had David's attention. "Let me warm up your coffee and I'll tell you what I'm looking for."

"Before we get into that, we need to talk real business, you know the stuff that pays the bills? *Fat Boy* will be delivered in two weeks. I've decided to test it right here on your wreck site. It came to me in my sleep. Why not kill two birds with one stone."

Scott grinned. "That was easy. Too easy, in fact. What's the catch?"

"You need my help. The pictures you're getting from *Rover* are grainy and there is a ton of silt down there. The new version can dive to three times this depth and has upgraded electronics and ground penetrating capability that can see clear down to bedrock. You say you're a mile deep, that shouldn't be a problem for *Fat Boy*. I'm going to head back this afternoon so I can get it ready."

Scott thought about the fuzzy images from the wreck and the signal disruption. He knew David was a perfectionist when it came to his inventions. "*Rover* sprung a leak, didn't it? This isn't about finding the ships, but you can't stand to see me suffer while I do it." Scott grinned. "Seriously, you think I need the new equipment to finish the job."

"The electronics were damp and I had to pull a control card. Another dive could have been catastrophic. But the truth is, we can test *Fat Boy* just as easily right here."

Scott filled David's cup with black coffee and waited while David added enough flavored creamer and sugar to make it into a sea-going version of a seven-dollar Starbucks double latte. "Are you ready for the rest of my story?" Scott asked.

David took in the aroma of his drink and took a sip. "You don't have any whip cream aboard, do you?"

"Rough it," Scott said, and

proceeded to explain why he thought the sub may have treasure aboard.

David let him finish and said, "You still don't know it's a Nazi U-boat. I'll get excited when we see a positive identification or can even identify the other ship as *Carissa*. Right now, you have two wrecks in the same debris field. Other than that, you don't really know what you're looking at."

After lunch David managed to get the circuit board dried out and made a repair to the microscopic leak that had caused the video disruption. Over lunch they had agreed they needed definitive proof they were not looking at two random wrecks that happened to be in the same spot in the ocean. Recovery of anything from that depth presented unique challenges and tended to be very expensive as well as time consuming. They needed to be certain further investigation was worth the effort.

"Let's concentrate on the submarine," Scott said, as they launched *Rover* back into the water. "If it's not a U-boat, there's no reason to go any further."

"You said the identification should be on the conning tower. I don't recall seeing it," David said.

Both men wore headsets that gave them a wide-angle view of what *Rover* caught on camera, but they had not yet lowered them over their eyes.

"We have about twenty minutes before it reaches the bottom," Scott said. "I think I'll call Patricia and let her know I'm going to stay out here a few more days. The weather is perfect and we're right on top of the wreck. I'd like to finish this up."

"I'm sure she'll be thrilled I showed up," David said. "After that trip to the South Pacific, I thought she'd never speak to me again."

"Come to think of it, she does refer to it as her vacation in hell, but I think she blames me more than you."

"We're not to blame. It was Richard Nendel. He's the one who talked me into the trip," David said.

"Nendel! As I recall, you both flew up here and twisted my arm until I caved. That was a dumb-ass idea that nearly got us all killed." He was talking about their search for Amelia Earhart's missing plane.

"Come on, you could never pass up an adventure. We all thought it would turn out better than it did."

"It's the curse of being a treasure hunter. If you're not optimistic it would be pretty depressing. Speaking of Nendel," Scott added, "I'll bet he could run down captured documents concerning Nazi U-boats operating in the Pacific during the war."

"I spoke with Richard the other day. You know he's retired now; I'm not sure he still has access to government archives."

"He's too young for retirement. If we prove this find is a Nazi U-boat, I'm sure he'll want to help us sort out the facts. We should ask anyway."

Scott lit up the satellite phone and made the call to his wife.

Patricia answered on the first ring. "Scott, I was just thinking of calling you."

She sounded worried, prompting Scott to ask, "What's up? Everything okay?"

"It's nothing really. How are you doing? Are you still planning on coming home tonight?"

"That's why I'm calling. We're making another dive right now, but David is flying home to prep the new *Rover* for testing. He's named it *Fat Boy*, you know after the atomic bomb? In the meantime, I want to take advantage of this weather."

"David's with you? Did he bring Fay?"

"Not this time. What were you going to call me about?"

Patricia hesitated before she

spoke. Should she bother him with this when he was out at sea?

"Patricia, are you still there?"

"Really it's nothing. We'll talk about it when you get home."

"You're not going to leave me hanging; come on, spill the beans. Did you wreck the Jeep?"

"I interviewed two scientists at Pacific Marine Science Center. I wanted to use an oceanographer in my next novel and we spent most of the time talking about tsunamis."

"Tsunamis? Makes sense, Oregon is at high risk at some point. Did they say something that concerned you?"

"Only that a tsunami is inevitable and we are living right on the beach, so we'll lose everything when it happens."

"Inevitable is not imminent. As a writer, I'm sure you know the difference, besides we're out of the warning zone. I checked before I built."

"I knew you'd make fun of me."

"I'm not making fun. I'm just saying, we can't be spending all our time worrying about something that will probably never happen. It's highly unlikely to occur in our lifetime."

"You don't know that, but I'm glad you're aware of the risk. Why haven't we ever discussed it?"

"You're right, we should have. I have an evacuation plan in the top drawer of my desk. I was going to go over it with you, but I didn't want to worry you. We can look at it when I get home."

"You have a plan and never discussed it with me!"

"Honey, I'm sorry. I meant to, but honestly I forgot all about it."

"Every mile along the coast there are signs entering and leaving tsunami zones and you forgot? Gil said it could happen today."

"Who's Gil?"

"Gil Trask, one of the scientists I talked to."

"Give me his number."

"Why?"

"Because I'll call him and give him hell for scaring the crap out of you."

"Now you know why I didn't want to bring it up."

"Go to my desk, get the plan out, and read it. If a tsunami happens before I get back, follow the plan. You'll be fine."

"What about you?"

"I probably won't even be aware. Other than on a mountain top, I'm in the safest place there is."

"But a tidal wave?"

"Not this far from land. Really, I think it's good that you're looking into this, but I wouldn't lose any sleep over it."

"Easy for you to say, you have saltwater running in your veins."

"Ha, I'm glad you haven't lost your sense of humor."

"Scott, she's on the bottom," David called out.

"Who is on the bottom?" Patricia asked.

"Gotta go, Honey, I love you." Scott hung up.

David flipped his headset down and Scott did the same while taking the control box from David.

"You sure you don't want me to pilot it?" David asked.

"I've been working with this for months. I even run it in my dreams. I can handle it."

"You seriously need to get a life."

"Says the man who keeps inventing these things."

On the panoramic screen in their headsets, they could see everything the submersible encountered, but at this depth the view was limited to how far the lights penetrated the darkness. In addition, the water appeared murky. Essentially, they were flying blind, poking along the debris from the wreck, hoping to catch a glimpse of any detail that could identify the submarine.

"*Fat Boy* has GIS capability and a remote operating mode. You can set a grid on the ocean floor and it will give you a 3D map of the area down to a few millimeters," David bragged.

"GIS, really? Isn't that the software they're using to map the ocean floor?"

"My version of it," David said. "Actually, it combines side scan sonar, ground penetrating radar, and visual optics into a single image that looks remarkably like a photograph. Once we process the data we can move through and around the image in three dimensions in the computer. That's why we needed to upgrade the computers on board."

"Really? We could use that feature right now," Scott said. "I could use a better map of the sea floor. The NOAA charts show it as an undersea mountain range."

"See, I told you you'd want the new model." David couldn't contain the grin on his face. "I'll let you know once it gets into Newport. Meanwhile, stop licking your chops and pay attention. How do you even know this is the right sub?"

Scott maneuvered *Rover* along the hull, inching his way from the nose along the length until he came to a tangled mess of broken and torn metal. The submarine was nearly cut in half.

"If the other ship hit it, it must have been moving at full steam," David said. "That's some serious damage."

One of Scott's theories was, that the ship and the submarine collided, but Scott shook his head. "No way a collision could have caused that kind of damage." His voice took on a disappointed tone.

"Where's the conning tower?" David asked.

"It's missing. That's what I told you earlier. It's got to be around here somewhere. All we can do is keep looking."

"You could check out the other ship. If you can identify it as *Carissa*, it would at least—"

"Not good enough," Scott cut him off. "The Coast Guard was even skeptical it was a Nazi U-boat. If it was Japanese, the identification would also be on the tower. We're a bust if we can't find some positive identification."

"Maybe a World War Two marine expert could identify the wreckage from what we have," David suggested. "Some of the video shows pretty good detail."

"Maybe, but the Germans supplied Japan with submarines early in the war. They could have copied the German plans."

"I agree the sub is the key to the mystery," David conceded. "I hope you find the tower. I need to scoot, so good luck."

David removed his headset and handed it to Scott. They hugged, and in a few minutes, Scott watched as the helicopter lifted from the deck and circled before disappearing over the horizon.

Scott spent the rest of the day piloting *Rover* in and around wreckage, but the conning tower was still missing. Discouraged, he brought *Rover* to the surface. There was nothing more he could do.

Waldport, Oregon

Patricia, with a glass of wine in her hand, stood at the railing on the deck watching the sun disappear over the ocean. It was a spectacular view, and she lingered there a few minutes after the sun had disappeared, imagining where Scott was, and if he was watching the same sunset. In her hand was the tsunami plan she had found in Scott's desk drawer. *Red clouds at night,* she thought. But she knew the clouds couldn't forecast a tsunami. She hoped it was true that Scott was far enough out to be safe from a seismic wave event or whatever the term was the Marine Science Center preferred. She recalled how she had noticed every tsunami warning marker on her way home from the meeting and sighed. *I can't believe Scott knew the risk and still built our home here,* she thought. But the ocean seemed so tranquil at the moment, it was hard to imagine something so beautiful could turn into something so destructive.

She had gone through the plan. It was quite simple, too simple, as far as she was concerned. It didn't mention valuables, heirlooms, family pictures, or the painting of her grandfather hanging on the living room wall. What about her computer and the back-up drives for all of her books? Basically, Scott's plan said, "if you feel a strong earthquake jump in the car and head inland, preferably not along a road that bordered the river." Didn't all of the inland roads follow a river? And where was Bay View Road anyway? Did he really want to go someplace where he had a view of the destruction? Tomorrow she would be sure to go over the details of his plan so she could suggest improvements when Scott got home. Meanwhile she would pack a bag with essentials and make a point to find high ground above the danger zone. Until then she wasn't certain she could sleep.

Chapter 5

June, 17 Pacific Marine Science Center

When the phone rang, Gil Trask lifted his attention from his computer. He and a colleague had been going over some of the latest GIS renderings of the ocean floor a few miles offshore. His colleague, Dr. Danna Collier picked up Gil's phone and answered. "Pacific Marine Science Center, Dr. Trask's office." She looked at Gil and gave him an evil grin. She had seniority over the younger scientist and often let it play out in childish ways. She also fantasized she and Gil as lovers, but her attempts to get his attention had failed. The truth was, she had always been awkward around men. Her first marriage had ended in divorce, something she wanted to forget. She had even taken back her maiden name to hide it.

She listened for a few seconds while Gil grabbed for his phone. "It's that romance writer again," Danna said, holding the phone to her chest.

"Give it to me," Gil said. He could feel his face flushing. Even though Patricia was married, he had a schoolboy crush on her. Someday he hoped to find someone like her. He was pretty sure Danna wasn't it.

Continuing to play, Danna kept the phone from him and said into the receiver, "Dr. Trask is in a meeting. May I tell him what this is in reference to?"

Gil reached over and hit the speaker function on the phone. "Patricia, you are on speaker. What can I do for you?"

"Gil, I hate to bother you, but something you said in our meeting the other day confused me."

"What was that?"

"You told me a seismic wave would likely be no more than a few meters high. I've been doing some research and our house is at an elevation of a hundred feet. I think we are out of the tsunami risk area. Are we still at risk?"

"I'm sure your insurance company is better equipped to answer that than I, but if you can give me your specific location, I'll be glad to check it out against our warning zone map. Elevation is just one of the factors contributing to a risk determination."

"Insurance company? I should have thought of that. I'm sorry for bothering you. I'll contact them."

"Honestly, I don't think it's a tsunami you have to worry about," Gil said. "Almost all the beach houses are built on sand. They are more likely to be destroyed in an earthquake. There's a phenomenon called liquefaction that turns the soil into quicksand."

"Thanks, that's a relief," Patricia said, sarcastically. "I feel so much better now."

Gil laughed. "Sorry for that. Put a good evacuation plan together and I'm sure you'll be okay. Most of the casualties in a seismic wave event are caused by people who are not prepared."

"I'm trying to do that," Patricia said. "There was something else, though."

"Anything, I'd be glad to help."

"Would it be okay if I used you as a character in my novel? I mean a fictitious character modeled after you."

"I'm flattered," Gil said. "I've never been a character in a book as far as I know. It's okay on one condition."

There was a long pause. "You know I'm married," Patricia finally said.

"No, I don't mean that. I just don't want to be portrayed as a bad guy."

"How about I let you read the manuscript before it's published. If you don't like your character, I'll make changes."

"Really? I didn't know that was how it's done. Make me look good and you can call me any time."

"Bye," Patricia said. She couldn't help but smile. She could almost see him blushing over the phone.

"You have a crush on her," Danna said.

"Crush? I do not, but she is pretty."

"'Make me look good. Call me any time'," Danna mocked. "Give me a break. The bimbo writes romance novels, for god's sake. She probably has the I.Q. of a doorknob."

"She was a TV news reporter before becoming a novelist," Gil countered. "I think you're jealous."

"God, how can anyone compete with that?" Danna put her hands up framing her face and swayed her head. "She wasn't anything but a talking head."

"I didn't know it was a competition," Gil said. "You are aware she's married."

Danna blushed and put her index finger in her cheek and said coyly, "Then there's still hope for us?"

"Us? Come on, look at this," Gil

said, changing the subject.

Danna stood behind him and leaned in close. When her hair bushed his cheek, Gil hit a key. "Here, I'll put it on the big screen." He transferred the picture from his computer to the monitor on the wall.

The sixty-inch monitor lit up with the multi-colored grid from the GIS. It showed the mountains under the ocean, fifty miles out from their office.

"That's the area I took core samples from last year," Danna said.

"I know. I read your paper. Based on your samples you postulate there have been over forty subduction zone events that we know of."

"Up from the eight previously reported," Danna added. "Actually forty-one. The average time between subduction quakes is two hundred-forty-three years, not 500 as previously reported."

"And every one of them was accompanied by widespread coastal flooding?" Gil said, looking up at her. "We haven't been able to verify that with the coastal geology."

"It's because all of the subduction events were not followed by a tsunami. I explained that in the paper." She nodded in thought. "The last known subduction quake was over three hundred years ago. That one produced a significant tsunami."

"That's what I was getting at," Gil said, rising from his chair and walking up to the screen on the wall. "See that mountain. It drops down over a mile and its peak is still a thousand feet underwater. This long slope has a massive layer of silt built up over centuries. If it gives way when the next subduction quake hits, it could produce a wave over a hundred feet tall."

"That's why you couldn't answer her question," Danna said.

Gil gave Danna a concerned look. "How do you answer a question like that? If we have a major landslide in addition to subduction ground movement, all bets are out the window. Ninety-percent of the tsunami zone warning signs in this area will be incorrect."

"All the coastal cities from Seaside to Bandon will be lost," Danna said, "including this building we're standing in."

"I think we need to bring this to the attention of Homeland Security," Gil said, grimly.

"Good luck telling the mayors of the coastal cities our earlier data was incorrect," Danna said, then added. "Understated is more accurate. Two hundred-forty-three-years is an average number between major tsunamis off the

Oregon Coast. We went almost nine hundred years without a subduction quake in the past."

"Yeah, but your report shows even subduction quakes have happened more frequently than previously thought. That raises the odds we'll get another one in our lifetime." Gil turned from the monitor.

Danna studied the charts that mapped the depth of sediment buildup along the underwater mountain. "I hate to be the bearer of any more bad news, but it wouldn't take a subduction earthquake to make a landslide on that underwater mountain," Danna said, following him back to his desk. "It wouldn't take much of a quake to put that sediment in avalanche mode."

Gil turned and went back to the monitor. "There aren't any core samples along the slope. Without it there's no telling how deep the sediment is." He pointed to a wide chasm at the base of the mountain. The data showed it as a bottomless pit, a blank area on the screen caused from lack of data. "If this is an unrecorded fault it could trigger a landslide." The wide crack extended inland from the subduction area.

"If it is, then this adds to the possibility this area could be in a lot more danger than we've previously believed," Danna said. "Two bits of bad news in one day. Do you want to do the report, or shall I?"

Gil considered it for a moment. "We need to make sure we're not jumping to conclusions. We could be opening a big can of worms."

"Maybe," Danna said. "But we need to make it credible enough that we get the team out there for another look. Our equipment wasn't rated for anything deeper than five-thousand feet. Where can we get equipment that can gather data at more than that depth?"

"I'll look into it," Gil said. "Good work on the paper, by the way. Without the data you provided, we wouldn't even be considering this."

Danna was pleased with the praise. "Thank you, Gil, I'm looking forward to reading your latest paper. What are you calling it?" She answered her own question "Oh, yeah, *The Cascadia Subduction Zone and the Link to the Cascade Volcanic Arc.* You may want to work on that title."

Chapter 6

June 18, Newport, Oregon

"You've been crashing at my place for two nights," Danna said to her brother. "It's time you find a job."

"What are you, my mother?" Paul said.

"If you don't like it, go live with her."

Wanting to change the subject, Paul walked over to the table and picked up one of the papers. "When are you going to be finished with this stuff? I want to get it back before Mom misses it."

"You don't know anyone who speaks German, do you?"

"Matter of fact, I don't, but I have a suggestion, if you really want to find out what's here."

"I can't wait to hear this," Danna said, rolling her eyes.

"A buddy of mine has a computer that translates. He writes text books and has them translated into foreign languages. He showed me how he does it."

Danna couldn't help herself. "You have a friend who can write? I'm impressed, but I already thought of that and have been using Google Translate to pick out key phrases. You'll be happy to know we are the descendants of a Nazi sympathizer. He may even have been a spy for Hitler."

"Cool," Paul said. "We have someone famous in the family."

"More like infamous," Danna said. "They used to shoot spies back in those days. But it kills any chance of getting an article published."

"A spy novel then; I think it sounds great," Paul said.

"Why do you think Mom kept this from us," Danna said. "I'll tell you why, because it would ruin us. Our family would have to move. You don't go around bragging about this sort of thing."

"You may be right," Paul paused for a moment. "Why do you think Mom kept the trunk? She could have destroyed all this."

"I think we need to ask her," Danna said,

"Don't include me. You want to tell her we got the trunk from her attic, leave me out of it."

"Coward," Danna said.

June 22, Aboard *Hunter*

David was in constant communication with the helicopter operator as the twin rotor heavy lift chopper lowered the cigar-shaped object into the water beside the ship. It looked identical to the *Rover* model Scott had been using. Like the old one, the object was about the length of a car, but it was only two-feet in diameter. This one was three feet in the middle resembling a pregnant cigar. David had given it the name *Fat Boy*, but to Scott it looked more like a blimp. The name was displayed in black script along one side, but was difficult to read because of the bright background color. *Fat Boy* had several ports and hidden compartments, but its most distinguishing feature was the color. It was painted bright day-glow-orange. In the sunlight it hurt your eyes if you stared at it. David had explained it presented a greater contrast against the ocean water. There was no doubt about that.

Scott was in the water in full wetsuit and diving gear waiting for *Fat Boy* to reach buoyancy so he could detach the cables. Slowly the helicopter unreeled the cables which were attached to mounting lugs on the nose and tail of *Fat Boy*. After the submersible was floating in the water, Scott climbed up on the slick object and detached the first cable. It released with a snap and he fell backward to avoid getting hit by the heavy hook as it sprang through the air.

David spoke to him through his intercom. "Scott, are you okay?"

"I'm fine. Where did you find that helicopter pilot? He could use some flying lessons."

"He's used to lifting logs out of the forest. It was the best I could do on short notice. You sure you're okay?"

"I'm good. Tell him to give me a little-more slack on the next one."

With both ends disconnected *Fat Boy* floated about half submerged, bobbing up and down with the ocean swells.

"Hop on, I'll give you a ride," David said.

Scott slipped up on the back of the remote operated vehicle and held onto the eyebolt where the hook had been attached. David ran the manual controls and took him in a wide circle cutting through the water at breakneck speed. Scott struggled to keep from being tossed in the ocean.

"Like riding a whale," Scott yelled, as he mimicked a cowboy riding a bucking bronco. Scott had actually ridden an Orca one time, but that's a story for another day.

"Okay, enough fun for today," Scott heard through his headset. "Let's bring it in and put it through its paces."

That afternoon Scott and David sat in the War Room running the deep-dive submersible through a set of maneuvers designed to test its ability to operate without direct control from the ship. In effect they were sending *Fat Boy* on a mission that it would carry out on its own. It had passed all the preliminaries. They were now ready for a major dive.

"I hate to eat humble pie," Scott said, "but you're right."

"What was that?" David asked, putting his hand to his ear. "I didn't quite hear you."

Scott shook his head, ignoring him. As *Fat Boy* sent streams of data to the super computer in the War Room, a 3-D image of the seafloor started to emerge on the large monitor. It was more detailed and covered a larger area than the physical charts he had been working with. By piecing together details and making hard copies, Scott was able to get a three-dimensional perspective of the shipwreck area. The scan captured hidden data, showing the depth of the sand in and around the wreck down to bedrock. He made color prints and taped them along the full length of one of the walls, giving him a unique perspective of the wreck and everything in the debris field. The data showed what was visible on the sea floor and also items that were buried in the sand. For the first time, Scott could see that the submarine was resting on the edge of an underwater cliff. The blank area on the other maps now showed the edge of a deep chasm about ten feet from the submarine hull. There was only one place left to search for the missing conning tower. It had to have gone over the edge into the abyss.

"Let's see if it's down there," Scott said, pointing to the area on the screen that still hadn't been mapped.

David worked his magic on his computer and the robot floated over the edge.

"*Fat Boy* is over a mile deep and still diving," Scott said. "The sail of that sub has to be at the bottom of that canyon."

"It's seeking an iron-based alloy that I added to its database," David said. "I programmed it with an analysis of the steel from one of Hitler's U-boats."

"You don't leave anything to chance, do you? Where do you go to find out the alloy makeup of a World War Two submarine?"

"Richard Nendel. It's good to have a friend in high places. When I mentioned what we were doing, he could hardly contain himself. He wants in on the search." David smiled, obviously proud of himself for coming up with something so obscure as the metal composition of a U-boat hull. "He's trying to talk his wife into a trip out here."

"He's retired. What's the problem?" It was a rhetorical question. Scott knew the problem was depression. Richard had seemed adrift after he lost his appointment when the new administration took office.

"I offered to bring him into my wing of the company," David said, "but he said his wife wouldn't leave the D.C. area."

"Don't believe him," Scott said. "We need to keep pushing. He'll come around. Maybe he could be swayed to join me. His access to historical data may be more valuable than his contacts with the Navy. Maybe if you offered to pick them up in the company jet, we could get him off the fence. Either side of the business, he'd be a great asset."

"It's worth a try."

"It would be great to see them again. Patricia would be thrilled. You can bring Fay and we'll throw an Independence Day party. You can all stay at our place. We'll make it a working vacation."

"I don't think mentioning work in the same sentence as vacation will get the girls on board," David said. "You better let me do the talking."

"Vacation, then; I'll have Patricia call Janet. We all go back a long way. It'll be fun."

Dave agreed. "I'll give Fay a call, but right now, we have a hit." He pointed to the blinking red light in the corner of the screen. "That's an alloy match, my friend; we found something deep down in that fissure."

"She's thirty-five hundred meters deep," Scott said. "We couldn't have found it with *Rover*."

"Over two miles down," David said, doing the calculation in his head. "What do you make of it? Is it the missing piece of the puzzle?"

"It's the conning tower, all right, but it's under a layer of silt. Is there a way to clear away the sand so we can get a visual on it?"

They were looking at a sonar image buried under three-feet of silt. The shape was unmistakable but there was no way to see if it had identification.

David turned *Fat Boy* on its nose and blasted the area with a strong water-jet. "You have to be careful doing this maneuver," David explained as the cameras became useless in the now murky water. "The water-jet is powerful enough to send *Fat Boy* in a tailspin. You notice I've turned on the thrusters to counter the action."

"I can't see anything," Scott replied.

"We'll have to wait until it clears before we can check for a number."

David picked up the satellite phone. "I'm going to call Nendel while we're waiting. I don't think Janet will need Patricia to convince her a vacation from Virginia this time of year is a good Idea."

"I agree," Scott said. "Tell the old fart he's crazy if he doesn't join us on this."

"I'll let you call him an old fart. He may be older than us, but I'll bet he can still whip both our asses."

"Speak for yourself, wimp," Scott said, laughing.

David put the phone on speaker and spoke up as soon as it was answered. "Scott says you're an old fart and a wimp if you don't take us up on the offer I'm about to make."

"David, is that you?" It was a female voice.

David sunk down in his chair.

Scott let out a hoot.

"Is Richard able to come to the phone," David asked. "How did you know it was me?"

"I hear Scott in the background. He put you up to that, didn't he?" Janet said, laughing.

"I apologize for my part in Scott's juvenile and obnoxious behavior," David said. "By the way, you're on speaker and Scott can hear you, so you better not tell him what you really think of him."

"Hi, Scott," Janet said. "In spite of what David says about you, I love you anyway."

"Hi Janet. We're not home right now or I'd let you talk to Patricia. I understand you're tired of traveling."

"Did Richard tell you that? I think he got spoiled working for the White House. You want to clue me in on what's up and I'll get the old fart off his duff and to the phone."

Scott filled her in on the plan.

"A Fourth of July party. I can't wait. I'll get Richard, and you can bet we'll be there."

"I'll send a plane for you and Richard," David chimed in.

"You don't have to do that," Janet said.

"No problem. Consider it done."

"Here's Richard. You boys stay out of trouble, and we'll see you soon."

As they were talking, the picture on the large monitor cleared up. The first thing out of Scott's mouth when Richard answered was, "Holy shit,

Richard, you won't believe what I'm looking at!"

"Don't tell me you found it! Son-of-a-bitch, I swear, you boys have all the fun."

"You can get in on this," Scott said.

"Richard, it's David. I never thought I'd be this excited to find a sunken ship that wasn't filled with treasure, but this is an incredible find. The number is unmistakable, U-2500. It's as clear as if it was painted yesterday."

"I wish I was out there to celebrate with you. I'll do a little research and see what I can find on that U-boat."

"Do it quickly. I'm flying back to pick you and Janet up. It won't be until next week, but we should have most of the info from this site gathered by then. We need to know everything there is on U-boats operating in the Pacific."

"Janet agreed to it?" Richard asked.

"As long as you two have been married," Scott said, "you really ought to communicate better."

"If I recall, you're the man who pissed his wife off over a vacation in the South Pacific."

"Careful man, she's still miffed at

you for talking me into it."

"Me? See that's what I'm talking about. You blame me because you don't have the balls to take ownership of your own decisions."

"I need to get back to work. You and Janet are staying at our house. Patricia will love the company, and I can't wait to see you guys."

"Keep this news to yourself," David said. "We'd like to make the discovery public on our terms. Every Nazi hunter on the globe will be homing in on this place if our find really does change the history books."

"My lips are sealed. Great work, you two."

June 25, Newport, Oregon

Danna had spent the night before thinking about a phone conversation she had overheard in the office. Patricia Westland had called Gil and invited him to a party. The party was enough to get her attention, but the next thing that came over the speaker phone was what had really caught her attention. Could it be true that Patricia's husband had pictures of the area where the wreck was found. She had to figure a way to find out more without looking too conspicuous. She had to get invited to the party, but how?

June 26, Pacific Marine Science Center

Danna arrived early to work and immediately went into the break room and made a pot of coffee. She watched for Gil to walk past. He always showed up at least thirty-minutes before the rest of the staff. When she saw Gil walk by, she poured a cup of coffee and followed him into his office. Standing at his door, she said, "Good morning, Gil. I'm glad I caught you." She handed him the cup. "I just made it."

"Thanks," Gil said, taking the cup. "What brings you in so early?"

"There's a great firework display in Waldport on the Fourth. I wonder if you would like to join me?"

"You mean a date?"

"It doesn't have to be, but yeah, I thought it would be nice."

"Actually, I've already accepted an invitation." He thought for a moment while taking a sip of coffee. "You can join me, if you promise to be on your best behavior."

"That's a terrible thing to say. Why wouldn't I be?"

"It's at Patricia Westland's house. I know what you think of her."

"I'm over that, silly man. I wasn't

serious. I'd love to go with you."

"My parents will be there," Gil added. "It's not a date. You'd just be along for the ride."

"I already met your dad, but I bet your mom could tell some stories about you." She broke into a wide grin.

"Best behavior, remember?"

"Got it. I'll play dumb. You can use me as arm candy."

"I'm about to take the invitation back," Gil kidded. Danna wasn't bad to look at, and she was smart, but he couldn't imagine them in a romantic relationship.

"I'm leaving," Danna said. "Enjoy your coffee."

After she left, Gil stared at his coffee and set it aside. "She probably spit in it," he said, under his breath.

That afternoon, both Danna and Gil were called into their supervisor's office. Their boss was a senior scientist with half-a-dozen diplomas framed and mounted on the wall behind her desk.

Sheila Winter was usually a hands-off boss. Gil hadn't spoken to her more than a dozen times since he'd been hired. For her to call him into her office was somewhat intimidating.

"I hope you consider this report a work in progress," Sheila Winter said, removing her glasses and letting them dangle from a cord around her neck. She had the report they had submitted claiming the area was in danger of a non-subduction tsunami. Gil had relied heavily on Danna's expertise and had been reluctant to add his name as an author.

"Of course," Gil said. "That's why we made a request to get GIS data and core samples of the mountainside."

"The communities of Newport and Waldport are at greatest risk." Danna added, "If the silt is as deep as I think it is, a cubic mile of land would be displaced. That could trigger a tsunami without a subduction event."

"There's also an unmapped area that looks like it could be an undocumented fault," Gil added. "This stretch of coastline could be at greater risk than we previously thought."

Sheila Winter looked up from the report. "I've contacted the Marine Geology Department at OSU and they won't have equipment free until after the shallow water survey for the Department of Fisheries is complete. Any data you hoped to obtain won't be available for eighteen months."

"That's too long," Gil said. "We're talking a minor earthquake in the area could put us in danger."

"I read the report," Winter said, "but without the equipment, we don't have data, and without data, this is all speculation. I'll let you know if anything changes."

Gil let out an exasperated breath. "Newport and Waldport will get a double whammy if there is a subduction event."

"Arguing won't change the facts," Winter said. "None of this leaves this office." She handed the report back to Gil. "We're scientists who deal in facts."

They turned to leave when Winter called out, "Danna, we need to talk."

Gil returned to his office. He was frustrated. He knew his boss was right, but that didn't make it any easier to swallow. He called his father from his office for advice.

"She's right, son," Jason Trask said. "We're asked to make predictions all the time without enough data. It always turns around and bites us in the ass. Soon enough, you'll get your data and you can issue a meaningful report."

"It's frustrating," Gil said.

"I know, son. Life often works out that way. Your mom and I will see you on the Fourth. I assume you are going to Patricia Westland's party. Your mom threatened to divorce me if I didn't bring her."

"Really?"

"Not really, well, maybe. We'll see you there?"

"I'm bringing Danna," Gil said. Then he added, "It's not a date."

"Danna? Okay, son. See you there."

Gil hung up the phone and looked up. Danna was standing there with a disappointed look on her face.

"How long have you been there?" Gil asked.

"You may not want to take me to the party," Danna said.

"What?"

"I've been fired."

"Fired? Are you kidding me? What for?"

"Don't worry, it didn't have anything to do with you."

"What then?"

Danna tightened her lips and clamped her jaw to keep from bursting out in tears.

"What happened?" Gil insisted.

"You know my latest report?"

"Yeah. It was great. A good piece of work. I told you that."

"A grad student at Oregon State was

using it as a basis for his research and discovered some errors. His professor is accusing me of forging references. I guess they are making an example out of me."

"That's hogwash. Anyone can make an innocent mistake. You wouldn't knowingly—"

"I appreciate your support, but honestly I knew I was making a giant leap when I published. I used some names that I thought would add credibility. I just got ahead of myself." She hung her head. "I'll never get a job in this part of the country again. Winter will make certain of that."

"That's terrible," Gil said. He honestly felt sorry for her. "Our date is still on. A party will cheer you up."

"I don't know, Gil, are you sure?"

"I'll pick you up at two. Be ready."

Chapter 7

July 4, Waldport, Oregon

It was a perfect day on the Oregon Coast. The sky was mostly blue with high wispy clouds and a slight offshore breeze making the day warmer than usual. Richard Nendel and his wife Janet had arrived with David and his wife Fay the day before. All six were sitting around the breakfast table at the Tanner house overlooking the ocean.

"David and I brought the California weather with us," Fay said, pouring coffee for everyone. "What a gorgeous day."

"You should talk about weather," David said. "I agree it's better than the fifty-below zero temperatures where we met."

"Being chased by the Russians in Antarctica is a heck of a place to pick up a girl," Scott said. "Patricia could add that to one of her stories."

"You're blaming me for Antarctic weather," Fay said to David.

"You have to admit, it was pretty cold," Scott chipped in. "But in your defense, I don't think there is enough sunshine in California to counter the - 70° temperatures we encountered down there."

"Thank you, Scott." She gave David a smirk.

"David, you and Fay meet in Antarctica?" Janet asked.

Fay stirred sugar in her coffee and gave David a loving gaze. "I was doing research on freshwater marine organisms; at least that was what I was supposed to be doing. Russia had discovered a freshwater lake deep under the Antarctic ice and I was part of the team that was invited to help catalogue the organisms." She shook her head and looked around the table. "Big mistake." She sipped her coffee. "As it worked out, we nearly all got killed. If it wasn't for David and Scott and that crazy machine they were testing, we'd all be dead. Patricia, where were you at the time? I don't remember you being part of that adventure."

"Believe me, I was a part of it," Patricia said. "So was Janet. Scott and I may not have been married at the time, but I worried every day Scott was down there. Janet can testify to that."

"She's right," Janet said. "Just because we weren't on the front line doesn't mean we weren't in the war."

"Sorry," Fay said. "I didn't mean it that way."

"You called Sub Zero a crazy

machine," David protested. "That crazy machine saved your life, and the CIA bought half a dozen of them. Last I heard my under-ice passenger vehicles are still keeping the Russians in check in that part of the world."

Fay leaned over to David and gave him a peck on the cheek. "It was just a figure of speech. Everyone at the table knows you are a genius." She paused for a second and winked. "And a sweet one, too."

"Dear God, it's too early in the morning for that," Janet said.

Richard reached for a second helping of bacon and Janet slapped his hand. "You know what the doctor said about bacon."

"Damn, I thought all the lovey-dovey talk was distracting you," Richard said.

"Richard, do you have a cholesterol problem?" Patricia asked. "I could have fixed egg whites. Are you on a special diet?"

"No problem with cholesterol," Richard said. "My doctor says I have an abundance of it."

"All those years of Navy food," Scott said. "The war-machine runs on bacon grease and gravy."

"Yeah," Richard said, with a nostalgic look. "Navy food was great, wasn't it?"

"Here's to old sailors," Scott said, lifting a glass of orange juice to Richard.

"Can we change the subject," Richard said. "All this talk about getting old is getting old. Any of you ever hear that song George Burns used to sing, 'I wish I was nineteen again', well I agree with him."

"Who's George Burns?" Patricia asked.

"My point exactly," Richard said. "I fell asleep last night and I woke up in an alternate universe. You young folks really missed out on a lot."

"Alternate universe?" Janet said. "That's his definition of waking up in a strange place and he can't find the bathroom."

Richard ignored her. "You kids are doing things we couldn't even imagine. My generation put people on the moon with slide rules and monkey wrenches and your generation doesn't even know what a slide rule is. My doctor, who was still in diapers the day I graduated from Annapolis, tells me I can't eat bacon. What happened to the world I grew up in?"

"You're sounding kind of grumpy, old man," Scott said. "Did you get enough sleep last night?"

"I slept fine," Richard said, "and my memory is fine, too. Patricia, does Scott still sleep with a gun under his pillow?"

"You sleep with a gun under your pillow?" Fay gave Scott an incredulous stare.

"Patricia didn't feel comfortable with a gun," Scott said, grinning. "Now I sleep with a big knife."

"Seriously," Richard said. "He nearly killed me when we were serving together in the Gulf. You don't want to startle this guy when he's sleeping."

"What can I say, you can never be too prepared," Scott said.

"Scott sometimes suffers from PTSD," Patricia explained. "It's a folding knife. No big deal."

Fay shook her head and Janet tried to stifle a grin.

"You all are putting me on," Fay said.

"It's just, you've never been married to a fighter," Janet said. "It takes a little getting used to."

Patricia spoke up. "I invited some scientists over for the barbeque this afternoon. I thought it might be interesting. Do you know we're sitting on top of the Cascadia Subduction Zone? We could all be wiped out by a giant tsunami at any moment."

"If you're trying to cheer me up, it's not working," Richard said.

"Patricia is researching her next book," Fay said. "I think it's a wonderful idea to intertwine a romance novel with impending disaster from a tsunami."

"I'm not sure my editor is thrilled with the idea," Patricia said. She glanced over at Scott. "But I am learning a lot about the inherent risk of living on the beach."

"We live on the beach in Southern California. Are we at risk, too?" Fay asked.

"The San Andreas fault runs along the California Coast. What's to worry about," David said, sarcastically. "Come on, you guys, there isn't any place on the planet that's one-hundred percent safe."

"Geez, we came all the way out here to listen to this?" Richard said. "I don't know about you ladies, but I want to hear about the Nazi submarine Scott and David found. When can I see it?"

Scott smiled. "Finally, a subject I can get comfortable with."

"I can't believe you're still upset because I said your tsunami evacuation plan was inadequate," Patricia said.

"That's the reason I didn't go over it with you in the first place." Scott looked around the table for support. "A tsunami is right up there with a nuclear bomb. You aren't going to get enough time to do much more than get to high ground and hope the wave isn't big enough that it takes all your property with it."

"I read about some guys just south of here who were in the tsunami from the Alaska quake back in 1969," Patricia said. "They had enough time to get to higher ground, but they thought they'd stop long enough to take a picture. They never found their bodies."

"In their defense," David said, "no one down here felt the Alaskan earthquake. No one expected a tsunami. There weren't warning sirens."

"But we have warning systems in place now," Patricia said. "There's no reason for anyone to be hurt if they plan well enough. My plan calls for me to escape with my most precious items."

"She wants to make a moving van our getaway vehicle," Scott said. "I keep reminding her our lives are the most precious thing we have. The rest is just stuff."

"It seems like there's room for compromise," Janet said. "Richard, having spent time in the Coast Guard, knows the value of planning ahead." She looked at her husband who had managed to grab another piece of bacon and was chewing on it.

"There, it's settled," Scott said, pushing away from the table. "If you ladies will excuse us, Richard, David and I are going to my office and catch up on some old war stories."

"I'd like to add something concerning tsunamis," Richard said, pushing away from the table. "I agree with Patricia, it's imperative everyone is prepared. In the case of a nuclear bomb, and a tsunami, if you aren't prepared you might as well bend over, grab your ankles and kiss your ass goodbye. Patricia, do what you have to do to make certain you and your family are safe; especially this knucklehead you married."

"Thank you, Richard. That's why I invited these guys over. They were very helpful bringing the reality of the danger to my attention."

"My plan will work," Scott called out over his shoulder as he left the room.

Scott's office walls were covered with pictures of the shipwreck. Richard walked over to the window overlooking the ocean. It too, was covered with multi-colored pictures of the wreckage. "Incredible, how did you get this kind of resolution?" he asked.

"They're high-definition, computer-generated images from, sonar and radar data run through my processor," David said. "Pretty impressive, if I do say myself."

"This is the sail of the Nazi sub," Scott said, holding up an 8X10 color image. "Believe it or not, this picture was taken through three feet of silt and *Fat Boy* found it from the magnetic signature of the U-boat metal alloy you provided."

"Ain't technology great," Richard beamed. "The analysis I gave David was in captured documents. We're damn lucky the Russians didn't end up with all of it. It feels good that I could help."

Scott continued, "The analysis told us it was the same alloy, but we wouldn't have had this, without Fat Boy." Scott held up another print. It showed the silt blown away and the U-2500 designation.

Richard grabbed the print from him and stared at it, shaking his head in disbelief. "Promise me I can be part of bringing it up. My preliminary research said a U-boat with that number never existed. This could add a new chapter to the history books."

"Don't get your hopes up," David said, "it's resting two-miles deep on a ledge in a trench that apparently doesn't have a bottom. If it's disturbed it could be lost forever. It's too deep to bring up anyway."

"According to the German records we captured, there is no U-2500. The first Type Twenty-one U-boat was designated U-2501. This number is missing from the records. This is a mystery that needs to be solved. Type Twenty-one U-boats were not introduced until late in the war. It was incredibly advanced compared to the other underwater boats of that time. Why it's here is a huge mystery." Richard was as excited as any of them had ever seen. "What about the rest of it?" Richard asked. "Can we bring it up?"

"It's in pretty bad shape," Scott said. He pointed to a picture on the window. "It looks like it took a major blow. There's speculation it was rammed by a Merchant ship, but we can't verify that without a lot more information."

Richard looked at it closely. "This damage was caused by a major explosion. No collision could have done this much damage."

"Not even a ship loaded with eighteen-hundred barrels of aviation fuel?" Scott asked.

Richard shook his head.

"The mystery deepens," David said.

Later that Afternoon

Scott, David, and Richard were on the deck having beers and enjoying the weather when Patricia appeared with

Jason Trask, his wife Carlene, son Gil Trask, and Danna Collier. "Boys," Patricia said. "These are the scientists I was telling you about at breakfast." She introduced them all around.

Scott reached in a cooler and pulled out some beers. "Can I interest any of you in a beverage. I have several brands of beer. The wine is in the kitchen."

"I think I'll try the wine," Carlene said, taking a beer and handing it to her husband.

Danna took a light-beer and Gil helped himself to a Heineken.

"You have a beautiful place," Gil said.

"I built it before Patricia and I were engaged. I think it was the reason she finally agreed to date me. Patricia says you are all geologists."

Carlene said, "I'm retired, but the rest of them are still out there saving the world."

Danna gave Gil a look. He made a gesture of zipping his lips.

"I have a lot of respect for geologists," Scott said. "My job would be impossible without the work you have done mapping the ocean floor."

"Patricia says you found a ship right out there," Danna said.

"Scott's a treasure hunter," David chimed in. "It's right up there with a professional gambler. He gets lucky every once in a while."

"That must be exciting," Danna said.

"Patricia says you think you found a German submarine," Gil said.

Scott looked surprised. "I'm trying to keep it quiet."

Richard interjected, "I learned when I was running NSA that it's impossible to keep a secret if you telephone, telegraph or tell-a-woman."

"What's a telegraph?" David asked.

"All right, enough of the old people jokes," Richard said. "Just because I reached the big six-oh, it doesn't mean I'm over the hill."

"He was alive when the Dead Sea was just sick," Scott said. He paused a moment in reflection. "I know it's not politically correct to be kidding Richard about his age, but we can't help ourselves. He's such an easy target."

Jason said, "We don't talk about age at our house either. Carlene thinks I should have retired ten years ago."

"See Scott," Richard said, "One day you'll be sorry you ever kidded anyone about their age. Life has a way of getting even with you."

Carlene touched Danna lightly on the arm. "I'm going to go join the women on the other end of the deck. You want to come with me?"

Danna hesitated for a moment. She wanted to stay and hear about the discovery, but she left with Carlene.

"Cute, Richard. Now you chased the women away," Scott said. "Why don't you fill the newcomers in on the historical significance of the find."

"And the area of the discovery," Jason said. "Gil and I were discussing that section of ocean a few days ago. Gil thinks there may be an undiscovered fault in the area. I understand it was pretty deep where you found the sub."

"Part of it is in a fissure," Scott said, "so deep we couldn't see the bottom from our sonar soundings. We were mainly interested in the conning tower that is resting on a ledge about two-miles down. No telling how deep the ocean is right there."

"Most of the seafloor over fifty miles out hasn't been scanned with modern equipment," Gil said. "The latest technology can map down to nineteen-thousand feet. I'm pretty sure what you are looking at is less than two miles deep."

"My equipment is accurate," David assured them. "The tower is resting on a ledge in a fissure and it has to be more than three miles deep. Have you got maps later than the 1965 NOOA charts we're working from?" David asked. "It doesn't even show the crevice."

"I'll have to take your word for it," Gil said. "We have some charts as late as last year, but most of the work recently has been closer to shore. Our grant is to chart Oregon waters. That limits us to three miles out. Any chance you could share some of the information with me?"

"You know I wouldn't mind having you look at some data we have and give us your opinion," Scott said. "We want to keep this find quiet, though. It may have historical significance and we don't want to be fighting with the Government over whether we have the right to be diving on a wreck that took place in World War Two; at least, until we know what we're looking at."

"As long as you're beyond Oregon territorial waters," Gil said. "What does the Government care?"

"International territory extends out two-hundred nautical miles. Any economic activity inside of that is Federal or state regulated. Someone always has their hand in the till."

"You put in all the effort to find something they didn't even know was there," Gil said. "Why would the Government want any more than their share of the tax on the profit?"

"I agree with Gil," Richard said. "If there isn't any money to be made, you probably won't get any attention from anyone but a few history buffs."

"Call me paranoid," Scott said. "Don't forget the families of shipwreck victims, and Germany; they may be against disrupting one of their ships lost in the war. And if we find out the U-boat sank an unarmed Merchant ship the families could sue Germany for restitution. From the record, the war with Germany was already over. Nothing is simple now days."

David took a sip of his wine. "As you can see, recovering treasure, whether historical or the real thing, has political, as well as economic considerations. We spend millions researching and then have to worry about others making a claim on what we found. Nothing under the ocean is as simple as it seems on the surface. Pun intended."

"I understand why you want to keep it a secret." Gil looked at his father. "I'd still like to see the area of the ocean floor where you found the wreck."

"Come on," Scott said. "The coals on the barbeque have a few minutes before they're ready. Maybe you can help solve the mystery."

"Scott, where are you headed?" Patricia asked, seeing the men heading back into the house.

"We're checking out the shipwreck," Gil said.

Danna asked Patricia, "Is that just a guy thing or are women welcome, too?"

Scott overheard. "Everyone is welcome," he said. He glared at Patricia. "It seems the cat's out of the bag anyway."

"What did he mean by that," Fay asked.

"I think I goofed," Patricia said. "I might have mentioned Scott and David had found a shipwreck, but Danna said she heard about it and there was an article in the paper the other day, at least an account of a ship that went missing back in the war. How's that for coincidence?"

"What do you mean it was in the paper?" Fay asked.

"Here, I'll show you," Patricia said, "I saved it for Scott." She handed it to Fay.

"David is so secretive about his projects," Fay said.

"At first I thought it was about the ship Scott had found, but it's an historical piece," Patricia said. "It's about a ship they think was sunk by a Japanese submarine. I don't know what all the fuss is about, anyway," Patricia added. "Scott found the sub a week before the article showed up in the paper. The two are not connected."

"I hope not," Fay said. "David is a stickler for keeping things secret."

"You don't know the half of it," Janet said, overhearing them. "Try being married to the head of the NSA. Richard and I told each other everything until he got that job. Now we never talk."

"But he's retired now," Patricia said. "You're together most of the time."

"Thank God for David's call," Janet said. "I think this trip is lifting Richard out of his depression. Since he retired, it's like he's given up on life."

Until now, Danna had stood close by listening to Patricia, Fay, and Janet talking about their past. The newspaper article Patricia gave Fay was the same one she had read. Maybe there was a story in this after all. "If you will excuse me, I'm joining the men," Danna said.

"We'll go with you," Patricia said. "No telling what those guys are up to."

Patricia, Fay, Janet, and Carlene followed Danna into Scott's office.

The men were crowded around the window of photos.

"Wow," Scott said. "I think this is the most people I've ever had in this room at one time." He pointed to a map taped to his window. "Most of what we've discovered is in a five-mile stretch of ocean in this area nearly sixty miles west of Cape Perpetua. Fifty-seven miles due west from where we are standing, to be exact."

Danna's eyes lit up. "That's the area Gil and I were talking about just the other day. If that slope gives way in an earthquake it could produce a hell of a wave."

"A tsunami?" Patricia asked.

"A tsunami," Gil said. "But it would take a pretty good earthquake in that region to cause a landslide, besides we don't have all the data to predict that."

"So, you decided to invite us all over to a tsunami watch party," Janet said, joking. "I thought it was for fireworks on the beach." She raised her eyebrows. "Or maybe treasure hunting?"

"There's nothing to worry about," Gil said, shaking his head at the excitement. He scanned the faces in the room and sneered in a menacing tone. "Unless there is an earthquake, of course."

"Then take a look at this," Scott said. "David where's that video you were showing me?"

David brought up the video showing

the small earthquake and the movement of the sand down the slope.

"You're lucky that mountainside didn't let go," Gil said.

"He's kidding," Gil's mother said.

"Maybe a little," Gil conceded. "If we thought there was undue risk, we would have declined the invitation. To be honest, I checked the Tsunami Zone map." He looked at Patricia and nodded, "like you asked me to, and you are sitting pretty high above the ocean, well out of the tsunami risk area."

Danna made her way to the window and studied the pictures taped to it.

Carlene was a petite woman with a hint of a southern accent. She had worked beside her husband for several years and for the USGS even longer and was still thinking about an earthquake. "Major earthquakes in this part of Oregon are extremely rare," she said. "You can't go through life worrying about such things."

"Have you identified the other ship as the *Carissa*?" Danna asked, still looking at the pictures.

"Not yet," David said. "We have new equipment and are looking for anything significant that might positively identify it. As you can see the bow of the ship, where you would normally see the name, is a tangled mass of corroded metal.   No identifying marks are evident."

"So, if you can't raise it and there's no physical treasure, why spend the money to investigate it further?" Janet asked. "What's all the excitement about?"

"It's the submarine that has our interest," David said. "I think we'll at least try to answer the question of why it's there."

"I would like to know why *Carissa* sank," Danna said. "My great-grandfather was on that ship." She was thinking about restitution. If the submarine caused the death of her great-grandfather, wouldn't the family be able to sue for wrongful death? Her mind was racing with ideas. "Is there any evidence the submarine torpedoed it?"

Scott eyed Danna with concern. He had completely misread her interest in the wreck. "I'm sorry for your loss. We'll try to be as respectful as we can. As of now we haven't seen any remains."

"And like we said earlier," David said, "there's not much value in bringing anything to the surface. We can mark the GPS location of the wreck and treat it as a grave site. World War Two historians may want to investigate it further, but there's no value in us doing much more."

"I want to know why a German

submarine that wasn't supposed to be in the Pacific Ocean and a Merchant ship are part of the same debris field," Richard said. "If we can solve that puzzle, I'll be satisfied."

"And if we get to eat before the fireworks start tonight, I'll be happy," Scott said. "I hate to break this up, but I need to get the meat on the grill before the coals die."

Over dinner on the deck overlooking the ocean, Gil turned to Danna on his right. "I understand your interest in the shipwreck. A family member on a ship that's been missing for almost eighty years, it must be exciting, and sad at the same time, to think it may have been found."

"I was more interested in going on a date with you," she said, coyly. "I like the way you explain things in less technical terms so lay people can understand."

Gil wasn't buying the compliment as sincere. "You mean, in a way that doesn't insult the intelligence of our hosts."

She shrugged. "See, that's what I mean."

"When are we scheduled to get eyes on the sub again?" Richard asked. "If we can see what's inside, it may provide some clues to our questions."

David said, "I think it would be more help if you stayed here and continued looking for info on the U-boat. You said you couldn't find a record it was ever commissioned. Why do we have one off our coast?"

"And what makes you think I can find anything more?" Richard argued.

"You're the one with the NSA database at your disposal. Are there war records the public isn't aware of? German messages or Japanese for that matter? You said it yourself, this is a real mystery."

"I'll make you a deal. Let me go out with you tomorrow and I'll pull as many strings as I can to get more information. Frankly, I think the answers to our questions are inside that submarine."

"I need him to come along," Scott said. "Another person who can drive a ship will be a big help. We agreed to keep the crew to a minimum."

"Why don't we all go?" Patricia chimed in. "If you insist on working over the weekend, let's just extend the party."

"We do have a long holiday," Gil said.

"Carlene and I have plans," Jason said. "We have a class from OSU meeting us at the observatory tomorrow. You folks have fun on your cruise." He got up from the table. I hope you'll excuse us not staying for the fireworks, but we have a long drive. Thank you for your hospitality. Scott, I hope you and Richard get the answers you are searching for. You know as well as anyone the sea doesn't give up its secrets easily."

Scott stood and shook Jason's hand. "Sorry to see you leave. Maybe I can visit the observatory sometime and you can show me what you do."

"Anytime. Be glad to give you a tour."

The others watched as Jason and Carlene left.

Scott glared at Patricia. "About going out on the ship," Scott said. "I don't think—"

"I'm not doing anything tomorrow," Danna butted in, looking at Scott. "Should I pack for an overnight trip?"

"Just for the day," Patricia said. "I'm sure the boys could use a day off, before going back to treasure hunting."

"Hey, don't I have a say in this," Scott protested. "*Hunter* is a research and recovery vessel, not a party boat. And Patricia, I thought after the trip to the South Pacific you never wanted to get on a boat again."

Patricia made a pouty face. "I

never get to see you anymore. Maybe it will give me some ideas for my new book."

"Give me a break," Scott said.

"Well, it is research," Patricia said. "Lighten up, it will be fun." She looked at Fay. "Isn't that right."

Scott knew it was hopeless. "I'll let Don know to pack more food. I hope you're not expecting free drinks and a dance band." Don was his first mate.

"Free drinks and wine," Patricia said. "I'll bet we could find a band if you want one."

"No!" Scott said.

"Wine won't be a problem," David said. "I have my own collection on board."

Chapter 8

July 5, 6:00 a.m., Newport, Oregon

The dock at Yaquina Bay was shrouded in fog as Scott and his crew prepared *Hunter* for the one-day voyage. As of now, none of the guests had arrived. The sun, filtered by the fog, was nothing but a white orb, and barely visible. Scott watched his three crew members loading supplies.

He had a lot of confidence in his crew. They had all been with him from his early treasure hunting days before he partnered with David. Now that he was a full-blown business, they had assumed rolls suited to their individual skills. It was a far cry from the early days aboard the first boat he called *Hunter*. That was a forty-foot fishing trawler converted into a treasure recovery ship. He had purchased and refurbished it after his second tour as a SEAL. In those days everyone was required to know the other person's job. When David came aboard and they partnered, he was treated as an extra hand and expected to pitch in. The first boat had been replaced by a larger, more technically advanced vessel they could actually call a ship. Each crew member had a specific assignment.

His first mate was Don Blanchard. He was in his late twenties, a college dropout turned fisherman. Scott had hired Blanchard for double the state minimum hourly wage and a small percentage of any treasure they found. Don had proved himself a capable pilot and Scott trusted him to do most of the navigation once they were out at sea. On the last significant find, Don had been well-rewarded and had even bought his own boat, and tried treasure hunting on his own, but he didn't have the research skills or the capital and soon gave up the hunt for treasure on his own. He never stopped working for Scott whenever *Hunter* was at sea and had never disclosed the side business to his boss.

His engineer was Tad Davis, a short, stocky, ruggedly handsome sort with jet-black hair and deep brown eyes the ladies found irresistible, if you believed his flamboyant accounts of his late-night interludes. Scott hired him because he was a top-notch diesel mechanic. He could get into places none of the other crew cared to go and was at home in the bowels of a ship with the diesel fumes and greasy floor. In the early days he had saved Scott and the crew from tragedy when they experienced engine failure at the worst possible moment, coming in over the bar. Even the Coast Guard was impressed with his quick analysis of the problem and how quickly he got the engines started again. For that, Scott told Tad he had a job for as long as he was in business. Tad could also drive the ship if they were in open water, but spent most of his time in the engine room below decks.

The third regular member of Scott's crew was Bobby Ford. When Scott had originally hired Bobby, his resume had sold him as experienced at sea, but it was soon evident Bobby's skills were more suited for the kitchen. Bobby was befuddled easily when faced with a problem, but he was an excellent cook and kept Scott and the crew well fed. They called him Cookie among themselves, but didn't dare use the nickname to his face. If they did, who knows what could end up in their food?

The rest of the crew were run-of-the-mill seamen with various levels of skill, all temporary employees he picked up from time to time from a local labor pool. Today Scott had three additional crew to help with the guests. He still wasn't too keen on the idea of having so many on board when he was trying to make the most out of the favorable weather, but he had to admit, he and Patricia hadn't spent enough time together lately, and he was willing to put up with a little inconvenience, if it would make her happy.

"The ship's ready, Skipper," Don said. "I've already notified the Coast Guard we'll want them standing by when we take her over the bar."

"Thanks, Don. We'll get underway as soon as the guests arrive."

"They're supposed to be here by now." Don said, checking his watch. "We're about to miss the tide."

"I'll call Patricia and see what the holdup is."

A few minutes later, Scott watched from the top of the gangplank, as Richard Nendel called up, "permission to come aboard, sir?" Scott laughed and waved Richard and Janet aboard. Gil and Danna were close behind, and when all were aboard, Scott showed them to the cabins. The two Captain's Quarters were more lavish and larger than the crew cabins, something David had insisted on when they had the ship outfitted. Patricia and Scott shared one of the Captain's Quarters, David and Fay the other. Scott had tried to offer his room to Richard and Janet, but Richard refused, insisting he was a crew member, not the senior officer. When the lavish quarters were first constructed, Scott had argued against them, but David had the money to do whatever he liked and Scott knew it was fruitless arguing with him. If David wanted luxurious quarters for Fay and him, on the rare occasion they were aboard, it was his call. The rest of the guests and crew had smaller cabins, each equipped with two single bunks. Not the best accommodations if you wanted to have a romantic getaway.

Scott had insisted the ship be built for work, not pleasure. *Hunter* was a research vessel with a few of the amenities of a pleasure boat, but way down the ladder from a yacht and certainly not decked out like a cruise ship. Originally, David had wanted to equip the ship like a luxury yacht, but Scott had convinced him it would be difficult to get serious work done if the crew thought they were on a pleasure boat. Scott was willing to forgo some creature comforts and spend the money on the latest in navigation and electronics technology for operating efficiency and safety. In a pinch, *Hunter* could virtually pilot itself.

The Coast Guard was on standby with a rescue craft at the ready when *Hunter* approached the channel leading out to the ocean. It wasn't a requirement that they be there, but Scott considered it important to have them available when he had passengers aboard. During this part of the voyage, Scott relieved Don and took over control. Don, David and Richard were standing next to him as he powered through the waves. Fortunately, the fog had lifted and visibility had increased to a mile. All his attention was on keeping the ship in the channel. Large ocean swells entered the channel and crashed in a spectacular water show on both sides of the ship. At this moment Scott's complete focus was on getting the ship out to sea without incident.

In one of the cabins below deck, Danna and a crew member were having a heated conversation. "How come you never mentioned your grandfather was aboard the *Carissa* and was lost at sea?" Bobby Ford asked.

Bobby was a tall lanky man in his early thirties. His eyes shifted nervously as if he was watching for any other passengers who might see them talking.

"Why would I? And it wasn't my grandfather, it was my great-grandfather," Danna hissed. "I didn't find out until yesterday I would even be here. If I would have known you were on board, I wouldn't have come along. I don't want you telling the others we have a past, Gil might get nervous."

"Nervous? About what?"

"About us. He doesn't know I was married before, and I don't want you screwing things up like you always do."

"I've cleaned myself up. Everything I've done since we split, it's been for you. I was hurting; you didn't have to divorce me."

"Do me a favor and skip the theatrics. You didn't have to do drugs; besides I have my own problems now. I lost my job. I have to move away."

"Pardon me if I'm not surprised. You always thought you were better than everyone else. Who did you screw this time?"

"I mean it. Keep your distance from me."

"It's a small ship. Our paths are bound to cross."

"So help me, Bobby, you screw this up, I'll throw you overboard."

"You always did look cute when you were angry. How about I just tell your boyfriend right now? Lay it all out on the table. Danna Collier was once Danna Ford. Was it so bad you couldn't even keep my name?"

The ship hit a huge wave head-on, causing Bobby to lose his footing. He lurched toward Danna, who managed to move out of the way, allowing him to hit the deck, hard. She grabbed the nearest thing she could find and hit him on the head. Unfortunately, it was a pillow and he got up laughing.

"Sorry, Princess, you never were a good fighter." He left the cabin in a hurry. As he turned down the corridor he was suddenly face to face with Gil. "Be careful, she's not who you think she is," Bobby said, angerly.

"What?"

"Ask your girlfriend." Bobby left Gil with a befuddled look on his face.

Gil stopped at Danna's cabin door and started to knock, hesitated, and returned to his cabin.

On the bridge, Richard watched intently as Scott maneuvered the ship through the narrow channel and into the rough water where the river currents mixed with the Pacific waves. On either side of the ship, a wall of rocks provided a breakwater extending a quarter-mile out into the ocean. "I taught him everything he knows," Richard said, as they hit the darker water beyond the breakers.

Scott shook his head.

David scoffed.

"Don't look at me like that." Richard said. "It's true."

"I was wondering why he knows so little," David said. "Now, I understand."

Scott laughed. "I ought to have each of you walk the plank." Scott got on the radio and thanked the Coast Guard for standing by. "I'll take it from here. Have a safe trip back."

"Roger, *Hunter*. See you on the return trip," came the reply.

Scott handed the helm over to Don.

Patricia knocked on Danna's cabin door.

"Come in," Danna answered. She was still distraught over her confrontation with Bobby.

Patricia opened the door and stuck her head inside. "The girls are gathering in the kitchen for tea," Patricia announced. "You're welcome to join us."

"Thanks, I'll be along in a few minutes." She needed to get to Gil before Bobby ruined everything.

"Are you all right?" Patricia asked.

Danna looked up. "I'm fine. Maybe just a little sea sick."

"I can get you some Dramamine."

Danna raised her hand. "I'll be fine. I just need to rest a moment."

In the "War Room", as Scott liked to call the conference room on the ship, were charts and monitors that allowed them to map the wreckage as the underwater search vehicle worked its way through a preprogrammed set of instructions. Scott was showing Gil, Richard, and David some footage that had been taken a few days earlier. "I agree with Richard. I'd give my left nut to get inside that U-boat," Scott said.

"Just to set the record straight," Richard said, "I didn't promise to give up any part of my anatomy. I'm just curious."

"Then I think I can help," David said. "We have some new technology."

"In that case, I take back the left-nut comment," Scott said.

"What have you got?" Richard asked.

David brought up a video on the large screen. "This is file footage on *Rover X-2*, the Navy designation for *Fat Boy*. They weren't amused at my nickname. I put the video together for a specific presentation to the Navy, but it will show you something we might be able to take advantage of. Scott, you haven't seen this yet, but I think you'll agree, we can make use of *Fat Boy's* added features."

"Stop the sales pitch," Scott said. "None of us are buyers. Get on with the show."

David started to fast forward through some of the footage and stopped with a nose-on view of Rover. It looked like a bright orange ball on the screen.

"Looks like a beach ball," Richard said.

David ignored him and continued with his pitch. "What I am about to show you has to remain in this room. The Navy hasn't seen this yet and I want them to get the full impact when I show it to them."

"Okay, enough drama," Scott said. "Get on with the program."

David started the video again. "If we can find an opening in the hull at least twelve inches in diameter, I can launch this AUD. It's less than eight inches in diameter and can operate for up to thirty minutes. It's programmed to memorize every move it makes and when it runs low on battery power it returns back to the mothership. In this case *Fat Boy*. The information it gathers is then relayed to the computers in this room. I designed it to search for bodies, but it will record anything it encounters. The one drawback is it can't be guided."

A port near the nose of *Fat Boy* slid open and the robot glided out.

"AUD stands for Autonomous Underwater Drone, I assume," Richard said. "So, it works without outside input. What keeps it from roaming off target?"

"It's not without a brain," David answered. "It can be preprogrammed to stay at a certain depth and not wander far from its launch point. It keeps in constant communication with *Fat Boy*."

"What keeps it from getting stuck," Scott asked, "if it's wandering about on its own?"

"Active Acoustic Positioning, or AAP. It constantly sends out soundwaves in all directions which tell it where obstacles are located. Similar to the echoes a bat uses to keep from running into objects. Watch this." David forwarded the video showing the AUD maneuvering through the fuselage of a downed underwater aircraft. The tiny disk-shaped device looked a lot like a Frisbee, slightly thicker and about the same diameter. It hovered at times and zipped around avoiding contact with objects, hesitating just long enough to snap an image before moving again.

"To save battery life, it snaps a digital picture rather than continuous video, but it can store five-thousand frames."

"So, it takes pictures. Does it know what it's looking for?" Richard asked.

David smiled. "I haven't gotten that far yet. Maybe the next model can store an image and search for it, kind of like facial recognition. Unfortunately, the pictures this one takes will probably be ninety percent useless."

"You mentioned the Navy using your devices?" Gil said. "The Marine Science Center could use this technology right now. I think there is an uncharted fault in this area that could trigger an underwater landslide."

"I'm sorry, Gil," David said. "I can't talk about other uses. It's still classified."

David paused for a moment to gather

his thoughts. "Like I said, right now I've designed this for underwater recovery missions, but the Government has several uses that are classified. I've had inquiries from nearly every branch of government including Homeland Security."

"He knows what they are, but if he told you, he'd have to kill you." Richard joked.

"Don't mind him," Scott said. "His jokes are even older than he is." He turned to the others. "We'll be making our first dive right after lunch. Lunch is in the mess hall. For those who don't know military speak, that's the dining room." Scott smiled. "After lunch, we'll be meeting on middeck near the helipad and hopefully get some work done on this trip."

Chapter 9

Aboard *Hunter*

Bobby Ford had worked for Scott off-and-on over several years. Since the season for treasure recovery in Oregon coastal waters was limited to about four months a year, his employment had been temporary and intermittent, but it was the best he could do considering his rocky past.

In the short time he and Danna had been married, he had dropped out of collage after experimenting with drugs, leading to full-blown addiction to methamphetamine. He had tried several times to kick the habit, but the drugs had always won. The marriage fell into chaos and that was the bottom for Bobby. He entered a rehab facility and, shortly after treatment landed the job with Scott. For this he was grateful.

As the ship's cook, Bobby was free to stock the kitchen and design the menu. He liked cooking for the crew members. Their tastes were pretty basic and they never complained. Today lunch was rib-eye steak, baked potato, and a tossed dinner salad.

The conversation over lunch was an eclectic mix of subjects. Richard was anxious to see inside the U-boat and speculated on what they would discover.

Gil was interested in the location of the conning tower and whether the fissure Scott described as bottomless was the fault he had suspected was at the base of the underwater mountain.

Patricia continued to pick Gil's brain concerning her tsunami evacuation plan.

Janet quizzed Patricia about the coastal community where she and Scott lived. She liked the weather and hoped they might relocate. She had finally had enough of the hectic life around Washington DC, and thought a move back to Oregon would be good for Richard.

Danna was quiet. She listened politely to the conversations; all the time preoccupied with the thought that Bobby may have spoken to Gil. The last few hours Gil had hardly spoken to her. She also saw her world falling apart. She was on a ship with people who didn't seem to have a care in the world. Why would they? They seemed to have everything, the perfect life. Everywhere she looked she saw what she would never obtain. It wasn't fair.

"Danna, what do you think about the possibility of a tsunami?" Patricia asked, trying to engage her in the conversation. "You work with Gil, you must have given it a lot of thought."

"If you knew what I do, it would

scare the hell out of you," Danna said. "We have just started to understand subduction events and their frequency. I've just found out they happen over three times as often as previously thought, and this area is at risk for a non-subduction related tsunami."

"That's the first time I've heard that term," Patricia said.

Danna continued, "Earthquakes cause tsunamis. It's well known that subduction earthquakes are more likely to cause a tsunami because they happen under the ocean and displace a lot of water, but there are instances of underwater landslides and even above water landslides that have resulted in tsunamis. Some as large as a subduction related seismic wave. Off our coast there is a mountain range with a slope that could give way, resulting in such an event." She raised her eyebrows. "I've asked for the equipment to research it further, but been told they can't get to it for another eighteen months."

"I'm sure they would free the necessary equipment if they were in agreement that it is as dire as you say it is," Fay said.

"I guess we'll never know," Danna said. "They won't believe the risk is there until all the facts are in and they won't release the equipment until nearshore mapping is completed. If it was me, I'd move to higher ground."

"Why didn't Gil tell me this?" Patricia asked.

"Because Gil didn't want to frighten you."

"Maybe it would be better if Richard and I locate to San Diego," Janet said, looking at Fay.

"You sound like you and Richard are seriously considering taking the offer to join the company," Fay said. "David will be thrilled."

"So will Scott," Patricia added, welcoming the change in the conversation.

Bobby, Tad and Don were at a table away from the guests having lunch. The ship had reached the rendezvous point and was holding its position on autopilot.

"It's going to be a pretty lean winter for us," Don said. "I'm beginning to wonder if this kick Scott is on is worth it."

"You mean, searching for wrecks with only historical significance?" Tad asked. "I've been wondering the same thing. How are we going to make any money diving on World War Two shipwrecks? There are hundreds of other wrecks along the coast that are known to have gold and silver aboard."

"Guys like us can't win," Don said. "I tried locating a wreck that was a shipment of gold from Chili during the Great Depression. The equipment to find it is way too expensive for the little guy to afford. I nearly went bust. Guys like Stafford and Tanner have made it impossible for the little guy to win."

"Scott has been good to us," Bobby said. "I didn't hear you complaining when we brought up the gold from *Isabella*."

"You made my point. That ship had gold on it. What we are spending our time on right now won't net us a cent. Unless Tanner gets his act together, I'm going to look for something that can give me year-around wages."

"We could tell Scott we need more money if he's not going to search for treasure," Bobby said. "I don't want to spoil the best job I ever had. We're eating steak and hardly breaking a sweat. Not many other jobs can offer you that."

"I agree," Tad said. "I could use some extra cash, but unlike the two of you I get to work when *Hunter* is docked. It will be a lean year, but maybe next year we'll hit it big. Life's a bitch, get used to it."

The wind had picked up and the sea was choppy as the guests assembled on middeck to watch the launch of *Fat Boy*.

"This is mostly boring for the next half-hour," David announced as the crane lowered the torpedo-shaped object into the water. "Once it's in the water, I suggest we all grab our favorite beverage and retire to the War Room where we can view in real-time what it sees down there."

"A man after my own heart," Richard said. "I know there's a bottle of Scotch with my name on it. Anyone else like Scotch?"

"Richard!" Janet said. "You know what the doctor said."

"He said I should cut back to one a day."

Janet lifted her eyebrows.

"If I'm only allowed one, it's gonna be the good stuff," Richard said. "Scott, do you still have that bottle of single malt I sent you for Christmas?"

"I think there's at least one drink left," Scott said.

"Damn doctor wants to take away all the good things in life. I can't smoke anymore, drink anymore, and God knows with a prostate the size of an orange, I can't chase women anymore, what the hell is there to live for?"

"He's exaggerating about chasing women," Janet said. "He wouldn't know what to do if he caught one."

"Is that right, Richard?" Scott

asked.

Richard gave his wife a look and smirked. "Remember that thing we did on the boat in the South Pacific?"

"Richard," Janet gave him a stern look. "That's not a conversation we should have right here."

Richard got the message and so did his wife.

After most of the guests had retired to the War Room, Fay was still at the deck rail looking at the spot where *Fat Boy* had disappeared. Danna approached her. "Patricia said you're a marine biologist. I helped chart some of these waters. You know we're sitting nearly on top of the Cascadia Subduction Zone?"

"You told us at lunch," Fay said. "What got you interested in geology?"

"Oceanography seemed a good field for a woman to get into at the time. San Diego has a huge marine community. You don't know of any good jobs down your way, do you?"

"Oceanography? I could ask around. Are you seriously looking to change locations?"

"If the opportunity was right," Danna said. She looked out over the ocean and said wistfully, "My great-grandfather was lost at sea somewhere near here. Scott may have found it."

"I overheard they may have discovered the ship your great-grandfather was on," Fay said. "It must be difficult to know you might see his final resting place in a few minutes."

"The truth is, I'm excited to link something physical with the family lore that surrounded his disappearance."

"Family lore?"

"Well, you know how stories get exaggerated through the years. Everyone who dies is suddenly the best person in the world, no matter what they did while they were alive."

"Do I detect a bit of cynicism?"

Danna smiled. "If you only knew." She put her hand on Fay's arm. "We should find a quiet place and trade war stories of what it's like to be a woman working in a male dominated world."

Fay laughed. "David is an angel and I don't feel like I've been dominated in the least."

"I mean, at work. I hear you taught at UC Berkley. Women have been suppressed for so long we can't even recognize when we're being stepped on."

"You sound like you've been hurt."

"If Patricia hadn't pushed Scott into agreeing to bring us along, we'd all be onshore discussing dishwashers or her boring romance novels. Why do we have to be excluded from the real action? What are the men keeping from us?"

Janet saw Fay was becoming uncomfortable with the conversation, even though she had been out of earshot. She approached Fay and Danna. "The boys say the real action is taking place in the War Room and we're all invited."

Danna sneered. "Tell the boys we'll be right there, if we're really welcome." She turned and left Janet with a confused look on her face.

"What's eating her?" Janet asked.

"Must have been something she had for lunch. I think one of the men may have pissed her off."

"That would be Richard," Janet said. "I saw them arguing earlier. He hasn't bought into the women's movement, or political correctness, for that matter."

"Surely, she didn't take Richard seriously," Fay said.

"It had to do with the war."

"Which war?"

"You'll have to ask him. David and Scott were there. I just caught the tail end of it. That girl has a problem."

"With men in general, I think," Fay added.

"You want to join them in the War Room or retire to the lounge and treat this voyage like the vacation it was supposed to be."

"Lead the way to the lounge," Fay said grabbing both arms and rubbing them. "It's getting cold out here."

Danna was the only female in the War Room. Everyone was gathered around the large monitor with the exception of David, who was sitting in front of his laptop at the conference table. She stood close to Gil, hoping to get a moment where she could talk to him. He seemed distant. She was certain Bobby had already opened his big mouth.

"There it is," David said, looking up at the monitor.

Richard raised his glasses and studied the screen. "Can you zoom in on that?"

"You see something?" David asked.

Gil and Danna were standing behind Richard and Scott looking at the same screen. Danna grabbed Gil's hand. "That's the submarine. They found it. They really found it!"

"I thought you'd be more interested in the *Carissa*," Gil said.

"Well, if they found the submarine, the other ship must be *Carissa*."

Gil was more interested in the geology of the area. "You notice how unstable that shelf is. Sediment seems to be drifting down constantly."

"There's a deep channel running along the subduction zone. I think they're right on top of it. There must be strong currents stirring things up," Danna said. "Or, do you think that could be the fault?"

Gil shrugged and uncoupled his hand from Danna. "There's no telling for sure. It's a pretty restricted field of view. The drifting sediment could be ground movement." Gill added. "Is it possible the sediment on that slope has reached it's angle of repose?"

Scott overheard Gil. He turned around and asked, "angle of repose?"

"The critical angle where nothing else can build up. Every bulk material has its own angle. Check out a pile of sand or gravel, round rocks form at a different angle from jagged rocks. Popped corn is different from wheat. It appears that slope is at the limit for the sand that's built up on it."

"Interesting," Scott said. "What's the significance to us?"

"If it gives way, you'll have a landslide that will wash the entire wreck into the abyss."

"It would be a shame," Scott said. "But there's no hope of getting that piece of history to the surface, anyway."

"You're not considering raising

it?"

"Too expensive."

"Holy shit, that is definitely a Type Twenty-one," Nendel said, looking at the image on the screen. "When you showed me the picture with the U-2500 designation, I was skeptical, but this confirms it. According to captured war records there were only one-hundred-eighteen built. Some historians have speculated that if the Type Twenty-one would have been built two years earlier, Hitler would have won the war in the Atlantic."

"History is filled with if's," David said. "Thank God that didn't happen."

"What makes the Type Twenty-one so special?" Scott asked.

"At the time, it was the most advanced submarine ever built. Years after the war, our nuclear subs used some of its advanced features. It ran nearly silent underwater, had three times the running distance underwater of its predecessors and the six torpedo tubes could be loaded in less time than it took to load one torpedo in earlier class subs. If they would have had this boat at the start of the war, all of Europe including Great Britain, might be speaking German today."

"It still doesn't explain what it was doing in the Pacific," David said.

"Unfortunately, like the Titanic, all we can do is record the pieces of the puzzle and hope to fit them together," Scott said.

David looked over at Richard. "Have you seen enough of the tower?"

"Sure, let's see the rest of it."

"There's a long shelf along the edge of the drop-off. Most of the wreckage is strewn along it," David said.

"David," Gil spoke up. "I don't want to interfere with your work, but is there a chance we'll be able to identify the other ship?"

"That's right, Danna's great-grandfather's ship," David said. "We can search for more identifying markings, but we haven't been able to find a name on the bow. Scott, what else should we be looking for?"

"It was hauling barrels of fuel. We should see some evidence of those barrels if they are not rusted away. I couldn't find anything else in my research that would help. An instrument, or perhaps the ships bell with the ship's name engraved on it would be a positive ID, but with the depth of the silt, that's a long shot."

"Like looking for a needle in a haystack," Richard said.

"It's okay," Danna said. "You can

keep searching the submarine for clues. It seems to be the bigger story."

Bobby Ford entered the War Room with a tray of drinks. He eyed Gil and Danna, avoided them, and set the tray on the table. He turned to leave.

"Just a minute, son," Richard said. "I want a Scotch on the rocks and make it the good stuff." He handed Bobby his empty glass.

Bobby removed the drinks from the tray and placed them on the table. "Anyone else?"

"I'll have a Heineken," Gil said.

"And a glass of Chardonnay," Danna said.

Bobby picked up the tray and walked out. The War Room had a bar in it. *Why can't they fix their own drinks?* He thought.

"Gil," Scott said. "If these two ships collided would you expect their remains to be strewn over this large of an area? I guess what I'm asking concerns the ocean currents in this area. Would they scatter the wreckage over this much area?"

Gil stepped up to the monitor. "The underwater currents are quite strong in this area. They move nearly parallel to the shore. I wouldn't be surprised if pieces were carried downstream for a considerable distance, but the wreckage looks more like an explosion to me, I don't know a lot about shipwrecks, but the damage looks more like these two vessels exploded."

"Richard came to the same conclusion," Scott said. "Have you ever considered turning in your diploma for a treasure hunter's badge?"

"If this is what treasure hunting is like, I don't think my bank account could stand the decrease in pay." Gil laughed. "I'm joking. I love my job. I'll leave the treasure hunting to the experts."

David laughed. "I couldn't agree with you more. We wouldn't be here if it wasn't for testing this new piece of underwater equipment. Treasure hunting requires a certain set of skills and a lot of money."

"I think I'm going to be sick," Danna mumbled. She turned and walked out of the room.

"I'm going to deploy the AUD," David said. "From here on out it's really going to get boring."

"I think I'll go see if Danna is okay," Gil said. "She didn't even wait for her drink."

"Speaking of drinks," Richard said, "Where is that lad?"

As they passed in the corridor, Danna stopped Bobby and grabbed her wine from the tray he was holding and continued on without speaking.

As Gil walked out of the War Room, he saw the two together. *They have some kind of a history, but what is it?* he thought. "Danna, wait up," he called out.

Bobby handed Gil his beer as he passed by. *Good luck, sucker,* he thought.

"Thanks," Gil said, taking it and continuing after Danna. He caught up with her. "You want to tell me what's going on?"

"What do you mean?"

"That guy, for one. You know him from somewhere, don't deny it."

"He's my ex, okay."

Gil was taken back by her curt answer. "Okay, I didn't know you were married before, but why keep it a secret?"

"Can we go someplace where we can talk in private?"

"My cabin is close."

They made the short walk in silence and Gil opened the door for her. Bobby, a good distance down the corridor watched them enter.

In the War Room, the large screen

looked like it was on freeze-frame.

"What do we do now?" Richard asked.

"We wait," David said. "It's going to take a while before the AUD runs low on juice and finds its way back to *Fat Boy*."

"We won't know what it found until it returns," Scott added. "Might as well join the girls and get ready for the return trip. We can head back in the next hour."

Bobby brought in their drinks. "Anything else, Skipper?"

"Let Don know we'll be returning to shore in about an hour," Scott said.

"Yes, sir."

Watching Bobby leave, Richard said, "Where do you find these guys. He looks like a zombie."

"Former drug problem," Scott said. "I thought he deserved a second chance."

"You better hope that snake doesn't curl up and bite you in the ass."

"Yeah, I know," Scott said. "I've heard all the stories."

Bobby stopped outside Gil's cabin and listened through the door.

"He was a loser," Danna was saying. She sounded like she was sobbing.

"You must have had something in common," Gil said.

"We were in college together. We were young and foolish. We weren't thinking about the future. He got into some bad drugs and couldn't shake them. It was too much for me. I filed for divorce."

"That's all?" Gil asked.

"What else did he tell you?"

"Don't get upset. He didn't tell me anything."

"There isn't anything else, understand? I'm beginning to wonder if spending this weekend with you was a good idea."

"It was your idea, not mine," Gil said. He stormed out of the room catching Bobby by surprise and nearly knocking him over when he opened the door.

"What the hell are you doing here?" Danna yelled seeing Bobby.

Gil headed for the upper deck. He didn't look back.

"Now, you've done it," Danna said to Bobby. "I warned you and you couldn't help yourself. I can have you fired."

"Please don't say anything to Scott. I need this job."

"Too late. I warned you and you wouldn't listen."

"Please. Danna, I'm begging you."

She followed Bobby and watched him disappear into a doorway. She noticed she was standing opposite the entrance to the War Room and it was empty. Her attention was drawn to a series of pictures flashing on and off the large monitor, looking like a slide show. Each frame stayed on the screen for a few seconds before disappearing and another one appearing. She walked in and watched as the slide show from inside the U-boat unfolded. She gasped, nervously, looked around the room to make certain she was alone, removed her smart phone from her pocket and snapped some pictures. She quickly walked out.

"Everything is secured," Don announced to Scott. "We're ready for the trip in."

"Good. Head for the harbor," Scott said.

The two of them were alone on the bridge and Scott decided to let him know that he and David had decided to discontinue the dive on the wreckage. "I want you to know, because it looks like I won't be using you for the rest of the season. It's too late to start another project this year. I know it's a blow, but all I can promise is, I'll call you if anything changes."

"You know I'll have to take employment if it comes up," Don said.

"I can keep you on retainer for another month, if that helps," Scott offered. "I got wrapped up in this project and I've spent way over what I intended. David is reining in the expenses until we deliver the prototype of *Fat Boy* to the Navy."

"You want me to break the news to Bobby and Tad?"

"That's okay. I'll do it. I'll be below. Let me know when we're ready to cross the bar."

Chapter 10

July 6, Waldport, Oregon

Scott, Richard, and David sat in deck chairs with drinks in their hands enjoying the stillness of the morning air before the wind picked up as it often did in the afternoon. The call of seagulls rose above the roar of rolling surf as half a dozen birds fought for the same piece of scrap they considered breakfast.

"I wonder if they understand each other," David said, lifting his bloody Mary toward the fighting birds.

"You mean, communicate, like we do; talk to each other?" Richard asked. "Honestly is that what you're thinking about?"

"Yeah. Can you imagine how difficult it would be to break a code if it was in seagull speak?"

"You got me there," Richard said.

"Maybe we could capture a bunch of seagulls and train them to be messengers like they did pigeons in the First World War," Scott quipped.

"I'm serious," David said. "They've found whales and dolphins have a very sophisticated language. They communicate with other members of their pod."

"It's a bird-brained idea any way you look at it," Richard said.

"Funny," David said.

"When are we going to get a look at the video from the AUD?" Richard asked.

"I saw a bit of it after we got in last night," David said. "I was tired, but what I saw was disappointing. I couldn't make out head nor tail of it."

"You mind if I take a look?" Richard asked. "I'm still trying to figure out what a U-boat was doing in this part of the world."

"And Gil's observation that it was an explosion makes a lot of sense, too."

"Wait a minute," Richard protested. "I was the first one who came up with that theory and I've done some thinking since then on how it could have happened."

"It doesn't matter who came up with it," Scott said. "You don't suppose both of them could have been taken out by another submarine in the area?"

"A Jap sub, I doubt it." Richard thought for a minute. "Scott, can I use your computer?"

"Sure, you want to let us in on what you're looking for."

"Archives of the Japanese war

records. We captured millions of pages of information, but only a fraction of it was ever translated. When I was running NSA, I remember coming across a mountain of Japan's Navy records. They were set to be digitized."

"Were they translated?" David asked.

"No, just a mountain of boxes they wanted me to declassify."

"How could you declassify something you couldn't understand?" Scott asked.

"I couldn't. I sent them back to the Navy. I need to get in touch with Admiral Donleavy." He stood up.

"Scott," David said, "we're done testing *Fat Boy*. I think it's about time to kill your project before it busts us."

"It isn't going to break us. I already told my crew we were done for the season. The Navy will buy a dozen Fat Boy's and we'll be okay."

"Then let me put it this way. This end of the business isn't helping pay the bills."

"You're forgetting the millions in gold we recovered from—"

"I know where you're going," David said. "We need to get on another find like that. Your obsession with World War Two isn't cutting it. Next year we need to be on something that can pay its own way."

Richard listened to the conversation and took Scott's side. "David, you can't rule out World War Two history. A lot of treasure was stolen and transported during the war and much of it is still missing. We haven't even seen what's inside the wreck."

"All I saw was a bunch of twisted metal. Even if we found something, the cost of bringing anything up from that depth is prohibitive."

"It's still a damn good mystery and everybody loves a mystery," Richard said. "Hell, you chased Amelia Earhart halfway around the world on a whim. I think you should at least let this play out."

"You don't want to go there, Richard," David said. "It was you who talked me into the Amelia Earhart boondoggle."

"Well, consider this shipwreck my whim," Scott said. "At least we can rewrite a few chapters in history. That alone will be worth the price of a little further investigation."

"I don't know why I put up with you two," David said, rising to his feet. He turned to Richard. "Use my computer to contact your friend and then we'll take a look at the AUD video. Maybe you can tell me what we're looking for. It looked like twisted junk metal to me."

An hour later they joined Richard in Scott's office. Ten minutes into the slide show from the AUD, Scott said, "What's that? Back it up."

David backed it up a few frames and then advanced the murky pictures frame-by-frame."

"Stop," Scott said. "Zoom in."

"What are we looking at?" David asked.

"That," Richard said, pointing to the screen. "Any way to enhance it?"

"I'm a private citizen, not the NSA. I'd have to run it through a separate digital enhancement program."

"I still don't know what we're looking at," Scott said. "I thought the pictures would be clearer."

"It's that constant drift of silt from the mountain," David said. "It's clouding everything."

Scott continued to stare at the picture on the screen. "If that's what I think it is, it's the Emperor of Japan's seal," Scott said.

"On a bar of gold," Richard added.

"We're too close to the screen," Scott said. "Step back a few feet and take a look." The image was fuzzy, but he was sure he could make out the sixteen petals of the chrysanthemum crest Japan had adopted as their seal in ancient history.

"Stand aside. I need some room to work," David said. "I don't need the two of you leaning over me: Emperors seal? Bar of gold? Give me a break. It's way too cloudy to speculate."

"I don't think we're seeing things," Scott said. "Come on Richard. I'll pour you a drink and you can tell me about the Japanese war records you found. David can do his magic and catch up with us later."

They retired to the den where Scott poured two Scotch on the rocks from the bar and handed one to Richard.

Richard clicked his glass to Scott's. "Most of the war records have been digitized and, those that haven't been, but are considered worth keeping, are stored in the basement of the Pentagon."

"Digitized. That's great," Scott said.

"Donleavy told me the Pentagon ran out of budget money for the project. Very few of the records have been translated. I'm not sure I have enough pull anymore to get them released even if I knew where to start looking."

"We start by looking for any reference to German and Japanese payments in gold. We know Germany was selling war equipment to Japan, including submarines. Maybe this was some kind of a war payment."

"I don't know." Richard seemed unsure. "I guess I can see if they'll let me in the database. I'm going to have to give them a carrot, though. They need to believe I'm doing some serious research."

"Send them a picture of the conning tower and tell them it's on the bottom, off the Oregon Coast. That should get someone's attention."

"Are you sure? If the wrong people get hold of it, you could attract a lot of unwanted attention."

"Do it. I'll handle David. He isn't interested in the project anyhow."

"Until now," Richard said. "Did you see how he took over when we mentioned gold?"

Scott raised his drink. "You may be on to something there."

"Scott, you and Richard, come in here," David called from Scott's office. "I found something."

Chapter 11

Waldport, Oregon

"We need to make a dive tomorrow," David said, excitedly. "I need to scan every inch of the bottom where that U-boat was destroyed. We need to search every nook and cranny. How soon can we can get back to the wreck?"

Scott sipped his drink, amused at how quickly David had taken an interest. "Tomorrow is Sunday. I'm not sure I can get a crew together on short notice," Scott said. "I just told them they would be off until next summer."

"We don't need much of a crew," Richard said. "The fewer that know about this the better."

Scott eyed David. "I take it you're interested. When are you going to apologize?" Scott asked.

"I'm sorry, okay? Just get a crew together. This weather isn't going to hold." David was excited. "This calls for a celebration."

"Already started," Richard said, holding up his drink. "Scott and I are way ahead of you."

Fay heard the excitement and came into the office. "Celebrate. I'm always up for that. I'll get the girls. Can we go out dancing?"

"Get everyone in here," David said. "We struck a bonanza."

"As in gold?" Fay asked.

"Just get the others," Richard said.

The enhanced video showed more than the one piece of gold Scott and Richard had seen. Scattered along the deck were sixteen ingots, all bearing the imperial seal. From the size, Scott estimated each ingot weighed ten kilos, about twenty-two pounds. The video also showed the remains of a half a dozen bodies, all in the same area. The fragments of Japanese uniforms made it evident this wasn't a Nazi submarine, at least not when it went down. After showing the enhanced pictures to everyone in the room, David broke the news. "We're going to go back out tomorrow morning."

"So much for dancing," Fay lamented.

"It's been down there for eighty years," Patricia said. "The weather is turning. What's the rush?"

"I can have a recovery vehicle flown up here," David said.

"I thought we didn't have recovery capability at that depth," Scott said. "When were you planning on sharing this with me?"

"I'm telling you now. First, we

need to know the extent of our find. Sixteen bars are probably just the tip of the iceberg."

July 7, Aboard *Hunter*

The daybreak trip over the bar sent David to the rail to lose most of his breakfast. He was dressed in full raingear to protect him from the weather that had set in overnight and served double duty as the wind was in his face. A small-craft advisory had been issued by the Coast Guard, but David had insisted they not wait. *Hunter* was equipped to handle the most severe weather and the only part of the trip that was considered dangerous was the trip out of the protected waters of Yaquina Bay. The swells tossed the ship erratically making it difficult to keep on your feet. A wave broke over the rail knocking David to the deck and he went sliding along in the slippery wash. He scrambled back to his feet and quickly retreated back inside.

"I damned near went overboard," David gasped, ripping off his slicker.

Scott, trying to pour a cup of coffee, looked up at him and continued, without spilling it. "You wanted to get back out today and I'm supposed to feel sorry for you."

"I must have gotten food poisoning at breakfast."

"You're seasick. Didn't you put the patch behind your ear?"

David felt behind one ear then the other. "I may have forgotten."

"Go to your cabin and lie down. I'll come get you when we reach the wreck."

"You seem to be doing okay, Bobby," Scott said, looking over at the cook.

"I'm immune to seasickness. When I was fishing, we braved weather much worse than this." He had fished for a week and was fired. Scott didn't have to know that.

"I appreciate you coming along on such short notice," Scott said.

"No problem. I never expected to hear from you again after Danna talked to you."

"Danna?" Scott furrowed his brow. "Was she supposed to say something to me?"

Bobby hesitated before answering.

"Bobby, what about Danna?"

"We were married. She's my ex. You might say, she was a bit surprised to see me on your ship the other day."

"So, why would that be a problem?"

Bobby threw up his hands. "I don't know. I might have threatened to tell her boyfriend, Gil, we were married."

Scott shrugged. "He would have found out sooner or later. I don't see it as a big deal."

"So, she didn't say anything to you?"

"I said she didn't. Is there something else I should know?"

"I'm embarrassed to say. If you want to fire me you can."

"Is this about your drug use?"

"You know about that?"

"Of course I know about it. Your counselor recommended you. Are you using again?"

"No, but I'm not proud of that period of my life."

"Why would you be. It only matters to me that you stay clean."

Bobby breathed a sigh of relief. "Thanks, Skipper. That's a load off my chest."

"Go see if Don needs any help. We're pretty short-handed on this trip and we'll have to cover for each other. Tell him to call me if he needs to take a break. In this weather, it's all hands-on deck."

"Does that mean you're going to do the cooking, Skipper?"

"Don't push your luck."

Bobby fought his way to the bridge

and entered the control room where Don was swaying to the music of a rock band. Bobby didn't know the group. "Catchy tune. Skipper asked me to check and see if you needed anything."

"You got some hot coffee with you?"

"Matter of fact, I do." Bobby pulled a thermos from a pouch in his raingear. "You expect this weather to break?"

"If you believe the weather service, not a chance in the next twenty-four hours."

"I'll skip the oysters for dinner, then," Bobby said.

"Did you get a look at David?" Don asked, grinning. "My lawn isn't that green and I watered it all summer."

"What do you think is so important, they have us out in this stuff?" Bobby asked. "I thought this job was a bust."

"You know as much as I do. I got the call yesterday and Scott said it was urgent." He looked off in the distance. "It has to be something big, to be out in this crap."

Bobby filled Don's spill proof cup and handed it to him. "Keep warm and on course. I'll let Skipper know you're fine."

"Tell him we're going to need a twenty-four watch tonight. This storm isn't about to let up." He took a sip of coffee. "And tell him I will need some relief in an hour or so. This coffee is going to want to join the elements at some point."

"Aye, aye, el Capitan." Bobby gave him a sloppy salute.

"Get out of here."

An hour went by and then another. Scott hadn't shown up to relieve Don. They were approaching the GPS location of the wreck. "Scott, I need some relief up here, you copy?"

"Roger," Scott answered over the ship-com. "Be right there."

"You must have been doing something pretty important to let me stay up here until I almost pissed my pants," Don said, as Scott entered the wheelhouse.

Scott grinned. "After you take a whiz, check in on David in the War Room. I think you'll agree what we found was worth the wait."

Scott took control of the ship. The swells were large enough to roll *Hunter* from side to side in spite of the automatic stability control system. He doubted the ship would settle down enough to launch *Fat Boy* any time soon.

A few minutes later Don entered the War Room. "Scott said we're on to something."

David turned from his computer. Richard was sitting in an easy chair watching the large overhead screen which showed the same picture that was on David's computer. They were reviewing the enhanced video frame-by-frame.

"It's gold," David said, trying to play down any expectations the crew might have. "Recovery is questionable. The location and depth are at the limit of our equipment." He paused showing the gold bars with the Emperor's seal embedded in them. "It's worth taking another look at it. Why do you think a submarine would be carrying a load of gold?"

"Does it matter? Gold is gold." Don walked over to the wall monitor to get a better look. He was weaving and bobbing, having a hard time staying on his feet. "The question in my mind is whether we'll be able to make a recovery in this weather?" He studied the bars on the screen. "Is this all there is?"

"We won't know until we do a detailed search of the sea floor along the entire wreck."

"That could take days," Don said, disappointed. "Maybe weeks."

"We won't have recovery equipment here for another few days anyway," David said. "In the meantime, if we can launch *Fat Boy,* we can do a thorough scan along the bottom."

"Why not just recover what we've already found? Scanning the bottom could take another two weeks." Don said. He had worked out the time from their other attempts to map out areas of wreckage. A grid scan had to be meticulous and always took a long time.

David shook his head. "Even if we find it, we may not be able to recover any of it this year. Depending on the size of the find, we could redirect some equipment and recover all of it next year. We're at the end of the season, this year."

"You must have an idea how much more there is," Don said.

"Right now Richard and I are trying to find a record of what it is and why it's here. Speculation is useless. Would you mind returning to the bridge so Scott can join us down here?"

Don knew he was being dismissed and wanted to let David know he didn't take orders from him, but he thought better of it. On the way back to the bridge, he stopped by the mess and asked Bobby what he was fixing for lunch.

"You can't be hungry already?"

"Did you see the video from the U-boat?" Don asked.

"I leave the technical stuff to the experts," Bobby said. "I figure we're after something big if we're doing it in this weather. I'm not much of a history buff."

"It's gold my friend, at least sixteen bars, twenty pounds each. That's three-hundred-fifty pounds. A cool five point five million dollars at today's price and they're talking about leaving it until next year before attempting recovery. We're here to see if there's more so they know how much equipment they'll need next year."

"You mean we're not going to get our share, this year? That sucks."

"You bet it does. First, he tells us to take a hike until next year and then brings us out in this storm, for what? A great big nothing, that's what."

"Scott knows what he's doing better than anyone," Bobby said. "If he wants to wait until next year, we need to trust him."

"Maybe, but that little beady-eyed bastard he's partners with, doesn't know shit. He comes aboard and struts around like he owns the place. I'd like to toss him overboard, just on principle."

"He's partners with the skipper. I think he's the money guy, so he may, in fact, own the place. We're having prime rib for lunch, but it's going to be late if you don't get out of my kitchen."

"Think about it," Don said, in parting. "More than five-million-dollars right under our feet."

Newport, Oregon

Danna spent the day going over her options. Getting up and not going to work gave her a strange empty feeling. Since college, she had never been without a job. Before she graduated, she had already secured a job with the Marine Science Center along with a guarantee she could continue her education at government expense. She had always been busy. Her brief marriage had threatened her job and her doctorate, but she had managed to work her way through it. She was an ambitious woman and proud of it. She was the only family member to graduate college, something she reminded her brother of often. Losing her job was a blow to her ego and a problem she had never seriously contemplated until now.

She heard the lock turn in her door and looked over at her brother as he let himself in. She hadn't broken the news to him.

"Hi, sis. Are you sick, or something?" Paul asked.

"What do you think about moving?"

"Moving?" Paul repeated. "Why?"

"I lost my job. I'm thinking of moving to California, or possibly to the East Coast."

"What about Mom?"

"Screw her. She was never around

when we were kids. That guy she married can deal with her."

"And you want me to move with you? I got friends here."

"What if you could take them with you?"

"You're talking crazy. You're not seriously thinking about leaving?"

Danna picked up her phone and swiped through her pictures and showed the picture of the gold bars scattered on the deck of the sub.

"What am I looking at?" Paul asked, staring at the small screen. "Are you sure this is the picture you want to show me?"

"Gold bars! Millions of dollars' worth."

"I don't see it, but I'll take your word for it. Where is it? The picture is pretty blurry."

"It's at the bottom of the ocean in the submarine that sunk the ship our great-grandfather was on."

"You mean the Nazi spy that Mom didn't want us to find out about?"

"Forget that. Who cares if he was a spy? Somehow that submarine and the *Carissa* sank at the same time. Think about it. As surviving family, we're entitled to that gold as reparation for our pain and suffering. No one knows it's there."

"Pain and suffering? We didn't even know him."

"I'm telling you what our lawyer would claim."

"Lawyer? We don't have a lawyer, do we?" He went to her refrigerator and grabbed a beer. "How did you get the picture?"

"That's not important. The question you should be asking is, 'how are we going to get it?'"

Paul popped the tab on his beer and downed half of it. "How deep is it?"

"Nine thousand feet."

"Now I know you're crazy. It costs a lot of money to retrieve something from that depth."

"What if we didn't have to bring it up."

"Someone else knows about it," Paul said. "You think they are just going to give it to us?"

"You're friends with Don Blanchard, aren't you?"

"Blanchard, yeah, I guess so. I know him. I worked for him a few days when he was trying to locate a ship that sank off the coast. He never found it."

"You know he works for Stafford-Tanner Enterprises now, don't you?"

"If you say so. I'm having trouble following this. Can I have another beer?"

"Help yourself," Danna said. "Don works for Scott Tanner and I was on the ship when they discovered the gold. I estimate it's worth over five million dollars."

Paul twisted the top off a bottle of Blue Moon and tossed the cap into a trashcan across the room. "Three points. Must be my lucky day."

"Are you listening to anything I'm saying?"

"Yeah, five million dollars. It's still at the bottom of the ocean. What do you want to do, wait 'til someone else brings it up and steal it?" Paul laughed and took a swig of beer.

"Exactly," Danna said. "It won't be that hard to steal it. I know precisely where it is and they don't know I know about it."

"Where does Don Blanchard fit in? You think he's going to take the gold and then hand it over to us?"

"Don runs the ship. If he can get the rest of the crew to go along with him, I'm telling you this can work. Did I tell you Bobby works on the ship, too?"

"Bobby. You're ex, Bobby? Now I know you're crazy. Bobby wouldn't kiss your ass if you covered it with honey."

"I got something on him. He'll go along."

"How do we get included in the cut?"

"That's where you come in. Think about it, we can all be rich in South America."

"South America?"

"There's no way to steal it and stay around here. Trust me, I've thought of everything."

Chapter 12

July 10, Pacific Marine Science Center

Gil took a call from his father on his office phone. "Dad, twice in as many weeks, are you and Mom okay?"

"We're fine. This is purely business. We've been monitoring ground movement on South Sister. I think we have magma rising in that area. Have you noticed anything unusual in the subduction zone?"

"A few minor earthquakes about fifty miles out. That's pretty normal."

"Just checking. You're sitting in the path of a tsunami if anything happens."

"Dad, I'm well aware of where we're located. We have a well thought out evacuation plan. I'll e-mail it to you, if you don't believe me."

Jason laughed. "Stay safe, Son. Let me know if you see any seismic events less than nineteen miles deep." Jason had the same information Gil could get right in front of him.

"I'm sure you'll be aware of it before me, with all the seismic equipment you're locked into."

"Maybe. You're our kid; your mom and I have to worry about you. You aren't serious about that girl, are you?"

"Danna? Is that what this is about?"

"Your mother didn't think too highly of her."

"She thinks any girl I date isn't good enough for me."

Jason laughed again. "You're right about that. I love you, Son. Take care."

Gil hadn't seen Danna since the day on *Hunter*. She said she was thinking of leaving the area and looking for a job. He figured she was gone.

That evening, over a beer and home-baked pizza, Gil thought about the conversation he'd had with his father. He hadn't introduced very many girls to his parents since graduating college. Danna hadn't really been a date, but she was in the same field as he, and he thought that would be a plus in a relationship. Still there was something about her he didn't trust. Her story about her great-grandfather and the *Carissa* was one that had caught him by surprise. He had thought her parents were from Costa Rica, not from this area. While he munched on a wedge of pizza, he opened his laptop and started a search for Merchant ships lost in World War Two. If he could access the company records for *Carissa*, he could see what her great-grandfather did aboard the missing ship.

Aboard *Hunter*

Hunter had been out for three days when Scott, David, and Richard met in the War Room to discuss their findings, or lack of discovery of any additional gold bars. With half the search completed, they had expected to find at least a few more by now. The recovery equipment was setting in a warehouse near the dock in Newport and they needed to make a decision: Stop the search and go for the recovery of the sixteen bars in the remaining days of summer, or keep searching and possibly lose the window for any recovery this year.

"I was able to find something of interest," Richard said, pouring a double Scotch on the rocks and settling into the only recliner in the War Room. "Hitler sold several submarines to Japan in the late Thirties, well before they bombed Pearl Harbor. When the War in the Pacific was heating up, the Germans agreed to sell Japan some of their later models to see if they could turn the War in the Pacific in their favor." Richard took a sip of his drink and swirled the ice around in the glass. "I'm speculating on the rest of this. Suppose, when it looked like an invasion of Japan by Allied Forces was imminent, the military put together a plan, much like the one Hitler had, to establish a new government in South America. Germany on the Atlantic seaboard and Japan on the Pacific. With a plan like that, they could have taken over the continent."

"That's completely unbelievable," Scott said. "First of all, there's no historical record of any Japanese presence in South America. Secondly, the Emperor was still in Japan when we won the war."

"There were some atrocious war crimes the Japanese military would be tried for," Richard said. "Suppose a group of Japanese generals, seeing what Stalin and the US were doing to Hitler's generals, decided to flee the country. I don't have any proof of it, but it could have been a plan to evacuate those who committed the worst crimes. Just suppose, and I know it's a stretch, just suppose Hitler's generals and Japan's generals were close enough that they were aware of Hitler's evacuation plan. This U-boat could have been part of an elaborate scheme to save themselves."

"They did find some of the most notorious players in the Holocaust had escaped to South America," Scott said. "But why the German markings on the submarine?" He poured a Scotch on the rocks for himself and took a stool at the bar. "Why would Japan keep German markings on their sub?"

"I thought of that too," Richard said, taking another sip of his drink. "If that sub was delivered at the last minute, it would have had a German crew. They could have loaded the gold and made a run for it."

"I'm still not buying it," Scott said. "The uniforms we saw were Japanese, not German. What do you think David?"

David was buried in his computer. He looked up. "About what?"

"Haven't you been listening to any of this?"

"I followed most of it, but I agree with Scott, there are a lot of holes in your theory. The only thing you can say for certain is Hitler delivered U-boats to Japan. Sixteen bars of gold wouldn't be enough to fund a new nation even back in nineteen forty-four. And, let's face it, there's no record of a Japanese presence in South America, because there isn't any. I still want to know how it sank."

Richard downed his Scotch, got up and joined Scott at the bar. He put a few more ice cubes in his glass and poured another drink. "I think I know the answer to that, too."

David joined them at the bar. "I hope it's more than pure speculation. This is starting to read like a novel. I would like some facts."

Richard raised his hands defensively and pursed his lips. "It's still speculation, but something we can give some credibility to, if we can get another drone in the sub."

"Tell me what we're looking for," David said.

"Wren torpedoes, the Germans called them Zaunkŏning. This model of torpedo was designed to lock in on the loudest noise after it ran four hundred meters. The boat had to maintain complete silence after launch or it could lock in on it instead of the target. There were at least two confirmed instances of German subs being sunk by their own torpedoes during the war. The Type Twenty-one was designed to be an escort-killer. It was very effective against a fleet of Merchant ships until we developed the *Foxer*, a noise making decoy. The timeline all fits."

"Let me see if I can put together a scenario that includes the *Carissa*," Scott said. "If I remember correctly, *Carissa* radioed they had spotted a German U-boat in heavy fog. It's possible the sub was on the surface recharging its batteries, not concerned with being seen because of the fog cover. Merchant ships of that era didn't have radar. *Carissa* chugs by and catches them by surprise. Now the U-boat commander is concerned their location will be reported and the Coast Guard will send PBY sub-chasers after them, not realizing Newport didn't have any PBYs in service at the time. The U-boat commander needed to act quickly and to sink *Carissa*, but they have to wait for the *Carissa* to be far enough away that they can launch a torpedo—"

Richard added, "The U-boat commander isn't worried, because he has the latest and greatest equipment. He estimates the speed of the tanker, waits the appropriate length of time and fires."

Scott finished his thought. "Not knowing the captain of *Carissa* has determined the U-boat must have been in trouble because it was on the surface, he turns the ship around to take a look and verify the spotting. The tanker and U-boat are on a collision course. The torpedoes have already been fired and the noise seeking torpedoes follow the tanker back to the sub and BOOM!" Scott hit his hand with his fist making a smacking sound.

"That was a day of bad luck for two skippers," David said. He poured a glass of wine. "Your explanation is as good as any, since we'll never know the truth, but I think there could be a simpler explanation."

David poured a glass of wine. "Since we are all speculating, my theory is the U-boat already fired its torpedoes, but the ship was closing in on them and the torpedo never armed until it was well past the *Carissa*. By then *Carissa* has spotted the sub and cuts its engines to run silent. Now the torpedo is searching for anything that makes noise. The U-boat loses the game of silence."

"Why did the *Carissa* sink?" Scott asked.

"The U-boat fired two torpedoes. As soon as the U-boat was struck, the captain of *Carissa* goes full throttle and, bang, the second torpedo finds it."

"Maybe the wreck will give up a few more secrets," Scott said.

"What about launching the AUD into another section of the U-boat?" Richard asked. "Are we all agreed we need to find out if it was armed with *Wren* torpedoes?"

"I was planning on it, anyway," David said. "There has to be more gold somewhere, but we still have to agree on a plan before we proceed."

Waldport, Oregon

Patricia, Janet, and Fay were having coffee, getting ready for a tsunami drill she had talked them into.

"This has been the most fun I've had in months," Fay said. "Janet, you've had an incredible life, hobnobbing with the politicians in Washington. Sometimes I long for a life outside of Southern California. If a tsunami drill seems like fun to me, I need to get out more often."

Patricia looked at her. "Fay, I thought you loved San Diego."

"If it wasn't for the Navy base nearby, David and I would be looking for a better environment."

"Believe me, Washington DC isn't the place if you're wanting to get away from the politically correct crowd," Janet said.

"I'm not talking about that," Fay said. "Southern California has no seasons. It seems like every day is the same as the next. I miss the snow in winter, the rain in spring, and the blossoms. When it rains in San Diego it pours down, maybe once or twice a year. No gentle sprinkle to water the flowers."

"We have the seasons here, for sure," Patricia said. "We have the rainy winter, the rainy spring, and the rainy summer." She laughed.

"What about the fall?" Janet asked.

"That's the one day that's free of rain."

Fay laughed. "Maybe there isn't an ideal place to live."

"Some are better than others,"

Janet said. "Some of my fondest memories are from the time Richard was stationed in North Bend, those were good old days, weren't they Patricia?"

"That was before David and I met, wasn't it?" Fay asked.

"Scott was still in the Navy stationed in the Gulf region." Patricia said. "We were just starting to date."

"Patricia and I haven't known each other much longer than you and David," Janet said. "Scott served with Richard for a short time. When Scott didn't sign up for another tour, we all happened to be on the West Coast in the same small town about an hour south of here. We became friends." She touched Patricia on the arm. "We were so young, back then."

"Okay, I'm about to cry," Patricia said. "Are we ready for the drill? Everybody have their suitcases packed with their essentials?" Seeing them nod, she shouted, "Earthquake! Grab your go-bag. We have to get to safety."

They all ran to their rooms and within a minute, gathered in the living room, ready to evacuate.

"Do you have your cell phones?" Patricia asked.

"Got mine," Janet said.

Fay lifted hers so Patricia could see.

"Let's go. We're taking the Jeep.

The roads could be damaged and we might need 4-wheel drive."

"Roger," Janet said, picking up her suitcase.

The three ran out the front door and tossed their luggage in the back. Fay and Janet climbed in the Jeep.

"Where's she going?" Fay asked.

A minute later, Patricia tossed two additional suitcases in the back, climbed behind the wheel, and they raced off. She turned south on Highway 101. "We are paralleling the coast for a way, but this is the quickest route to get to a safe elevation."

"Which is?" Fay asked.

"I'm not sure. Our insurance company said fifty feet elevation was out of their risk assessment zone. I'm shooting for three times that high to be safe."

"How do you know how high we are?" Fay asked.

Patricia pointed to the navigation screen in her dash. "This part of HWY 101 is just above one hundred feet. According to the evacuation signs, it's out of the tsunami danger zone." She put on her turn signal just north of Alsea Bay Bridge and turned east, following a road that paralleled the river, but at a higher elevation than the highway. They all watched as the elevation ticked up. In a few minutes she pulled off the road onto a gravel turnout and stopped. She checked her watch. "Elevation one-hundred-forty-seven-feet. That took twelve minutes. We may be in trouble if the roads are damaged."

"Or you could drop a few suitcases," Janet suggested. "You were the slowest one. Really. You emptied out the safe and cleared all your pictures off the wall and put them in a suitcase? Why don't you make copies of what you really consider valuable and store them in a vault somewhere safe?"

"Not a bad idea," Patricia said. "Now, let's get out and watch the wave roll in."

She opened the door and stood looking west over the bridge and out to sea.

"You know this is just a drill," Fay said, getting out and joining Patricia and Janet.

"Shhh, I think I can hear the wave coming in," Patricia said, putting her hand to her ear. "They say it sounds like a freight train."

"So does an avalanche," Fay said. "Personally, I don't want to be close enough to hear either one."

"And a tornado," Janet added. "I've heard they sound like a freight train, too."

"Okay, make fun of me. If there ever is a tsunami, I'll be safely watching it from here. You two are on your own."

"I hope this spot isn't on everybody's plans," Janet said. "One more carload of people and it would be pretty crowded."

Chapter 13

July 12, Aboard *Hunter* 5:00 p.m.

"We've mapped everything we can," David said. "The poor visibility made it impossible to see much on the visuals. I think it's time to go back and take a good look at the sonar data."

"I agree," Scott said. "I'm ready for a night in my king-size bed."

"You two are getting soft," Richard said. "What happened to the days when men would spend years at sea, sleeping on a hammock in the belly of the beast?"

"Like you ever saw that kind of service," Scott said. "As an officer, you had all the amenities of home."

"Not all," Richard said. "Not many women aboard ship in my day."

Scott shook his head. As long as he'd known Richard, he was a devoted family man and a loyal husband. "I'll let Don know we're going in. We should make port before dark."

Waldport, Oregon

Patricia set a deli plate, French bread and crackers on the table. "Everyone, help yourselves," she said. She looked at Scott. "You didn't call and let me know you were coming in today."

"I thought I'd surprise you."

"It was a surprise, all right," Fay said. "I think David is picking up some of Scott's bad habits. He didn't call either."

"Sure, pick on the guy who just found five point five million dollars in gold bars."

"That was the same amount you found a week ago. I thought there'd be more by now," Fay said.

"That's a lot of money, Fay," Janet said.

"It is," Richard said. "And we think we solved the mystery of how it got there."

"Speculation, Richard. We haven't found the torpedoes," David said.

"They'll be there," Richard said. "Once the footage is enhanced, they'll be there."

"More gold, too," Scott said, fixing a sandwich. Looking at Patricia, he said, "This is good, Honey. I was getting sick of ship food. The prime rib was a little dry, last night."

"You eat better on that ship than I do at home," Patricia said.

"You're never going to forgive me?"

"Never," Patricia said, smiling.

"What are you two talking about

now?" Richard asked.

"There are so many things," Patricia said. "I like to keep him guessing." She took a sip of wine. "The girls and I did have fun while you were gone, though."

"Yeah, we took a wine tour into the valley one day," Fay said, lifting a bottle of Willamette Vineyards Pinot Noir.

"And, don't forget the tsunami drill," Janet said. "We had to wait for Patricia to get four suitcases in the jeep. It made us late and we would have all perished."

"And I'm the one who writes novels," Patricia said. "That was a monumental exaggeration. It took us twelve minutes to get to our rendezvous point. With a little more practice, I'll make it in ten."

"No one ever accused Patricia of not being prepared," Scott said. "Speaking of being prepared, this was a rough trip for David. He chummed for fish most of the time. In his defense, the ocean did have a little chop."

"Not at the dinner table, Scott," Patricia said.

"I didn't say threw-up. Oh, yea, David upchucked nearly every day we were out to sea. He forgot his Dramamine."

"Jesus, Scott, give it a rest. Not

everyone has a cast iron stomach," David said.

"Navy men do," Richard said.

"I'm turning in," David said, checking the time on his smart phone.

"Me too," Fay said, taking David's hand. She looked back at the others and winked. "He's been gone almost a week."

Richard let out a sigh. "I remember those days."

"As I recall, you couldn't wait to get me in the sack when you finished a tour," Janet said.

Richard smiled. "I guess I'm not that old. I still remember that thing you did—"

"Richard," Janet interrupted. "I'm sure Patricia and Scott aren't interested in the details of our love life."

"Here, Old Timer," Scott said, handing Richard his drink. "I think that's your cue to shut up."

Morning at the Tanner residence came with the sound of thunder. It hit so close the walls of the house shook.

"What the hell was that," Richard said, jumping out of bed. He opened his bedroom door just as another flash of lightning lit up the entire house.

Scott came out of his bedroom, feet bare and buckling the belt to his faded jeans. He grinned at Richard, "Hell of jolt when it's right on top of you."

"This happens often?"

"Often enough Patricia sleeps through it. I'm going to make sure the windows and doors all got closed last night."

Newport, Oregon

Danna entered the Pacific Marine Science Center for the first time in a week. Not seeing anyone at the reception counter, she slipped through the gate and went to her old office and closed the door. The same storm that had moved in rapidly last night was pelting the area with rain and she removed her wet jacket and hung it on a rack. She had just opened her computer when there was a knock on the door.

After rapping softly a few times, Gil opened the door and peeked in. "Danna, you're back. I thought you were out of town."

She looked up at him. "I came in to clean out my desk and to clear up a few things."

"I need to apologize for my behavior on the ship," Gil said. "It shouldn't mean anything to me if you were married before."

"I should have told you," Danna said.

"Truce," Gil said. He stuck out his hand. "We're friends, right?"

"Friends," she repeated. "I'm going to be out of town for a while. I needed something off my computer."

"Is everything okay."

"Yeah, fine."

"Going anywhere special?"

Danna frowned and shook her head.

"Okay," Gil said. "Enjoy. You want the door closed?"

"Leave it open."

"See you." Gil returned to his office. *That was strange,* he thought. *Damn, I forgot to ask her.* He went back down the hall. Danna was putting on her jacket getting ready to leave.

"Danna, I forgot to ask, was that your great-grandfather on your mother's side or your father's side of the family that was on *Carissa*?"

"Why?" Danna looked at him curiously.

"It's nothing. I was interested and thought I'd see if I could find anything on the *Carissa*."

"It was my mother's grandfather, but it's really none of your business. I already know my family history."

"Then what was his name?"

"Jones. First Mate Edward W. Jones."

"Thanks," Gil said. He left her standing in her office. He couldn't explain what bothered him about her story, but he wanted to know more.

Waldport, Oregon

David, Richard, and Scott were in Scott's office at separate places working on their computers. David was running the digitized information from the sonar scans they had made along the bottom. There was a ton of information that had to be processed and the ocean wasn't giving up its secrets easily. "What's taking so long?" Richard asked.

"It just takes time," David said. "Without the super computer on the ship, you'll have to wait a few more hours. Why don't you leave and harass the women?"

Richard got up. "You think I'm harassing you?" He grabbed David around the neck, pulled him out of his chair and gave him a noogie, knocking David's glasses off in the process. "This is harassment."

"Stop," David shouted.

"Stop playing around, you two," Scott said. "We're supposed to be working and you two are acting like you're in junior high. If you don't feel like working, go play with your skateboards."

"I'm sending this guy back to Virginia," David said. How am I supposed to get anything done when he's acting like the schoolyard bully?"

"You know, I'm right here and you're talking around me," Richard said.

"He's got a point, Richard," Scott said. "Stop picking on my main man."

"I thought I was your main man," Richard said, bending over and picking up David's glasses. He handed them to David. "If Scott says you're the main man, I guess I owe you an apology."

David grinned. "I'm the one with the purse strings. That makes me the main man." David sat back down at his computer. "I should have some data in a few more hours."

The room grew quiet as everyone went back to work. A few minutes went by when David lifted his head. He heard snoring. He looked over at Richard who was leaning back in his chair with his eyes closed, breathing deeply. "Now would be a good time to get even," he said with a grin.

"Don't do it," Scott said. "Trust me, it'll be worse if you try and get revenge."

"I used to think highly of him,"

David said. "Sleeping on the job, really? We're not paying him, are we?"

"We need to cut him some slack," Scott said. "He's the same man we used to know, but he's bored out of his mind. He spent so many years serving our Country, he never learned how to play golf. Janet told me this trip has made a new man out of him," He leaned toward David and whispered, "they had sex last night."

"Thank you for planting that picture in my mind," David said, making a face.

"You're welcome." Scott smiled and went back to work.

***

Pacific Marine Science Center

Gil spent his lunch hour researching the crewmembers of the Merchant ship *Carissa*. He found First Mate Edward W. Jones with a picture taken in 1939. He looked at the Multnomah County records for any information he could find on the man and came across a court record in 1938 of a man named Wolfgang Werner Schmitt who had petitioned the court for a name change to Edward Werner Jones. He knew some German-Americans had their names changed during the war to avoid persecution. Jones had enlisted with the

Merchant Marines shortly thereafter. *This might be of interest to Scott Tanner,* he thought.

Chapter 14

Waldport, Oregon 8:07 a.m.

Patricia picked up the phone. "Patricia speaking."

"Patricia, it's Gil. I hope I didn't wake you."

"I've been up for hours," Patricia said.

"How's the evacuation plan coming along?"

"Still working on it. I need to pare down what I think is important in life. My go-bag turned into three large pieces of luggage."

Gil laughed. "I'm sure you'll figure it out. I really wanted to talk to Scott. Is he available?"

"Just a minute, I'll have him pick up in his office."

Scott picked up his phone. "Gil, what can I do for you?"

Gil gave him the information on the first mate on *Carissa*. "I thought it might help piece the puzzle together. A German is First Mate on the ship and a German submarine? You think it's a coincidence? I'll send you the link in case you're interested."

"It might just be a coincidence," Scott said. "We've established the submarine had a Japanese crew. Once we have it figured out, we'll have to get together and I'll fill you in on the details." He hung up and walked to the kitchen to refill his coffee.

"What did Gil want?" Patricia asked.

"He had information on Danna Collier's great-grandfather."

"The one who was on the *Carissa*?" Richard asked. "I overheard as I was coming down the hall."

"Her great-grandfather was First Mate Edward Jones. Turns out he was a German who changed his name before the war."

Richard went over to the coffeemaker and poured a cup of coffee. "Was he piloting the ship?"

"Probably. The message to the Coast Guard was sent by Captain Shunt. If nothing else, it may be another piece of our puzzle."

"You want me to get David out of the sack?"

David walked in the room in his pajamas. "I'm up. What's all the ruckus about?"

"Jones, the first mate on *Carissa*, was really Wolfgang Werner Schmitt," Scott said.

"A German," Richard said, as if it meant something.

"A German who thought it was necessary to change his name," Scott added.

"It may not mean anything," Richard said. "A lot of people change their names to fit into society more easily. After we entered the war there was no shortage of prejudicial treatment of German and Japanese-Americans."

"I followed up on the link Gil sent me and it's the timing that looks suspicious to me," Scott said. "Schmitt changed his name two years before Hitler declared war with us."

David finished mixing his coffee and tasted it. He added two more cubes of sugar. "Are you thinking the ship was turned back toward the U-boat without the skipper knowing?"

"That makes more sense than going back to investigate," Richard said. "Most Merchant ships would want to put as much distance between them and an enemy submarine as they could get." He thought for a moment and took a drink of coffee. "Of course, if I was at the helm and we passed by a surfaced enemy submarine, I might want to stay close enough that they couldn't arm their torpedoes. I might even cut my engines."

"That would be a pretty gutsy move," Scott said.

"Wartime protocol. If we knew about the *Wren* torpedoes, it could have called for cutting the engines and maintaining silence."

"So, we'll never know if her great-grandfather was a traitor or a hero," David said. "I don't see this information helping."

"Maybe he was a spy," Scott said. "Maybe he knew the sub would be out there and wanted to rendezvous."

"I hate puzzles that can't be solved," Richard said.

"Well, the enhanced video could answer some questions," David said. "I didn't get a chance to review it yesterday, but it's all done. I could use another set of eyes to review it."

"How about two extra sets. I think we're all interested in what we find." Scott topped off his coffee.

"I'll fix some breakfast as soon as Janet and Fay are up," Patricia said.

Seal Rock, Oregon

Ten miles south of Newport, Danna pulled her Toyota Tundra pickup up the drive of a house on a wooded hill overlooking the rocky shore. From the hilltop she could see twenty-miles out to sea where the horizon melded with the powder blue sky. She let herself in using the key her brother had given her.

She was the first to arrive. She went to the kitchen and put on a pot of coffee.

The house was owned by a couple from Arizona who used it as a vacation home to escape the unbearably hot summers in Phoenix. This year, they were unable to make the trip to Oregon due to a family illness. Paul was the groundskeeper and general handyman and had full access to the premises. It was a perfect place to meet and when he offered her the keys, she jumped at the chance. It was secluded and they wouldn't draw any attention from nosy neighbors. She stared out the window and dreamed that one day she would own such a place. She had been planning for a week and had made a blueprint of *Hunter* from the pictures she had taken and her memory of the ship from the brief time she had been aboard, but she had something better than a blueprint. She had Don Blanchard on their side.

The knock on the door startled Danna out of her muse. She looked out a side window and saw Don Blanchard and Paul. She opened the door. "Where's Tad Davis?" she asked.

"I'm not sure about Tad," Don said. "He wasn't even aware we discovered gold. He may be loyal to Scott. Bobby may be a bust too."

Danna gave Don a look of exasperation. "You said you could get them both on board. You either get him on our side or you'll have to take care of them."

"Sorry," Don said. "It is what it is. More money for the rest of us."

"You told Bobby how much money was at stake?" Danna asked, not believing any of them would turn down that kind of money.

"What do you think? No, I told him we wanted to take over the ship for the fun of it."

"No need to get mad," Paul butted in.

"Let me worry about Bobby," Danna said.

"You're not talking about hurting anyone," Don said. "Stealing the treasure is one thing, but…"

"Relax. We can pull this off without hurting anyone," Danna said. "Let's get down to business. Don, when are they scheduled to go out again?"

"Scott hasn't called me. I'll give you a ring as soon as I know anything."

"But you said they decided to go for it this year?" Danna wanted to make certain there wasn't a change from the last time they had spoken.

"That little shit of a partner of his was iffy on that, too, but I'm pretty sure they aren't going to leave five million dollars in gold sitting on the bottom when they have a positive location and the equipment to retrieve it is already sitting in a warehouse on the dock in Newport."

"Good," Danna said. "Here's what I think we can do. Don, be sure to interrupt if you see something that doesn't make sense."

Waldport, Oregon

"That thing must have gone down like a rock," Scott said. He was looking at a small area where gold bars were buried beneath the silt. The camera on *Fat Boy* gave no indication the bars were there, but the GPR images showed the distinctly shaped bars under a layer of sand.

"This is going to make recovery much slower," Scott said. "We're fighting a strong current and won't be able to locate the bars visually."

"I count 107 more bars, that's 123 all together." Richard said. "That's a lot of pocket change."

"Enough to make recovery this year a priority," David said. "Scott, when's the soonest we can get back out there?"

"Give me a day to get the crew together and the ship stocked. We can load the recovery vessels today if you want. Richard, check the weather for the next week and see if there are any storms coming our way."

"Breakfast is ready," Patricia called from the kitchen.

"A real treasure hunt," Richard said. "I can hardly believe you guys do this for a living."

"We do a lot of other things," David said. "Someday I'll take you through our facility in San Diego. You still have security clearance, don't you?"

"Last time I checked. I'm not too sure of the current president, though. He revoked the security clearance of a former CIA director the other day. He has the power to do that."

"Keep your head down and stay in the middle of the herd," Scott said. "You'd be a terrible loss to us if you weren't able to access government information."

Chapter 15

July 13, 7:45 a.m. Yaquina Bay, dock

"That's the last of the load, Skipper," Don Blanchard said to Scott. "Bobby and Tad are already aboard."

"We're going to stay light on crew," Scott said, "so I'll be your relief. You want to take her over the bar this trip?"

"I could use the experience," Don said.

"I'll be beside you. Once David and Richard are aboard, we'll cast off." Scott had a printed copy of the weather report. It showed a few squalls and some rain in the next week, but that was pretty normal for midsummer. No big storms appeared on the way. Today was clear and calm. *Any weather in Oregon is temporary*, he thought.

Danna watched from the shadows as *Hunter* left the dock. Moored on the other side of the bay was a twenty-three-foot boat named *Pacific Mist* waiting for her and her brother to pilot it out to sea once she got the call the gold was on board *Hunter*.

She was disappointed that both Tad and Bobby didn't buy into a takeover, and would settle for the meager share Scott had promised them as a bonus. At half a percent each, it amounted to between twenty and thirty thousand dollars. They could have quadrupled that if they would have gone along with her plan.

Feeling out Tad had been Don's assignment. He was to do it without going into the details of the plan and making sure Tad wouldn't rat on him for bringing up such a notion as taking the gold. After Don had found out Tad and Bobby didn't show interest, Don had quickly dropped the subject, not wanting to draw suspicion.

Danna had approached Bobby, thinking she could bring her ex along with a threat of exposing his drug addiction to Scott, but early in the conversation, Bobby called her bluff.

"Scott knows I was on drugs," Bobby had said.

Danna immediately made an excuse to get off the phone and hung up. She had devised another plan, a bit more complicated, but one that would work if they couldn't include all the ship's crew.

Of course, she couldn't tell the others what she was up to, that could risk the entire operation. As it was, Tad and Bobby would get nothing. More likely they would be killed. She had promised no guns, but with that much money at stake, she and Paul had purchased matching 9mm pistols which could easily be concealed. It was important that she keep her activities as close to normal as possible, but the wait was eating at her.

She went over the plan in her mind again as she watched *Hunter* disappear in a thin veil of fog.

As Don drove the ship across the bar, the stun gun in his pocket seemed to contact anything he touched, making him mindful of the task ahead. His part of the plan called for him to use it on the entire crew after they had brought up the last piece of gold and everyone had turned in for the night. He would then tie up the crew and take the ship out to a rendezvous point and disable the ship's engines.

Danna and Paul would be within five miles of the rendezvous point waiting for a satellite call from Don, assuring them he had secured the ship. She and Paul, in *Pacific Mist,* would meet up with Don on *Hunter* and the gold would be transferred to their small pleasure craft. From there they would travel south and bring the boat into the small port at Brookings where a heavy-duty van was waiting in the parking area. Transporting sixteen bars of gold could easily be done without anyone noticing. From there, the plan was to drive through California and into Mexico, where the gold would be melted and poured into smaller ingots that could be easily turned into cash. It was a simple plan. Five-million dollars would go a long way in Mexico.

After *Hunter* disappeared, Danna got back in her pickup and went for a cup of coffee.

Gil saw Danna as soon as he had entered the local Starbucks. She was stirring creamer into her coffee. "Danna, I didn't expect to see you here. I thought you were going out of town."

"I decided to stick around and finish up a few things. I had to give thirty-days-notice on my apartment," she lied. She was planning on skipping out the second she got the next call from Don.

"Are you sure everything is all right? Is there anything I can do to help you get a new job? I might know some people."

"My mom's been sick and I need to take some time off to help her. I'll look for something after she's well." It was another lie. The more she did it, the easier it was. People were so gullible.

"I'm sorry to hear about your mom," Gill said. "I hope it's nothing serious."

"The flue, I think. I have to get back to her. Are you through asking questions?"

"Just trying to be friendly," Gil said, under his breath as she walked out.

Paul Collier had worked as a deckhand on a fishing boat, a motorcycle mechanic, and a groundskeeper, all minimum wage jobs with little or no future. He had done drugs with Bobby when he was married to his sister, and then tried to back off the strong stuff when Bobby checked into rehab. He could, at times, be considered as a functional drug user, but other times it got completely out of control. The thought of having as much money as he wanted at one time made his palms itch. He couldn't wait to get to Mexico with his pockets overflowing with cash. For this reason alone, he had managed to get his life back together. The recreational Marijuana helped calm his nerves, at least that was what he kept telling his sister.

Aboard *Hunter*

Don set the autopilot coordinates for the U-boat location and sat back in the captain's chair going over his part of the plan in his mind. He had been with Scott long enough to familiarize himself with the equipment he would be using to bring up the treasure. While he didn't have any personal experience with the remote piloted underwater vessels, he had seen them operate. This was a different operation than he had ever been on before, though. The water was much deeper and everything would have to be done robotically. He wasn't certain how long that would take. Scott had told him to prepare the ship for two weeks at sea. He hoped it wouldn't take that long to bring up a few bars of gold.

"We need to set a new course," Scott said. "We're bringing up the bars that are buried south of the U-boat first."

It was the first Don had heard of the additional bars.

"How many are there?"

"One-hundred-seven additional bars spread out in a small area not far from the U-boat," Scott said. "They're buried under the sand so we missed them until now. We'll bring them up one at a time, and then retrieve the ones inside the sub."

Already Don's mind was trying to calculate the weight of the additional treasure and the time it would take to raise that many bars, one at a time. The trip suddenly went from a few days to maybe a week or more. *That's why all the supplies,* he thought, while trying to keep a neutral face.

"Where are they, Skipper?"

Scott gave him the new coordinates. "This find could make you a wealthy man," Scott said. "I hope you don't go off on your own again."

"You knew about that?" Don was embarrassed. "I think I learned my lesson on that one," he said, recovering from his shock. He was still trying to come up with a number. His share would suddenly be at least a quarter-million dollars. Suddenly, Don knew the plan would have to change.

"Can you take over for a few minutes, Skipper?" Don asked. "I need to go to the head."

Don went to his cabin and took out his calculator. "My god, that's over two thousand pounds," he mumbled.

He picked up the satellite phone, but couldn't get a signal. He didn't dare take it out on deck, he'd have to wait until dark to contact Danna with the news. As he sat on his bunk he started shaking and thinking. *Why let Danna and Paul in on the extra gold?* He was doing all the work and Danna wasn't even offering an even split. *Why did he need her at all?* He went over the plan and what would be required to modify it. He eventually came to the realization Danna's plan wouldn't work at all.

"Sorry about that, Skipper," Don said, returning to the helm. "I'm ready to take over, now."

"We're a few minutes out. Once we're in position, the sea is calm enough we should be able to maintain position on auto. You see anything change, give me a call. I'm going to be on deck helping launch the recovery vessel."

"No problem. See you in a few hours."

The recovery vessel David brought up from San Diego was a version Scott had never seen before. It reminded him of the first crab-like underwater robot David had invented, but was larger and more robust. The old vessel had operated flawlessly, but the long trailing antenna made it difficult to maneuver inside a sunken ship. There was always the chance of snagging the antenna-tether which could endanger the mission and a million-dollar piece of equipment. The new version had no tether and looked more like a puffer fish with claws. It had a basket on its back, similar to the original and enough LEDs to light up a stadium at night. "The lights will be of little use," Scott said. "You can't see your hand in front of your face down there."

"That's why you're gonna love the improvements I've made," David said. He pointed to an area on the end of the claws. "When the claws are wide open, they act as a metal detector. I can tune it to any metal from aluminum to gold. I developed it for underwater mining of manganese nodules. We can use that feature to locate the ingots underneath the sand. We can find the bar, reach through the muck and pluck it out without even seeing it."

"That is the coolest piece of machinery I've ever seen," Richard said.

"It does have one drawback," David admitted. "The claws are only rated for twenty-five pounds. Pulling a ten-kilo bar out of that silt might be too much for it."

David saw the disappointed look on Richard's face. "So, here's what we're going to do. We're going to use the water jet to move some of the sand away. That's going to ruin visibility and we will not be able to monitor what it's doing."

"How is that going to work?" Richard asked.

"We'll be flying blind," Scott said. "Use the metal detector to hone in on the gold bar and the claw to recover it. But I would like to send a basket down that we could load and bring up instead of bringing the robot up each time. Bringing the bars to the surface one at a time will take forever."

"That area is riddled with tangled metal," David argued. "A basket could get hung up on debris. Bringing up each ingot individually will be our safest bet. This is new equipment. We can't risk losing it."

"Sounds like you thought it through pretty well," Scott conceded. "Let's get it in the water."

An hour passed and then another without recovering a single bar. Scott saw the concerned look on David's face. Something was wrong.

"We should be bringing up gold," Scott finally said. "I've been watching you play with that control panel for two hours. You want to tell me what's going on?"

"I don't know," David said.

For David to say that, there had to be a big problem.

"Tell me what you know and maybe Richard and I can help."

"I can't find the gold. My coordinates tell me we're right on top of it, but there isn't anything there. I've been running diagnostics on the equipment, but I can't find anything wrong."

"That's impossible," Scott said, incredulously.

David let out an exasperated sigh. "I've never run across anything like this before."

Richard was trying to remember if he'd ever come across a situation where a location they had locked in on, had changed. He knew the GPS coordinates couldn't change. "The gold must have moved," he blurted out.

Both David and Scott looked at him like he was crazy.

"You're saying someone dove down and stole a field of gold bars a mile under the ocean," Scott said. "That's impossible."

"I heard you say that before," Richard said. "I didn't say someone stole them. They must have moved."

"What?" Scott asked.

"Don't go killing the messenger. I just know the accuracy of the GPS. In my experience it's not the problem. The only thing left is the gold had to have moved."

"We were here a few days ago," David argued. Then he grew quiet and frantically tapped the keys on his computer. "Shit!"

"Don't say 'shit' and not tell us what you found," Scott demanded.

"Earthquake. We had another earthquake. It must have moved the gold." He brought up the previous images from *Rover* and *Fat Boy* and transferred them to the large screen on the wall. He jumped out of his chair and pointed to the screen. "The gold is right here, or was right there on the side of the slope."

All of them were staring at the screen thinking the same thing. *Where would the gold be now?* The edge of the cliff was not ten feet away. *Could it be over the edge?*

David was thinking this might be the shortest recovery effort in history. "If it didn't fall over the edge, it will be damn close. Vibration and gravity will send it in that direction."

"Do we want to send *Fat Boy* down to check out the edge of the cliff?" Scott asked.

David shook his head. "We already have the recovery vessel down there. I just have to tell it to change the search field. If it's there, it will find it."

"If it's not?" Richard asked.

"We don't know how deep that chasm is. Finding it at the bottom is not something we can do this year." David's voice was heavy with disappointment.

"An earthquake explains a lot," Scott said. "We never would have found the sail of that U-boat if it hadn't landed on that ledge. It was probably separated from the rest of the wreckage by earthquakes."

"That means we're in danger of

losing everything," Richard said. "We better hope there isn't another earthquake."

"Thanks for pointing out the obvious," David said. He went back to his computer and punched in new instructions, hit enter and leaned back in his chair. "In ten minutes, we'll know."

As they impatiently waited for information from the recovery vessel, Scott patted Richard on the back. "Good call. We were both stumped."

"Remember that helicopter that went down in the Mediterranean?" Richard asked. "We had it on radar from three different ships so we had the crash site pinpointed to within a few yards."

"I remember," Scott said. "At four-thousand feet, it took two days to find the wreckage. That was from currents in the area."

"Bingo," Richard said. "Our data was correct, but once it was off our radar, it could have been anywhere by the time it got to the bottom. We'll find the gold."

"An earthquake is the only thing that fits our situation," Scott said.

"We got it!" David yelled at the top of his lungs. "It's bringing up the first bar."

"Anyone else want a drink?" Richard

asked. "I think this calls for a celebration."

Scott put his hand on Richard's shoulder. "It's all-hands-on deck, Admiral. We can celebrate when the hold is full of gold."

Richard frowned. "Am I on vacation or working, right now? I'm having a hard time distinguishing between the two."

"Working!" both David and Scott answered together.

Don watched the activity from the bridge. Each trip to the bottom and the return trip took an hour. Recovery rate was one bar an hour at best and closer to an hour and a half. At that rate, if they worked around the clock it would take a week to recover all the ingots. Of course, they couldn't work around the clock. The robot needed to be recharged between every other trip and the crew was too small for around the clock operation. *What am I going to tell Danna?*

With the discovery of over a hundred more bars of gold, Don had slowly been putting together another plan that would exclude Danna and her brother all together. The boat she said they had rented was not going to hold 2200 pounds of gold and three passengers and still be seaworthy. He really didn't like Danna or her brother, anyway. He needed another plan, but an alternate plan would require him to get Tad and Bobby back on board. Maybe the extra gold would be enough to back his original plan. Take control of *Hunter* and sail to a port outside US territorial waters.

In spite of the late start, by dusk five bars had been salvaged and placed in the hold. There were no security measures taken to place the bars in a safe. Everyone on board was part of the team and each entitled to a portion of the take. Scott had no reason to believe the three hired crew members would consider taking the ship and the treasure. His mind didn't work that way.

There was a special hold, however, that Scott had built into the deck which was equipped with a locking latch to keep the contents safe during a storm or rough seas. It was a simple lock that didn't even require a key. This is where the five bars rested as the team retired for the day.

A small front was passing through and Don set the ship's autopilot to hold their position so they wouldn't require someone at the helm, twenty-four-seven. With the engines rumbling and the running lights glowing bright for safety, Don left the bridge and joined the crew in the War Room. It was the first time Scott had gathered them all together to go over the recovery plans in detail and the first time Bobby and

Tad had been told about the extra gold bars.

Scott sat at the conference table and looked around the room. On his left was Richard and to his right, David. Don sat in a chair across from them with Tad on the couch on one side and Bobby in the recliner on the other. They were all drinking their favorite beverage and the room was filled with anticipation. Much of what they were about to hear, they had already speculated about in their own minds, if not to each other.

"We're in the first stages of recovering over two thousand pounds of gold ingots that were lost over seventy-five years ago," Scott began. "To save you the math, that's over forty million dollars at spot price. It could be more if there is historical value to a collector. Because of the unique nature of the find, it may go for auction at a significantly higher price." He stopped while the other's cheered. "There is a downside, however," he stopped for a moment as the room grew silent. He continued, "discoveries of this type are often disputed. From what we know about the find, we believe the gold originated in Japan, but it was on a German submarine. There is a chance both countries will make a claim on it."

"That's bullshit," Don said. "International Marine Law allows us to salvage treasure from an abandoned or deserted vessel. I'd say seventy-five years at the bottom of the ocean is pretty abandoned." He looked at Bobby and Tad who were clearly siding with him.

"I'm not going to argue the law with you," Scott said. "Sometimes the recovery is cut and dried, but more often, when a large sum of money is involved, there are those who will file a claim, even if it is a long shot. In this case the claim would probably be filed in the United States District Court in San Francisco. The gold could be held until the courts have decided if those filing a claim are entitled to a portion of it."

"That could take years," Bobby said. "What are we supposed to do while it's tied up in court?"

"We're talking about a lot of money. I think it will be worth waiting for," Scott said.

"Are we really talking years?" Tad asked.

Scott pursed his lips and nodded. "Unfortunately."

"The ships on auto, Skipper," Don said. "It's been a long day, I'm turning in."

He was clearly disappointed, maybe even angry, Scott thought. "Good idea," Scott said. "It's going to be long hours for the next week."

After the crew had departed, David went to the bar and poured a glass of wine. "That went over like a turd in the swimming pool." David said. "I told you to keep the bad news until we recovered everything."

"I had to let them know," Scott said. "They were already counting the dollars, I could see it in their eyes. Better to disappoint them now than have them get their hopes up and be disappointed later."

"You really think Japan will make a claim on the gold?" Richard asked.

"There's no way to keep a find like this out of the papers—"

"Or off the Internet," David cut in.

"How much will we be awarded for the recovery?" Richard asked. "We're entitled to something for recovering it. How do you expect to cover expenses?"

"Good question," Scott said. "The courts awarded the silver from a sunken Spanish galleon to be returned to Spain a few years back. The treasure hunter was out everything. These ingots clearly have the Imperial Seal of Japan on them. It would be hard to argue they didn't belong to them at some point in time."

"You mean, we could raise all the gold and Japan could demand all of it back?" Richard asked.

"Or Germany could claim it belongs to them. Suppose it was a payment for equipment," David said. "It was a German submarine. I could see where they might have a claim."

"And don't forget the *Carissa*," Scott said. "If it's determined the submarine launched a torpedo that sunk the tanker, there are the families of the crew who will want to be included in any settlement."

"What's the bottom line?" Richard asked.

"We've got the expense of recovery. At a minimum, we'll be granted enough to cover our salvage cost." David said.

"I'm beginning to wonder if it's worth the effort," Richard said. "I had no idea recovering lost treasure was so complicated."

"I've been telling Scott that all along," David said. "That's why I was so negative about this one, until I saw the full value of the bounty. Forty million is enough to fight a few lawsuits."

Chapter 16

Newport, Oregon

Danna watched the sun set over the Pacific and wondered why Don hadn't called. She gripped the phone hard enough her knuckles were white. When her phone finally rang, she almost jumped out of her skin, but it was her cell phone, not the satellite phone. She checked the caller I.D. "Hi, Paul. Before you ask, I haven't heard from Don, yet."

"That son-of-a-bitch," Paul said, angrily. "I was afraid he'd try something like this. He's out there with our gold and is cutting us out of the loop."

"Don't panic yet. Maybe something came up. Where are you right now?"

"I'm at the *Bayview Bar.*"

"I'll be right over."

★★★

Aboard *Hunter*

Don waited in his cabin, wishing the others would retire so he could make the call. He still wasn't sure what to tell Danna. The treasure was so large. *Could they carry that much extra weight in the boat Paul and Danna had rented?* He knew taking over *Hunter* and stealing that much gold would require Tad and Bobby's help. He needed them to run the ship, help load, unload, and transport the gold once they were in port. He needed more time. *Will I be able to keep Danna and Paul in check for another week?* he wondered. He opened his cabin door and listened for the sound of anyone prowling about. Not hearing anything but the normal background noise of the ship's engines and periodic creaking of the ship as it rose and fell with the ocean swells, he headed to the upper deck to make the satellite call to Danna. Standing on the bow of the ship, Don found shelter from the rain and wind under a canvas, made certain he had a signal and made the call.

Danna was with her brother sitting in a booth next to a window at the *Bayview Bar*. She was sipping on a rum and Coke and gazing at the shimmering lights reflecting off the bay. "This is it," she said to her brother, picking up the phone.

"Hello."

"Danna, Don here."

"I know who it is. You're the only one who has this number. What took you so long?"

"We need to change our plan."

"Don, so help me, if you're scamming me, I'll get even."

"Nothing like that. The treasure is much larger. We're now looking at raising one-hundred-twenty-three gold ingots, not sixteen."

Danna put her hand over the phone and forced herself not to break out screaming. "Wow. How are we going to smuggle that many bars into Mexico?"

"We can't. I've been racking my brain to figure out another plan. That much gold will draw a lot of attention and take some serious equipment to move. Where are we going to store it? You can see we need to come up with a better plan."

Danna waved her brother off as he was trying to get in on the conversation. "That's going to take a few more days, to bring up, won't it?"

Don laughed. "You got that right. They worked all afternoon and only brought up five bars."

"We only have the boat rented for a week," Danna said, "I'm going to lose my deposit. I can't cancel at this point."

"Ditch it. We need a larger one anyway," Don said.

"Are you kidding me! I already drained my savings on this project. How am I supposed to come up with a larger boat?"

"We're talking forty million dollars, Danna. I'm sure you can think of something."

"Okay, I'll see what I can do. Call me every night. I don't want to be second guessing what you're doing." Danna hung up.

"What's he trying to pull?" Paul asked.

"He says it will take a lot longer to recover because, wait for it, they found a lot more gold!" Danna raised her hands in the air like she had just scored a touchdown.

"Jesus, Danna, keep it down." Paul looked around the room to see if anyone was paying attention. He leaned across the table toward her. "How much more?"

"Lots. Enough that we need a bigger boat. Can you hotwire one of those luxury yachts?"

"How are we going to get one of those out of the harbor without being seen?"

"You know those things are moored ninety percent of the time. The owners won't miss it for a month."

"It's not the owners I'm worried about. You and I don't exactly look like the luxury yacht types and the Coast Guard will be watching vessels coming and going. No way will we get away with it. Besides—"

"Then we'll have to steal a yacht that's already out at sea," Danna interrupted. "There's forty million dollars up for grabs."

"How are we going to steal a boat out on the ocean?" Paul knew he would have to do the work. Boarding another boat without the owners knowing it was not only tricky, it was downright suicidal. Law on the high seas was shoot first and ask questions later. Boat owners were weary of other boats approaching. The idea stunk. He shook his head. "I'm not doing it."

Danna leaned into her brother. "We're talking at least forty-million dollars," she said again. "We need to find a way."

Don put the phone away. It was after midnight and he knew he was expected to be up at dawn. He was still wrestling with the task ahead. *Maybe they will steal a boat big enough to sail to a distant port.* There were a few places in Central America where they might make landfall without having to go through customs. A gold bar might be enough to bribe a customs' official in a third world country. Cartels slipped drugs through those ports all the time. He plopped on his bunk and fell asleep without undressing.

Later that day, Cascades Volcano Observatory, Vancouver, Washington

The earthquake was deep, over thirty miles below the ocean and a hundred miles off shore. The needles on the seismometers jiggled frantically for thirty-seven seconds and then stopped. It wasn't enough to alarm anyone on shore. Very few felt it. The director of the observatory, Dr. Jason Trask, wouldn't even know it happened until he arrived at work the following day.

Chapter 17

10:13 a.m. Aboard *Hunter*

Scott, David and Richard were taking a break while the equipment was recharging. They were all on the portside of the ship watching a pod of gray whales heading south.

"You seem preoccupied," Scott said.

David had been unusually quiet most of the morning.

"You ever get a feeling something is about to go horribly wrong?" David asked.

"All the time," Scott said. "More than likely it will, so cheer up and enjoy life while you can."

"I don't know what it is. We're on one of the biggest finds we've ever seen and it seems to be slipping away, literally. We have seven bars and are in danger of losing another hundred. They are marching toward the edge of that ravine like a herd of lemmings."

"Did something happen last night, I'm not aware of?" Scott asked.

"The bars have moved again. It's

like I'm chasing them. Every day they seem to be closer to the edge. I'm having nightmares about it."

Richard was watching the whales through a pair of binoculars, a good ten feet away from Scott and David. The drum of the ship's engines and the slap of the water against the hull were enough to shield him from the conversation. He had seen whales many times before, but they always fascinated him. The last whale disappeared and he lowered the glasses.

"We about to get started again?" he called to Scott.

"In a minute," Scott said. "David wants to send down *Fat Boy* to see if the submarine hull has moved."

Richard came closer. "Did we have another earthquake?

"We did," David said. "That's thirteen in the past week. But who's counting?"

"Thirteen? That sounds unlucky."

"Unlucky is if that U-boat reunites with the tower," Scott said. "That ledge the tower is on isn't large enough to catch the rest of it if it goes over."

"So, you're thinking we need to get those sixteen bars right now?" Richard asked.

"I think we need to know how bad things are," David said. "This wreck may have been down there for seventy-five years, but it isn't going to be accessible much longer. Another year and we'd never have found it."

"Then jawing about it isn't going to make things better," Richard said. "What can I do to help?"

"We're talking about sending *Fat Boy* down to survey the submarine while we continue to bring up the gold bars. It means you will have to retrieve the bars when they come up all by yourself. David and I are going to be busy for the rest of the day."

"I'm on it," Richard said.

The next day

6:10 a.m. Newport, Oregon

There's a lot of preparation needed to steal a watercraft, especially a large one. If you are planning on taking a voyage, there is a horrendous fuel bill and the record you took on that fuel. Next, there are the provisions for food on an extended trip. Last, but not least, you need to know how to operate and navigate the craft you are intending on stealing. Paul and Danna were smart enough to realize this and, therefore, had to improvise. Fortunately for the two, Danna had the training needed for planning, and this wasn't any different than any number of problems she had faced in her job. The conclusion was, they would let someone else do the hard planning for them. They would have to be invited to go along on someone else's voyage.

For much of the day before, Danna had hung out in the Bay View Bar watching people come and go until she found the perfect mark.

It was a ruggedly handsome man in his late twenties, with a weeks' worth of beard and dazzling blue eyes. Over a drink at the bar, he had told her about the voyage he'd be taking the next day. She had slipped him enough 200 proof ethanol in his last drink to put him out well into the next day if he was able to make it home that night.

As the sun rose, casting long, quivering shadows, on the still water, Danna waited for her moment to engage the couple aboard *Tranquility Bay*.

They were a pleasant looking couple in their late fifties, and he was on the phone, wondering why his hired hand hadn't shown up. The boat wasn't fifty feet long, like Don had requested, but at thirty-six feet it was seaworthy and able to carry a heavy load. Also, it could be piloted by one person. She could tell by the gestures the man was making, it was now or never. She sucked in a deep breath and approached the boat from the stern. "*Tranquility Bay*, an odd name for a boat," she called to the woman.

"It was my husband's idea," the woman said looking down at Danna. "It was where we stayed on our honeymoon."

"I'm Danna Collier," Danna said. "I work over there at the Pacific Marine Science Center."

"Oh, how interesting. Are you a scientist?"

"Oceanographer. I helped chart a lot of the water off our coast."

The woman turned to her husband. "Honey, get off the phone and come and meet this nice woman."

He stuffed his phone in his pocket and came over to his wife. "Danna, this is my husband of thirty-seven years, Fred Donald. I'm Merry. I know Fred Donald, two first names. We get that all the time. His family was originally McDonald, you know like the restaurant, but no relation, darn it. Do you think he's cute? My name is just as unusual. Most people think it's M-A-R-Y, but it's M-E-R-R-Y, like Merry Christmas, get it? My birthday is in December."

Will this woman ever shut up? Danna thought. "If I were ten years older, I'd try and steal him from you," Danna said smiling.

"I'm going to let you girls chat," Fred said. "We seem to be missing our deckhand." He slipped his phone from his pocket again.

"This is a beautiful boat," Danna said. "It looks vintage. You don't get the rich mahogany railings and solid teak decks any more. Seems everything is metal and fiberglass."

"Oh, you know your boats. We restored this ourselves. Everything is original, except the engines and the navigation. We had dual Volvo marine engines installed, because we like to take it out pretty far. Safety is the number one concern out in the ocean, my Fred always says."

"He's right, about that," Danna said. "May I come aboard?"

"Oh, where are my manners. Certainly. I can show you around."

Danna climbed aboard and Merry showed her around.

"This is perfect," Danna said.

"I know. We're so lucky. We're going out tuna fishing. There's a huge school of yellow fin a hundred miles out."

They were below deck in the galley, when Fred called down. "Merry, we may have to cancel. I can't seem to raise our deckhand. I doubt I can find anyone on short notice."

"That's terrible, Fred. I was so hoping to get a hook in one of those fish." She looked at Danna. "This trip was supposed to be our anniversary present. I'm so disappointed."

"Maybe I can help." Danna said. "My brother is a deckhand. He even knows how to drive a boat. I can call him and see if he's available."

"I don't know," Fred said, joining them. "I've used this guy for years. It's hard to find reliable help."

"Trust me, my brother is the best. I could come along if you're nervous."

"What the hell, give him a call," Fred said.

Merry put her hand on Danna's arm. "You are such a stroke of good luck. Are you sure you can take the time off work?"

"I'm on vacation," Danna said. "Why else would I be wandering around the docks this time of day?" She made the call. It just so happened Paul was on the docks too. He'd catch up with them in five minutes.

Paul lined up behind a fishing trawler twice the size of the boat he was piloting. He had never taken a boat over the bar by himself and wanted to be sure he didn't make a mistake that would cost them the boat or their lives. He had secured his Oregon boater's license a year earlier when he thought he might try fishing again. Fred had insisted on seeing it. This was his first time using the license for real. Everything he had learned for the test had been online.

"Are you sure about this?" Danna nervously asked, watching the fishing boat in front of them crash into a giant wave.

"Shut up, I need to concentrate."

Paul eased up on the throttle and waited in the trough of a wave, and as the bow started to rise, pushed the handle to full throttle. "Hang on!" he yelled, realizing he had timed it wrong and instead of riding the wave they plowed through it. The wave broke over the bow, sweeping around the bridge and flowing along the deck before running back to the sea. No sooner had it passed when they were riding the backside down like a rollercoaster and the next wave was threatening to break over them. This time Paul got lucky and nosed the craft up the wave and topped it just before it crested. They heard the diesel engines scream as the propellers came completely out of the water. Just as quickly they hit another swell, this one smaller. Paul breathed a sigh of relief as they headed for open sea.

"That was close," Danna said. "I thought you knew how to drive a boat."

"It's been a long time," Paul said. "We made it didn't we."

Earlier that morning, Paul had watched in the shadows as Danna carried out the plan they had devised the day before. He had seen the couple preparing the thirty-six-foot Chris Craft cabin cruiser for a trip. It was an older boat, but had been kept in pristine condition. The Mahogany trim gleamed in the morning sun. He had longed to own something like this, but had given up hope. Now he was captain of his own ship. Soon they would be sailing south with more gold than either of them could ever imagine. The weather was perfect and they had equipped the boat for several days at sea.

Danna recalled the conversation she'd had with the couple. "You remind me of our daughter," the woman said to Danna, giving a knowing glance to her husband. They had even offered to outfit them with a rod and reel so they could test their skills against the tuna. "It will be fun. If we can't hook a tuna, we'll go for halibut," Fred had said.

She hated killing them, but she had flipped through all the other options in her mind and it kept landing on the same page. They were in it too deep to turn back now.

As soon as the man had contacted the Coast Guard and cleared their position in line to shoot the bar, Danna pulled a gun on Fred and Paul took over the controls. She had already tied up his wife and stowed her below in the forward cabin.

She snickered at the thought. The boat was named *Tranquility Bay* after a coastal village in Italy where the couple had spent their honeymoon, now it would be the place they would die.

When the radio squawked "*Tranquility Bay*, this is Yaquina Bay Station, are you safe?" Paul panicked.

"Answer it," Danna insisted. "You were supposed to notify them when you were clear of the jetty."

"You do it, I got my hands full."

"They'll know something is wrong if I answer."

"Dammit, do I have to do everything?" Paul picked up the mike. "Yaquina Bay Station, this is *Tranquility Bay*. Sorry for the delay, we're clear of the jetty and headed for deep water."

"Roger, *Tranquility Bay*. Have a safe trip."

Danna still held the gun on Fred and was ready to use it. She pulled out a zip-tie and held it up to the man. "Put your hands together like you are praying," she said, making a loop in the tie. She slipped the loop over his hands and jerked the free end until the man winced in pain. She then marched him below and soon returned to the main deck.

"What are we going to do with them now?" Paul asked.

"What do you think?" Danna said. "We can't take them to Mexico with us."

"I don't want to kill them," Paul said. "They are a nice couple."

"You don't have to worry about it." Danna stuffed the gun in her pocket. "See, you don't have to do everything. I'll take care of them."

"But kill them?"

"We let them live, they know our names and our descriptions. They even know where I used to work, for god's sake."

"Do what you gotta do," Paul said. His face broke into a broad grin. "It's not like you need a job anymore." He couldn't keep the grin from his face. "We're just a couple of rich people on a cruise in our pleasure boat."

***

6:45 a.m. Aboard *Hunter*

"I've found a way to speed things up," David announced over breakfast.

"That's good," Don said, "because there's a storm coming in from the northwest."

"How bad?" Scott asked.

"Gale-force winds. Nothing we can't handle, but it sure would be nice to be onshore when it hits."

"How much time do we have?" David asked.

"Forty-eight hours, maybe sixty."

"Two days," David said. "It could be cutting it close."

"What's the plan?" Scott asked.

"We use *Fat Boy* as a transport vehicle to bring the ingots up to the surface. You know the compartment where the AUD is kept? We take out the drone and it's large enough to hold four ingots at a time."

"That's going to screw with its ballast," Scott said. "It will be too nose heavy to navigate. You think it will still be able to maneuver?"

"It did fine with you on its back. I'm just planning on loading the gold and letting it rise to the surface. We collect the gold in the lifeboat and bring it onboard."

"It's worth a try," Scott said. "What do you estimate we can get before the storm hits."

"All of it," David said.

"If I have a vote, I say go for it," Don said. He was for anything that would speed up the process. The sooner they got the gold on board *Hunter*, the better. They could transfer it to the smaller vessel and outrun the storm. He didn't relish riding out gale-force winds in a smaller vessel.

Scott looked over at Bobby. "Bobby, can you handle the lifeboat? It's going to take one man at the tiller and Tad can collect the ingots. David will run the robots; Richard and I will collect the ingots when you bring them in." He thought for a moment. "I'm not going to lie to you, this is risky. You drop an ingot and we all lose."

"No problem," Tad said.

"I can handle it if you can handle sandwiches and scrambled eggs for the next few days," Bobby said.

"Then, it's all-hands-on-deck," Don said, grinning. "I always wanted to say that."

"Eat a good meal," Scott said. "We're going to work straight through until supper."

All of them seemed excited. Cutting the time at sea and making port before the storm appealed to everyone. More gold meant more money. David was looking forward to getting off the ship, possibly more than anybody. He had suffered several bouts of seasickness and he had things piling up in San Diego.

8:01 a.m. Pacific Marine Science Center

Gil took another call from his father. It was the third call in two weeks, prior to that he could count on one hand the number of times his father had called him since he'd graduated from college. "Dad, every time you call, I'm imagining you or Mom are in trouble."

"I know you're not on top of earthquakes as much as your colleagues at OSU, but I think you should pay attention to what's happening along the subduction zone."

"I'm on top of it, Dad. It's a few minor quakes, most of them over ten miles deep. We've had them before and I've been in touch with OSU. They don't think we're seeing anything that amounts to a pattern, certainly not a swarm. It's unusual, but not unprecedented."

"You know I worry about you, Son. When I visited and we were talking about a tsunami, honestly, I couldn't see anywhere you could get to for safety. You know that bridge over the bay is almost certain to come down if you suffer a major quake?"

"Dad, I can't believe you're getting this excited over something that's not likely to happen in our lifetime."

"I promised your mother I'd call. If you get a major quake, head south, not over the bridge."

"It's already in the plan, Dad. We have an inland road picked out that will get us high and dry in less than ten minutes. You know, we're supposed to be the experts." Gil was smiling, thinking of his father calling him over this. He heard his father sigh.

"I'll let your mother know. By the way, are you planning on coming home anytime soon?"

"We all saw each other over the Fourth. Is there a reason you're asking? You're feeling all right, aren't you?"

"That wasn't much of a visit," his father said. "There were so many other people around."

"I promise I'll be home for Thanksgiving this year."

"I'm going to hold you to it."

"Bye, Dad." Gil hung up, confused by the call. His father wasn't one to panic easily, but there must be something he saw that nobody else did. *Better to be safe than sorry,* he thought. He checked the evacuation plan on the wall next to his office door. It was simple enough. There was a back road that paralleled Hwy 101 heading south. In less than a mile there was another dirt road heading inland. He shook his head. *No problem*, he thought, but just to be certain, he called the Oregon State Geological Center again to see if there was anything unusual occurring that he should be aware of, but they had no new information to share. He went back to his work.

His father, on the other hand, opened the Three Sisters watch site and checked the seismometers placed around the 10,358-foot, South Sister. The east side of the mountain had been bulging for years, but recently activity had increased, evidenced by nearly constant earth tremors of low magnitude. He checked the GPS locators and saw the mountain had moved another two millimeters on its eastern slope. Bend, Oregon, and the nearby city of Redmond were a community of nearly eighty thousand full time residents. They were directly in the path should there be an eruption.

Jason felt a subtle knot in the pit of his stomach, something was telling him things weren't like they seemed.

Chapter 18

Waldport, Oregon

The city of Waldport was populated with about 5,000 year around residents, and double that number in the summer months. Most of the permanent residents lived high above the downtown businesses on a ridge that overlooked the town and the ocean. These were the shop owners, fishermen and carpenters, handymen, and forest workers who plied their trade for a living. The airport, golf course and the high school also sat safely high on the ridge. But it was different for those who could afford property on or close to the ocean beaches. Those houses, as well as the downtown area sat barely above sea level. At high tide many of the houses could watch the waves break a hundred feet from their deck. Highway 101 passed directly through the city at an elevation of about thirty feet. There was nothing in that area that was safe from a tsunami, but to those who made the town their year-around home, it seemed like the town had been there forever. It had been established in the late eighteen-hundreds as a lumber port, but morphed into a fishing village and more recently as a quiet getaway during the summer months. It was a perfect place to retire. When the one traffic light in town was installed, it tended to be a nuisance not a necessity, but during the summer months, when the highway became jammed with travelers it became a welcome addition.

Today, as Patricia, Fay, and Janet headed across the Alsea Bay Bridge they were stopped by the light. Patricia waited patiently as the light blinked through its programmed sequence. There had been many times when she had wished it wasn't there, and this was one of them. "The city fathers thought this was a good idea," Patricia commented, waiting for the light to turn. Finally, it did and they drove another block and pulled in front of Peterson's Art Gallery. Even in the late morning hour, traffic was light. After spending an hour perusing the paintings, sculptures, and unique handblown glass items on display, they paid for their treasures and carried them back to the Jeep.

While getting into the driver's seat, Patricia glanced across the bay at the high cliff dotted with a few houses but mostly coastal pine and fir trees. The ridge was higher than the highest span of the bridge that stretched over the bay. She was standing on the sidewalk. The altimeter in her Jeep listed the altitude at thirty-three feet. She was trying to locate the spot where they had all stood the day before watching the imagined tsunami.

"Are you girls up for something different for lunch?" Patricia asked.

"We're just riding along," Janet said. "What have you got in mind?"

"There's a new Hawaiian restaurant on the wharf. I thought we might try it."

It took all of two minutes to make it to the restaurant on Alsea Bay. She parked the Jeep. On the wharf, just below them, an old man dropped a trap into the water hoping to catch a Dungeness crab. She and the girls got out. Again, Patricia's eyes were drawn to the high cliff across the bay. She stood for a moment staring.

"What are you looking at?" Fay asked.

"I've been wondering the same thing," Janet said. "What is it over there that's got your attention?"

"See that cliff across the bay?"

"That's where we went on your evacuation plan, wasn't it?" Fay asked.

"It is, and looking at it from here, it makes me a bit nervous?"

"It looks plenty high, to me," Janet said. "If a tsunami came, I'd much rather be up there than where we're standing right now. We can't be more than twenty-feet off the water, and look, you can see the surf. This is the last place we'd want to be in a tsunami."

"All this talk about a tsunami is making me sick of the ocean," Fay said.

Patricia, still lost in thought, walked around the front of the Jeep, opened the passenger door, and pulled a pair of binoculars from the glove box. She put them to her eyes and then handed them to Fay. "That cliff is made of sandstone. It's crumbling as we speak. Trees are falling off the edge. A big enough wave might undercut it and we'd be sucked right into the fray."

"That's a scary thought," Fay said, handing the binoculars to Janet. "You want to change your plan?"

"You bet I do. We're taking a drive after lunch and finding a new rendezvous spot."

Chapter 19

Somewhere Out to Sea

Two hours back, she had forced the couple to go to the rail where she executed them, putting a 9mm slug into their heads at point blank range. Fred fell backwards over the railing and hit the water, but Merry slumped to the deck. It was all Danna could do to lift the woman enough to send her into the water. She had never come close to killing anyone before, but she had never had a reason as compelling as this either. *When you put your mind to something, it's surprising how easy it is.* Strangely, the bodies floating in the water made her queasy. *I should have weighted them down,* she thought. *What if they float to shore?* She had waited a few minutes thinking she may vomit, but Fred disappeared, as did Merry. She swallowed hard and joined her brother at the helm.

Paul was staring at the screen on the navigation system.

"We should have spotted the ship by now. Are you sure you know how to read that thing?" Danna said, looking at the navigation system.

Paul continued to stare at the screen. There was a red dot surrounded by circles. Along the top of the display were several numbers and a few letters. The only thing he understood was the arrow with the large "N" in front of it.

"I think that points north," he said.

"Which direction are we headed?" Danna was getting impatient. There were no other vessels on the screen.

She looked out in all directions, but all she saw was empty ocean. The plan called for them to find *Hunter* and shadow it, waiting just over the horizon until Don called for them to move in.

"I may have mixed up north and south," Paul finally admitted.

"We've been on the water for six hours!" Danna shouted.

"I figured it out," Paul announced. "If I do a one-eighty, we'll be headed south. We are probably seventy miles northeast of Don's position."

"You had one job to do and you screwed it up. Why should I trust you now?"

"We need to stay out overnight anyway. We can navigate by the stars tonight. I'm sure we can find him."

"I'm supposed to believe you can navigate by the stars. The sun is right there. I think that's south." She shook her head. "What the hell was I thinking, letting you in on my plan?" She started opening drawers and pulling books from a shelf in a nearby cupboard. Finally, she found a book titled, *I Com Marine Commander Instructions*. After thumbing through the book, she checked her notes for the location Don had given them for *Hunter*. She pushed Paul aside and entered it into the GPS. On the screen, the location of *Hunter* appeared along with their current position.

"Paul, you're an idiot. We're nearly a hundred miles off course." She pointed to the screen. "See that dot. That's *Hunter's* location. Keep the boat going toward the dot. With any luck we'll make it before dark."

Aboard *Hunter*

Scott watched through binoculars from the deck as Tad leaned over the side of the lifeboat and muscled the four bars of gold from the compartment in *Fat Boy* as it bobbed up and down partially submerged. They had all agreed Tad was better suited to the task of leaning over the side and pulling the heavy bars from *Fat Boy*. It was a slow and cumbersome operation, and required a degree of agility and strength. David had been right about it being faster than the previous method. They had already recovered thirty-six bars in the time it had taken to retrieve four the day before. Once the bars were in the lifeboat, Bobby steered the lifeboat back alongside *Hunter* where Scott lowered a basket on a cable attached to an electric winch. There was ever-present danger a bar could be dropped with all the handling and everyone touching the gold was aware of the value. Each ingot was handled as it were a newborn baby.

Scott brought up the basket and placed the four latest gold bars in the hold with the others. The batteries on *Rover* were due for charging and David brought the recovery robot to the surface and around to an opening in the stern of the ship where it could be connected to a quick charger on the lower deck. Tad and Bobby followed it in and moored the lifeboat to the deck for a much-needed break. They headed to the mess where Bobby made sandwiches for everybody.

"You fellas enjoy yourselves. You have forty minutes and then we need you back out there," Scott said, taking a bite of a ham sandwich.

Scott left the mess with the sandwich in his hand to join David and Richard in the War Room. He met Don coming down the passage way in the opposite direction.

"Hey, Skipper," Don greeted. "I thought I'd take advantage of the guys coming in and see if I can grab a bite."

"Bobby made sandwiches. I'll be in

the War Room if you need me. I told Tad and Bobby they have forty minutes."

David was leaning back in his chair with a glass of wine in his hand and Richard was pouring a drink at the bar. They turned when Scott walked in.

"Pretty slick, huh," David said. "We'll have the last bar on the ship by this time tomorrow. Then, while you bring the booty back to port, I'm going to jump in the helicopter and beat-feet to shore before the storm hits."

"Sounds like a plan," Scott said. "Your little trick has more than cut our recovery time in half. I'd like to beat the storm in myself."

"Adding *Fat Boy* to the mix wasn't without a cost," David said. "Quick charging every few trips cuts battery life significantly. Both of the robot's batteries will be shot and need to be replaced before I put them through the paces for the Navy next week."

"I understand you needing to get back to the office," Scott said. "Maybe I can join you on this trip. You were a big help to me. I'd like to return the favor."

"I think you're going to have your hands full up here," David said. "When the press gets wind of the size of this recovery, they're going to go nuts."

"You sure you want to miss all the

fun?"

"I'll be long gone by the time you make port. I'll leave the fun stuff to you." He knew how much Scott hated the press.

"Do me a favor and stick around until we get back so we can celebrate with the girls," Scott said. "We've hardly spent any time with them."

"Maybe I can do some work from your office another day," David said.

"The house will seem empty without you and Fay," Scott said. "It's been a fun couple of weeks."

"What about me," Richard said. "You're going to miss me, aren't you?"

"My liquor cabinet will miss you," Scott said. "Next time you show up, bring a case of Scotch with you, and none of the cheap stuff."

"It's a deal," Richard said, lifting his glass.

There was a sense of nostalgia in the room. Treasure hunting for this year was coming to an end, as witnessed by the winds picking up and the dark clouds on the horizon.

"No doubt this is the most unusual salvage we've ever done," Scott said. "Not many folks can share such an adventure with their friends."

"Now you're going to make me cry,"

Richard scoffed.

"Yeah, I think married life is making you soft," David kidded. "We're not done here yet."

Snacking on sandwiches, chips, and soft drinks in the mess, Don, Tad, and Bobby also felt the end of the recovery was near.

"What's the count?" Don asked Bobby.

Tad answered first. "Forty."

"Whew," Don said, shaking his head in an exaggerated move of disbelief. "That's almost nine hundred pounds of pure gold. Did you take the time to look at those ingots? Over thirteen million dollars at market price. It's a shame we'll never see any of it."

"Scott said we'll get our share eventually," Tad said. "We need to be patient."

"Our share!" Don repeated. "We do all the work and they get all the money. The system is rigged against guys like us. We'll be lucky to see any of the proceeds, and you both know it."

Don eyed them closely. If he could get them to help take over the ship, it would make his job easier. He could cut out Danna and Paul; leave them far behind as he steered the ship to the nearest natural port. He had yet to figure out where that would be. While he was tending the bridge, he'd had plenty of time to devise another plan, but stealing the ship with the gold aboard required the other two crew members. There was no way he could capture *Hunter* without their help.

"It's the way it is," Bobby said. "We all made our choices."

"You're saying we don't deserve a bigger part of the take?" Don was in Bobby's face.

"Back off, man," Bobby said. "Talking about getting more of the loot isn't going to change anything."

"He's right," Tad agreed.

"There's three of us and three of them. We can have it all if we're smart," Don persisted.

"You're talking about taking the ship?" Tad was wide-eyed in disbelief.

"Why not? We know how to operate it."

"Because, we sail into any port in the country and we'd be arrested on the spot," Bobby said.

"What if we made port in another country, someplace where they would accept us?" Don watched them closely. They were listening and that meant they might buy into his plan. "We could go to the Cayman Islands or Central America. There are lots of places where we would never be recognized."

"What do we do with Scott, Richard, and David?" Tad asked. "Scott isn't going down easily. He used to be a Navy SEAL. I think those guys were pretty tough."

"That was years ago. We can take them by surprise in their sleep," Don said. He put his hand on his pocket and felt the taser.

"You're not talking about killing them," Bobby said, nervously. "I'm not signing up for killing anyone."

Got him hooked, Don thought reaching in his pocket. He pulled out the taser. It was the size of a smart phone. He activated it for effect. "We disable them in their sleep and tie them up with these." He showed them a zip-tie. "We can release them in the lifeboat once we're in control. It will only take a few minutes. We take them by surprise in the middle of the night; they'll never see us coming."

"Sounds like you've thought this all out," Tad said. "It might work."

"You bet your ass it will," Don said, raising his eyebrows. "The question is, are we ready to be multi-millionaires or going to be poor sailors the rest of our lives?"

"I'm in," Tad said, looking over at Bobby.

"If you're in I'm in, too," Bobby said.

"Then get back out there and get the rest of the gold." Don slipped the taser back into his pocket. *Man, are Danna and Paul going to be surprised when they get here and* Hunter *is nowhere in sight.*

★★★

Danna and Paul agreed to take separate four-hour watches through the night. They could see the dark clouds on the horizon moving closer, but were certain they could beat the storm. *One more day, and we'll have the gold aboard*, Danna thought. *Paul and I are the only ones entitled to it. Our family was devastated when great-grandfather didn't return.* She had never met her great-grandfather, but imagined she knew him from all the papers she had read. *He was a man ahead of is time*, she thought. *They owe us.*

★★★

Aboard *Hunter*

Scott entered the War Room. It had been a grueling sixteen-hour day. "I'm going to have a few beers and head for bed," he said, looking at David and Richard. They already had drinks in their hands. He grabbed a Blue Moon out of the refrigerator, twisted off the cap and took a long drink.

"Me, too," Richard said. "It's amazing to think we were able to raise thirty more ingots after lunch."

"At this pace, we'll finish up late tomorrow," David said.

"If we make port by sunset, that gets us home twelve hours before the storm hits," Richard said.

"I'll get the girls together and we'll have that welcoming party when you arrive," David promised. "Then Fay and I really do have to split."

"We have a lot to do tomorrow" Scott said, finishing his beer. "I'm turning in."

"I talked to Fay today," David said, raising his voice. He looked at Richard. Scott stopped by the door and turned. David continued, "In case you're wondering, both of your wives are doing well. They went shopping for those fancy handblown glass globes and had lunch Hawaiian-style."

"Honestly, are you really interested in art and hand-blown glass globes?" Scott asked, shaking his head in disbelief.

"He gets crabby when he doesn't get enough sleep," Richard said, lifting his glass. "Good night, Scott."

Chapter 20

Aboard *Hunter*

The next day was gray. A high layer of clouds had moved in overnight completely blocking the sun. The ocean had turned a dark slate green. Swells were increasing in size with a few whitecaps on the horizon. The wind was ten knots and gusting. All the signs of the approaching storm filled the air.

In spite of the weather, Scott was amazed at how anxious the crew was to get started. He figured everyone wanted to get home and beat the storm. The total count was seventy-four when they had finished the night before. Tad and Bobby were out in the lifeboat again. They were struggling to keep it in the vicinity of the spot where they expected to see *Fat Boy* breach the water. If they were in the wrong spot, the rising submersible could come up under them and they might capsize. He watched through binoculars in anticipation as Tad and Bobby struggled with the first four ingots of the day. Yet, they were smiling and joking. *They must be glad it's almost over,* he thought.

Over breakfast, Scott and David had discussed a change in the arrangement they had made with the crew. After seeing the disappointment on their faces when they were told the gold would probably be held in escrow until any disputed claims were settled, Scott had convinced David to make another arrangement. He hadn't mentioned it to them yet, so the laughter and enthusiastic manner in which Bobby and Tad were acting seemed a bit odd. At the moment, he wished they were taking their job a bit more seriously. The last thing he needed was a distraction as they finished up the operation. *It will be a big party on board ship tonight,* he thought, *but right now there is still a big job ahead.*

★★★

Tranquility Bay motored steadily toward the rendezvous point with *Hunter*. The overnight trip had been steady and uneventful with the wind at their backs. Danna grabbed a warmer jacket from the rack as she opened the hatch and climbed up on deck. She half expected to see *Hunter* on the horizon, but still saw open water in all directions.

"Still on course. I've got coffee, if you want some," Paul said.

"You're chipper this morning."

"We're about to be millionaires many times over," Paul said. "What's not to be happy about."

"For one," Danna said, "We need to find a place to take on fuel. The diversion you caused by your stupid mistake cost us a lot of fuel. Have you got money on you to pay for a fill up?"

Nothing his sister could say was going to dampen his mood today. "Now I know how rich people feel. All that wealth, but no cash to buy lunch. That's what credit cards are for. I know you have one."

"Credit cards? Mom really did drop you on your head when you were an infant. Credit cards leave a trail."

"Whatever," Paul said, rolling his eyes. "See that speck out there? That's our golden goose. You can get off my back, now."

Danna picked up the binoculars and checked out the ship. Sure enough, it was *Hunter*. "I'll fix breakfast. This is going to seem like the longest day in our lives."

***

Scott and David gathered in the War Room as the batteries in both vessels were in for recharging again.

"Water's getting choppier and the wind's picked up. I think that storm might hit early," David said. "Maybe we should cut it short."

Scott looked over at him. "You want to go to shore early?"

David thought about his helicopter tethered to the deck. "I said I'd wait until we have all the gold, but I can't chance it for more than a few more hours."

"You continue to run that robot from the War Room. Richard and I can handle it on the deck. We'll get every last one of them."

"Sounds like a plan," David said. "We still have to get the bars from inside the U-Boat."

He launched the recovery robot and made certain it was on the bottom. He swallowed hard and realized he wasn't feeling well. He placed the remote-control box on the table and sat down in one of the plush recliners and closed his eyes.

An hour passed before Scott discovered something was wrong. They had recovered eight ingots, but in the past hour nothing. Tad and Bobby used their radios to contact the ship. "We should have had another load by now," Tad said, over the radio. "What's the hold-up."

Don, as well as everyone on the ship, was tuned into the same channel and caught the message. *Hold-up*, Don thought. "There's no hold up, yet," he said softly. Tonight, they would execute his plan.

"I'm not sure," Scott said. "Richard, go check with David."

A minute passed before they heard Richard on the radio. "We got a problem," he said, "David has passed out. He's breathing, but he doesn't look good."

"Be right there," Scott said. "Tad, you and Bobby might as well come in and take a break."

"Roger," Tad responded.

Scott entered the War Room just as Richard lifted David up and placed him on the couch.

"I thought he didn't look good this morning," Scott said. "You think it's seasickness?"

Scott went over to the First Aid box and snapped an ammonia salt capsule and passed it under David's nose. David immediately woke with a start.

Scott grinned. "We thought you might be dead, but you were just playing possum."

"I don't feel well," David said.

"That's pretty obvious. What did you have for breakfast?" Richard asked.

"A café mocha," David said.

"Get him something to eat. He looks anemic," Scott said. "When are you going to learn those things will kill you?"

Richard left for the mess while Scott stayed with David.

"We've only brought up eight bars!" Richard heard Don say just outside the mess.

"We? It was Bobby and I who were freezing our asses off while you were in the wheelhouse with the heater turned on high. Don't give us any shit about only eight bars."

"Am I interrupting something?" Richard asked, coming through the door.

"We were just discussing the mission and our lack of progress today," Don said.

"David isn't feeling well and needs something to eat. Any suggestions?"

"I made a batch of muffins. They're good. Bran with raisins." Bobby got up and took a metal tray from the cooler.

"I'll take a few," Richard said. He put three in a plastic bag and took another to eat on the way.

"That was too close," Don said. "From here on out, we only discuss this when we know we won't be interrupted."

"Who made you the boss?" Tad asked. "And we never discussed how we're going to split the take. You better not be thinking you're going to get a bigger share than me and Bobby."

"We're splitting it three ways,

okay. You do your job and I'll do mine."
Don stormed out of the mess and went
back to the bridge. He heard a beep on
his radar and checked the screen. Sure
enough, there was something five miles
on the horizon. He checked to be certain
he wouldn't be heard and picked up his
satellite phone.

"Is that you on the horizon?" Don
asked.

"Finally," Danna said. "How's the
recovery coming along?"

"We're having a bad day. David is
under the weather and we can't operate
the robot without him. Right now, it
stands at eighty-two bars."

"We need to do this tonight. With
or without the rest of the gold," Danna
said. "In case you haven't noticed the
weather is changing for the worse."

"I agree," Don said. "I'll call you
after dark."

At this point there wasn't anything
to be gained by arguing with her.
Executing the plan tonight made sense,
but meeting up with Danna and her
brother wasn't going to happen.

Don stashed the satellite phone and
checked on the condition of the ship.
All systems were operating flawlessly.
He looked out at the dark, choppy water.
It was bad enough it wasn't safe for Tad
and Bobby to be out in the lifeboat. The

early arrival of the storm threatened to spoil everything.

He had tossed two plans around in the back of his mind. He kept going back and forth, trying to make up his mind which one would net the most money for him. The original plan with Danna and Paul had its faults, but so did his plan with Tad and Bobby. He could easily eliminate Danna and Paul after they had loaded the gold onto their boat and keep everything for himself. *Tranquility Bay* was small enough he could operate it himself. There was no way he was going to operate *Hunter* without help. Also, *Hunter* would be more difficult to disguise. He could change the name, but after it was reported missing, there would be an international alert. You couldn't just make a ship the size of *Hunter,* disappear. Every port in the Western Hemisphere would be on the lookout for her. He struggled with his options. The more he thought about it the more he thought he needed a third plan. One where he was the only one who ended up with the gold. He would have to split the gold three ways if he took *Hunter*, and only one way if he rendezvoused with *Tranquility Bay,* but the storm could ruin everything. The ship could weather a storm much better than a small craft. He made a body count. If they took *Hunter*, he would almost certainly have to kill Scott, Richard and David. They were all too well known not to be missed and a massive search would be launched once they didn't return to port. David had enough money his wife could post a massive reward for finding the ship. On the other hand, no one would miss Danna and Paul. One hundred percent of the gold and two dead bodies, or three dead bodies and a third of the gold. "Damn, what was I thinking," he said out loud, but he was still uncertain. He looked out on the horizon and saw lightning flashing in a dark squall.

David ate the muffin and was feeling better. They knew he would be okay when he asked for the second muffin. In an hour they were ready to go back to work.

On the way to the lower deck where the lifeboat was tied, Tad opened the hatch and looked at the stack of ingots. "Hard to believe gold can be at the bottom of the ocean for that long and still look as good as new," he said to Bobby. He traced the sixteen petals of the Imperial Seal with his index finger and thought, *this is the most beautiful thing I have ever seen.*

"The weather is getting worse," Bobby said, nervously looking at the chop in the water and feeling a gust of wind.

"I'll be glad when we have the rest of them," Tad said.

"Me, too, let's get this over with." Bobby cinched up his life vest and climbed in the tiny boat.

In spite of the weather, things were operating smoothly again. The storm had held steady and had stayed far enough away everyone could still do their job. Another twelve ingots had been brought up in the past three hours.

It was after noon and the robots had to be brought back to the ship for recharging again. The crew took a break, but Scott, on the lower deck, had a concerned look on his face. The lifeboat, lashed to the dive platform of the ship, was bouncing erratically against the platform and was in danger of being damaged. He went down a ladder and placed two foam fenders between the lifeboat and the platform. Waves were breaking over the platform even though it was well inside a protective opening in the stern of the ship. The two robots seemed to handle the rough water without a problem, but they were secure in their padded charging stations. The lifeboat, on the other hand, was close to being swamped. Satisfied things were safely secured he joined Richard and David in the War Room. "I'm thinking we should wrap it up and go in rather than ride out this storm," Scott said over lunch, which consisted of more ham sandwiches and muffins. Since Bobby had been helping recover the treasure, the quality of the meals had dropped considerably.

"The easiest part of the recovery is sitting in that U-boat underneath us," Richard said. "Maybe we should go for those before we hang it up."

"He's got a point," David said. "We can park a basket just outside the wreck and bring up all sixteen at once."

"It beats sending Tad and Bobby back out in that lifeboat," Scott said. "There were a few anxious moments I thought they were going to be swamped by the waves. I wouldn't be out there in this weather and neither should they."

"All agreed," David said. "We make one more dive, and head for shore."

"How about the helicopter?" Scott asked. "You still planning on taking off this afternoon?"

David hesitated. "Weather permitting," he said. He had pretty much written off the possibility when he saw the wind was gusting up to twenty-knots. "Let's get this done ASAP."

Scott found his crew in the mess. "Good news, guys. We're going to send a basket down and clean out the sixteen ingots in the submarine and call it quits. That's going to leave us a few ingots short, but it's not worth risking the crew, at least not in this weather. Bobby, you and Tad can stay onboard." He looked at Bobby. "Maybe you can come up with a good meal to celebrate. We hope to be back in port before nightfall."

Don, Tad, and Bobby exchanged panicked glances. For their plan to work, they needed Scott, David, and Richard fast asleep. There was no way they were going to overpower them while they were awake.

"That's great, Skipper," Don said. "We get to sleep in our own beds tonight."

"We'll be making the last dive within the hour. You know what you have to do. Tad, be sure to secure the lifeboat back on deck."

The crew watched Scott as he left. As soon as he left, they gave each other panicked glances.

"This doesn't change anything," Don said.

Tad jumped to his feet. "What the hell, man, this changes everything."

"Keep your cool, we can still pull this off."

"How?" Bobby asked.

"Tad, you can fake engine trouble long enough to keep us out here until dark, can't you? I know the skipper and he won't risk taking the ship across the bar after dark."

"Just long enough for him to decide to spend the night out here?" Tad nodded. "It might work. I can do that."

"Once everyone is asleep, we take over the ship and head for open water," Don lied. He had no intention of doing anything but load the gold onto *Tranquility Bay* and leave everyone tied up and drifting on *Hunter*. The ship would drift in the choppy sea for several days before beaching or crashing into the rocks offshore. He would destroy the radio and make certain there wasn't any means of communication available should any of them free themselves. By the time the ship was discovered, he'd be thousands of miles away. He stifled a grin. *Genius*, he thought. *I'm a rich fucking genius. What about Danna and Paul?* The question came to him almost out loud, as if someone else asked it. "They will help load the gold," he said. "Do I leave them on the ship or toss them overboard later?" He shrugged. "Doesn't matter."

As David had predicted, the recovery of the sixteen ingots went quickly and without problems. "Save the easiest for last is my motto," David said.

Scott, using an electric winch, brought up the basket containing 352 pounds of gold. "I'll take care of these," Scott said. "You get the robots back onboard and secured. Richard, tell Don to ready the ship for the trip in. We should be able to make it before sunset."

Two hours later

"Ship's ready to sail, Skipper," Don said, when Scott entered the wheelhouse.

"Good job," Scott said, "You can take a break. I'll take over."

"Sure thing, Skipper." Don left the bridge and headed for the mess. He wanted to be far away from Scott when the shit hit the fan.

When the constant drum of the engines died, David and Richard were in the War Room starting an early celebration. Richard stopped pouring his drink and said, "What the hell?"

Bobby and Don were in the mess and Tad was in the engine room. Don looked at Bobby and grinned. "It's starting."

Scott got on the ship com and called the engine room. "Tad, do you copy? What's going on?"

"I'm on it, Skipper. Give me a minute and I'll run diagnostics." He hung up and went back to reading an outdated issue of Playboy that had been thumbed through so many times the pages were ragged and smudged with engine oil and grease. He leaned back against the bulkhead. He knew Scott wouldn't wait long before calling back.

The call came sooner than he expected. He threw the magazine aside and answered. "It seems to be a faulty thermocouple, Skipper. The engines have overheated."

"This is serious," Scott said. "How long before we get the thermocouple changed out?"

Tad checked his watch. "Give me an hour."

"I can't give you an hour. I need it in the next fifteen minutes."

"I'm sorry, Skipper. There's no way that's going to happen."

"How about I come and help?"

"No need to do that. We'd just be bumping into each other."

"You want to be the one to tell the crew we're going to spend another night out here?" Scott asked.

"No, sir. That's why they pay you the big bucks."

"Smart ass," Scott said. "Call me the second you're finished."

Tad retrieved the magazine and found a clean spot to sit. He glanced over at the thermocouple with the sensor wire disconnected and dangling from it. He picked up the magazine, leaned back against the bulkhead again, and turned to the centerfold.

With no engines, they were dead in

the water, not the best situation in the growing storm. The ship was already rocking in a motion that made even his stomach queasy. "Don, return to the bridge," Scott called over the ship com.

"What's up Skipper?" Don asked, entering the wheel room.

"Take over the helm. I'm going to check on the progress in the engine room. It can't take this long to change out a heat sensor."

"I'm sure Tad has it under control," Don said. "What do you want me to do up here?"

"Stand by until we get the engines back online," Scott said. *What the hell is going on?*

"Skipper, does this mean we'll spend another night out here?"

"Not if I can help it," Scott said.

Without the noise of the engines, Tad heard the approaching footsteps and grabbed the loose wire. He waited until Scott was in sight and held it up. "Just finishing up, Skipper. Got the new thermocouple installed." He plugged in the wire. "There we go. Good as new."

"I think we already missed our window," Scott said, checking his watch. "Nice try." Scott was clearly disappointed.

"Sorry I let you down, sir."

"Nothing to be sorry about, you did your best." Scott patted him on the back. "Why don't you join the rest of us in the War Room. I'll give the others the bad news, but we can all celebrate tonight as I have a surprise for you and the rest of the crew."

Now that the engines were running, the ship was weathering the approaching storm with little difficulty. The state-of-the-art controls automatically stabilized the ship and kept the yaw and pitch at an acceptable level. Scott called everyone to meet in the War Room. They would make port first thing in the morning.

Scott looked around the room with a satisfied smile. Everyone including David and Richard were in a festive mood. "Good news or bad news first?" Scott asked, standing by the bar.

"Bad news," Bobby called out.

Of course, everyone already knew the bad news. They wouldn't be making port tonight. David had weighed the option of taking the helicopter in, but the wind gusts were erratic enough it could make for a risky lift-off. Clearances were simply not enough for him to risk it when they would be in port the next morning anyway.

"Okay," Scott said, getting all their attention. "We had a small engine malfunction which delayed us enough we can't make port until tomorrow morning. You'll have to endure the luxury of your shipboard accommodations for one more night."

"Give us the good news," Don said, raising his beer.

"The good news is, we recovered one-hundred-ten gold ingots. That's a total of twenty-two hundred and forty-four pounds of gold. At today's market we estimate it's worth to be right at," he paused, "David why don't you tell them."

"Thirty-five million dollars," David said.

"We'll be lucky to see any of it," Don said, just loud enough that Scott could hear.

Scott ignored him. "I know how hard it is to wait for the promise of your share, so—"

"Here we go again," Don interrupted.

Scott ignored him again. "So, David and I put our heads together and came up with something I think will please all of you. We decided to give each of you a check for your share of the gold as soon as we reach port. You won't have to wait for the money. We'll take the risk and fight the court battles. Each of you will be paid the full amount of your bonus regardless of the outcome."

"What if you lose in court? You're gonna take the money back, aren't you?" Don said.

Scott couldn't believe how negative Don had become. He just told them they were going to get paid even if he and David went bust. "You all keep the money, we take the risk." Scott said. He looked around the room, expecting a more positive response, jubilation, in fact. "If there a problem with that, tell me, now."

"That's one hundred and seventy-five thousand dollars for each of you," David added.

"Thanks, Skipper, and you Mr. Stafford," Tad said. "I know you didn't have to do that. That money can buy me a house and a new car."

Later that night, Don met with Tad in his cabin. "I know it sounds like a lot of money, but wouldn't you rather have all of it? We take the ship and we each get eleven million."

"Scott's right," Tad said. "A hundred-seventy-five thousand is more money than I expected to ever see at one time. It's a guarantee. I'm out of your crazy scheme. It probably wouldn't have worked anyway. Where are you going to hide a ship this big?" Tad was adamant. "I talked to Bobby. We're both out and you can't run this ship without us. Settle for the one hundred seventy-five

K and be glad we don't tell Scott about your crazy scheme."

Don could see he was going to lose this battle, and he couldn't risk Tad saying anything to Scott. "Your right," he conceded. "Tomorrow we'll all be rich. Keep this between us and we'll have a beer and laugh about it once the checks are cashed."

It was 2:00 a.m. and Don had yet to close his eyes. Tad and Bobby were out, time for plan B. He peeked out his cabin door and looked down the passageway in both directions. He was pretty sure everyone had turned in for the night. The only sound was the constant drone of the engines as the autopilot kept the ship from drifting away from the set location. Seeing the coast was clear, he made his way to the upper deck and made the call to Danna. "We're on. Stand by and I'll give you a call when it's safe to approach."

"Make it sooner rather than later," Danna said. "This weather is going to make it difficult to transfer the gold."

"I got it covered," Don said. "Bring the boat up to the lower deck where we launch the robots. I'll have the gold ready. Wait for my call."

Don went back inside and stopped at Tad's cabin door. He listened for a second and then quietly opened the door.

He saw Tad sound asleep in his bunk. He gripped the taser in his hand ready to use it. As he leaned over, Tad woke and looked straight up at him.

"What are you doing here?" The words had barely left his mouth when Don plunged the taser onto his chest. Tad's body froze for an instant before erupting into a debilitating spasm. Don was surprised how calm he was as he removed two large zip-ties from his jacket pocket and bound Tad's hands and feet. Next, he removed a sock from Tad's suitcase and stuffed it in the unconscious man's mouth. *One down, four to go.* He had chosen Tad for his trial run, because, next to Scott, he was the strongest one he'd have to disable. The ease at which it went down gave him confidence to tackle Scott next, but he wasn't kidding himself; Scott could be a problem.

Outside Tad's cabin, Don took a deep breath. Scott might not be as easy as Tad. He needed insurance. He knew there was a shotgun under the bar in the War Room. The gun would come in handy if Scott offered too much resistance. Don hated the thought of killing anyone in cold blood, but he knew there was always a risk. A shotgun blast might wake the others and he needed to catch each of them by surprise. He desperately wanted to carry out his plan without using it, but he went to the War Room and removed the shotgun from its holder under the bar. He rummaged through several drawers until he found a box of shells. He loaded the gun and pumped the action to chamber a shell. Suddenly, he wished he had thought this out a little better. He had both hands full, one with the shotgun and the other gripping the taser. He couldn't use them both at once. The more he thought about it the more nervous he became.

Two minutes later, he felt awkward and nervous as he turned the latch on Scott's cabin door.

Chapter 21

Don Blanchard listened to Scott's soft rhythmic snoring as he stood in the doorway. In the dim, red, glow of the ship's inside nightlights, he carefully placed the shotgun up against the bulkhead and slowly made his way toward the bed. With the taser clutched tightly in his right hand he surveyed Scott's quarters. He had never been in there before. The room was larger than the crew quarters and it took several steps to cross to the bed. Just as he was leaning over to jab the taser into Scott's neck, the ship rolled, causing the shotgun to slide off balance and crash to the deck. Even though the gun didn't discharge, the noise was enough to wake Scott, who had always been a light sleeper. Scott opened his eyes, but Don was ready and plunged the taser down contacting Scott in the jaw. He had missed his target but the high-voltage jolt of electricity was enough to paralyze the much stronger man. Scott's body shook violently, became stiff, and then went limp. Don wasted no time in binding Scott's hands and feet using the zip-ties from his pocket. He searched for a gag and found a sock on the floor. It would do. He stuffed it in Scott's mouth.

As Don reached to pick up the shotgun, he couldn't stop his hands from shaking. There was no backing out now. He was committed. He had to finish what he'd started.

One by one, Don neutralized everyone on board. Bobby was the last one and the easiest. He had everyone tied and gagged and he never had to use the shotgun. He breathed a sigh of relief and made his way to middeck where the gold was stored.

In the storm, moving the heavy ingots from middeck to the lower deck proved to be more of a task than he had imagined. With the increasing wave action, the rolling of the ship, and the constant downpour, each trip became more difficult. An hour passed and he had only transferred half of the gold. He was out of breath, bruised and sore from falling several times. It was time to get help. He considered untying Bobby and forcing him help, but reconsidered. Paul would be a willing helper. He called *Tranquility Bay*.

"My god, Don, we've been on pins and needles waiting for your call. Is everything okay?" Danna asked.

"Everything's fine. I need a little help getting the gold to the lower deck. Go ahead and bring the boat in."

The cabin cruiser looked small as it came up behind the much larger

Hunter. After it had docked and they had lashed it to the larger vessel, it was still resting ten-feet below the lower deck of *Hunter.* The cabin cruiser was too large to fit inside the bay where the lifeboat and robots had operated from. Even with several foam fenders for protection, the two vessels seemed to dance to their own set of music and crash together loudly every time a wave whipped by. Don lowered a ramp, but it too gyrated with the opposing movement of the vessels.

Danna looked up at the wobbling gangplank and began to doubt the sagacity of their plan. She hadn't considered how difficult it would be to mate up with the larger vessel.

"We'll use the hoist to lower the ingots to the boat," Don called down to Paul, "but first I need your help getting the rest of them."

Paul scrambled up the ramp and his eyes opened wide when he saw the stack of gold. "Man, let's get the gold aboard and get out of here. I'm not sure we can stand the full brunt of this storm."

"The rest of the gold is up there," Don said, pointing to the deck above them. Paul, mesmerized by the number of ingots, picked one up and inspected it in the light. He ran his fingers in the impression of the Imperial Seal. "These are beautiful. And each one is worth over three hundred thousand dollars?"

Danna scrambled up a ramp and joined them. She picked up an ingot. "My god, they're heavy. How many more are there?"

"Enough that I don't want to spend the night talking about them," Don said. "We need to be long gone before daylight. We don't want to be seen."

"What did you do with the rest of the crew?" Danna asked.

"Can we have this conversation later?" Don said, angerly. "Paul follow me."

Paul followed close behind Don as he made his way to middeck, and Danna, wanting to be in on everything, followed close behind. When they reached the hold, she looked in and gasped. There was more gold than she had imagined.

Chapter 22

4:37 a.m. Aboard *Hunter*

Scott awoke confused and struggling against his restraints. He vaguely remembered seeing Don's face, before everything went black. *No, not Don*, he thought. He had trusted the man, taken him under his wing, and trained him to run his ship. He was terribly disappointed, but more of a concern was his fate along with David and Richard. *What was the plan? Of course, it is the gold, but how?* Taking the ship would not be easy and Don couldn't do it by himself. Bobby and Tad had to be in on it. If they were, there was no telling how this would end. *They will have to kill us all. Are they really capable of that?*

Scott struggled against the restraints, cursing himself for not seeing this coming. His hands were behind his back, his feet were tied at the ankles. The last time he had felt this vulnerable was when his scuba gear got hung up inside a sunken vessel in the Mediterranean. His SEAL team had been sent in to check for survivors after a collision during training exercises with the Turks. Right now, none of his options were good. He didn't have a well-trained force watching his back. No one would be coming to his rescue. If he was going to get out of this fix, it was up to him to figure out how. Without knowing how many others were involved, he had to assume the worst. His crew had orchestrated a mutiny, and judging from his condition, they had been successful. He twisted the restraints until they cut into his wrists, but they didn't budge. His hands felt cold from lack of circulation. He was helpless without the use of his hands. He struggled to get enough oxygen into his lungs. The gag in his mouth tasted like the morning after an all-night drinking party.

Scott's mind kept racing through a list of impossible options. He had to focus. The shotgun was the only firearm on board. Don knew about that and probably had it with him. If they were planning on killing him, why hadn't they done it? He tried with no avail to push the gag from his mouth using his tongue, but it made things worse. He started choking as the sock crept deeper in his throat. His mind was spinning. "*Prioritize. Focus on one problem then the other. Relax, you can do this,*" the voice of an old drill instructor he hadn't thought of in years was telling him.

The steady hum of the engines and the lack of motion told him the ship was still holding in place. He still had time to save the ship if he could get free. He cursed the plastic strap that was binding his hands. He knew breaking it was useless. The police hadn't turned to zip-tie restraints so people could easily free themselves. They were more difficult to get free of than standard handcuffs. About the only way to free himself was with a knife. He let out a slow controlled breath.

He contorted his body and felt under his pillow for his knife, worked his fingers around it, and struggled to open it. That was the easy part. Holding the knife and cutting through the restraint was arduous and took all his concentration.

His grip slipped and the sharp point of the blade stabbed into his wrist. He let out a muffled cry and clamped down hard on the gag in his mouth. He felt his warm blood trickle down onto his cold hands and the slippery fluid made his grip on the knife even more difficult. It took all his concentration to saw at the restraint without losing his grip on the handle, and he was beginning to feel it was never going to give. He pulled and twisted and sawed some more until, in an instant, it broke, sending the knife skidding across the cabin floor. He immediately went for the gag and pulled it from his mouth and rolled off the bed to the deck. In the red glow he couldn't see where the knife had gone. With his hands free, he put pressure on the worst wound and continued his search.

Outside the weather was steadily worsening. The wind was whipping waves against the ship and the spray was shooting up the hull and sending torrents of salt water over the deck.

One of the ropes securing *Tranquility Bay* worked its way lose from a cleat and Danna scurried back down the ramp and frantically tried to secure it. The boat was bouncing furiously against the fenders.

"You better get that line tied off before you lose everything," Don yelled down at her.

If she couldn't get it secured there was danger the boat would be damaged or worse, swamped by the breaking waves. She found the rope but was no match for the choppy water. Try as she might, she couldn't get the rope wrapped back around a cleat.

"You're the slowest pack mule I've ever seen," Don barked as Paul delivered another ingot to the stack.

Every step had been an effort and Paul had fallen three times on the last trip. "Get off my back, that was the last one."

"Good, get down there and help your sister secure the boat. I'll get the hoist ready to lower the gold."

Paul barely touched the ramp as he jumped down on the deck of *Tranquility Bay*. He fell hard at the feet of his sister.

"Get off your ass and help me," Danna shouted above the roar of the storm and the crashing hulls.

Don pushed a toggle on the tethered control box to raise the gold. The electric winch moved slowly, and as the netting surrounding the ingots tightened around the gold, the cable stretched to its limit, threatening to snap. The boom swung sharply as the full weight of the load lifted from the deck. Don grabbed the boom and pushed it with both hands, swinging it out until the load was dangling above *Tranquility Bay*. He started to lower the load and stopped abruptly when he caught movement out of the corner of his eye.

From his cabin, Scott had gone straight to bridge to see if Don was there. He had every expectation of finding Bobby and Tad with him, but the bridge was unmanned. He headed to middeck where the gold was stored. He had watched as a man he had never seen before struggled to pick the last ingot out of the hold. He followed him in the shadows and watched him place it on the stack with the others. Don was standing over the gold like he owned it. The plan was becoming cleared by the second. He wasn't witnessing a mutiny, but a theft. Don had orchestrated a scheme to take the gold. He was waiting for the right moment to attack, and when Paul scampered down the ramp, Don was alone.

Catching Scott's lightning fast movement, Don dropped the control box and lunged for the shotgun a few yards away. His hand reached it, just as Scott was on him. Scott had failed to see the gun hidden in the shadows and Don whipped it around with one hand and fired carelessly. The recoil of the 12-gauge shotgun jerked it out of his hand, sending it sliding away as a wave washed over the deck.

The blast drew the attention of Danna and Paul. They stopped trying to secure the boat and looked up at the scuffle. But they heard a loud crash and realized they had a bigger problem. The boat was bouncing so violently in the rough water they could barely stay on their feet. Paul fell to the deck and stared up at the pallet of gold perilously dangling above him. It seemed to be a very thin thread keeping the gold from dropping on top of him. He scrambled out of the way and was soon back on his feet. If the cable broke, the gold would crash through the deck taking the boat, him, and Danna with it. He had to get to the hoist and lower the gold. The hell with Don, who was still engaged in a fight for his life.

At the moment, the gold hung tight, swinging in a lazy motion like the pendulum of a grandfather clock. It appeared to be secure for now, but things were rapidly getting out of hand. The ramp was jumping and dancing making it nearly impossible to use, but it was the only path to the winch control box.

"Do you have your gun?" Danna shouted to Paul. She was frantically holding on to the bowline, trying not to let go, but when Paul pulled the pistol from his pocket she let go and both of them scrambled up the gangplank. Danna lost her footing and was about to go over the edge when Paul grabbed her by her rain jacket and helped her back to her feet. A few seconds later they were both on *Hunter*.

Scott had seen none of this. He had been preoccupied with Don.

Paul was first to set foot on *Hunter*. Scott was on top of Don about to coldcock him when Danna took aim and pulled the trigger. At the same time there was a loud crash distracting her. She turned toward *Tranquility Bay*, fearing the worst. The chop of the water had increased to the point where the suspended gold was crashing into the deck with each wave. Twenty-two hundred pounds of gold was acting as a battering ram, threatening to shatter their only means of escape. Something had to be done immediately or they would lose the boat. Their plan was falling apart rapidly.

"Get the gold on the boat, I'll handle this," Danna said, training her gun on Scott and Don. She fired another shot, but was too late. The shot went wild and the next punch put Don out cold. Scott slowly stood up with his hands raised.

The ship was barely stable enough for them to maintain their footing. Paul, unfamiliar with the winch, stared at the control box for a moment trying to figure it out.

"Get the gold on the boat!" Danna yelled, raising her gun at Scott to make sure he didn't try anything.

"What's your plan, Danna?" Scott asked. "I don't think you thought this out very well." He pointed with his head. "He doesn't know what he's doing."

"I'll get it," Paul said, pushing a toggle switch forward.

At that moment the ship fell four feet. It was as if the ocean had dropped out from under them. They heard a loud crash as the gold smashed through the deck of *Tranquility Bay*. Paul lost his balance and tumbled across the deck. His head hit the railing and he rolled off the deck.

Danna hit the deck hard. The gun went skidding away. She scrambled to recover, but Scott, who had been brought to his knees, tackled Danna twisting her arm behind her.

Suddenly Scott felt a pain in his back and splinters went flying. Don had recovered and grabbed an oar from the lifeboat. He had swung it like a baseball bat shattering it across Scott's back.

Don immediately realized he should have aimed for Scott's head. Scott rolled off Danna and jumped to his feet.

Holding the remaining piece of the oar, Don went after Scott again, but Scott was too quick for him. As Don lunged and swung with all his might, Scott moved just enough for him to miss sending Don pirouetting off balance like a drunken ballet dancer. Don tried to catch himself, but his momentum was too great and he hit the railing backwards and tumbled over the railing. He crashed against the suspended pallet of gold, bounced to the side and disappeared in the choppy waves.

When Scott's attention was drawn back to Danna, she was on all fours in a frantic search for the gun.

"You get up and you'll join Don and the other guy," Scott said, standing over her.

Chapter 23

5:03 a.m. Waldport, Oregon

The earthquake was strong enough to wake everyone in the house. Dishes flew from the cupboard and the dresser, in the master bedroom where Patricia was sleeping, skidded along a wall and smashed through sliding doors that opened to the deck.

Patricia woke, too frightened to speak. She was frozen in place even though everything in the room was moving violently. It was as if it was never going to stop. When the bed smashed against the outside wall nearly tossing her through the window, she figured it out and scrambled to the floor.

Janet woke in a freefall to the floor. It was like waking in the middle of a nightmare. The window in her room shattered when a statue of a ballerina Patricia had been given on her twelfth birthday hit it head first. It sounded like a gunshot and the open window let in a more terrifying rumble sounding like rolling thunder. It continued for another three minutes and thirty-seconds, but it seemed like forever.

When the house stopped dancing, Janet got to her feet and tried to open the door to her room, but it was hopelessly jammed. "Patricia, Help!" she called.

Before the earthquake, Fay had just gotten up to use the bathroom. She had smashed hard against the bathroom wall and ended up in the bathtub. The toilet broke from the floor and the water in the tank and bowl splashed in a wave across the room. A broken hose snapped and sprayed water everywhere like a spitting snake on steroids. Of the three, Fay, the only one who had witnessed a serious earthquake before took a minute to get her wits about her and had the good sense to stay where she was until the shaking had stopped.

The light in the bathroom flashed just before the electricity went out, and with the overcast outside, it was too dark to see. She took deep breaths and let them out slowly, an exercise she had learned as a child to calm her nerves. She heard Janet calling for help.

Patricia heard Janet's screams also, but was too befuddled to think straight. She was on her hands and knees feeling around the room for her suitcases when Fay stumbled in her room.

"Patricia, are you okay?"

"I need my go-bag," Patricia said. "We need our go-bags."

"We need to get out of here," Fay

said. "Do you know where I can find a flashlight?"

"Kitchen drawer," Patricia said.

Fay made her way to the kitchen and started rummaging through the drawers. Most of them were already open to their limit and the contents scattered on the floor. Dishes and glassware had fallen from the cupboards and shattered on the tile floor. She was barefoot and walked gingerly trying to avoid major obstacles. All the time, Janet was screaming in the background, and Patricia seemed totally out of her mind. *I've got to get control of the situation,* Fay thought.

Not finding the flashlight on the floor, she fumbled through the drawers. Finally, her hands felt the familiar shape of the object. She grabbed it and turned it on. The beam showed major structural damage. She wondered how she had found the kitchen with all the mess. She headed back down the hallway towards the bedroom. Her only thought was getting the three of them to a safe place as quickly as possible. She failed to notice how eerily quiet it had become outside. She struggled to walk on the twisted and buckled floors. She tried pushing on Janet's door and it wouldn't budge.

"Janet, can you hear me?" She called through the door.

"Get me out of here," Janet screamed.

"Calm down. I'm going to get you out. Are you hurt?"

"No, I just want out."

"First you need to find your clothes and get dressed. I'm going to find something to break through the door."

"Fay?" Patricia was standing behind her. She was still in her in her nightie. Her suitcase was in her hand.

"Get some shoes on. You're not going anyplace dressed like that," Fay said.

Patricia didn't move. She stood staring at Fay.

"Hurry," Fay said, "I'll take care of Janet."

"Where are your clothes?" Patricia asked.

From the time Fay was a child she had liked the free feeling of sleeping unencumbered. It wasn't until that moment she realized she was completely naked. She shined the light on herself and started to laugh.

"Take the flashlight." Fay handed it to her. "I'm going back to my room."

A break in the clouds let a sliver of moonlight creep into oceanside windows. Fay threw on a pair of slacks, a sweater, and slipped into a pair of flats, the first things she could find. She glanced out the shattered window and realized the ocean was missing. A cold breeze was fluttering the curtains. She saw the deck was still attached to the house, but tilted at an awkward angle. *It might be the only way to get to Janet*, she thought. She scrambled across the bed and climbed out on the deck. Living on the ocean for years, the continuous pounding of the surf was almost like a tranquilizer for her. Now it was deadly silent, causing an uneasy feeling to well up inside her. Pushing the fear aside, she tested the railing to see if it was secure, and made her way along it to Janet's room. She saw the window was broken out.

"Janet, this way. We can go along the deck and through the kitchen."

Janet had already dressed and had a suitcase with her.

Patricia arrived at the kitchen the same time Janet and Fay entered through the door from the deck.

"You think there will be a tsunami?" Patricia asked.

"There's no ocean out there," Fay said. "That's a bad sign."

"Oh my God," Patricia said, scanning the light around. "Everything is a mess."

"We need to get out of here," Fay said. "Remember the plan."

"We'll take the Jeep," Patricia said. "Grab your go-bags and let's go, just like we rehearsed."

"It's too late if you don't already have your go-bag," Fay said. "We've wasted at least ten minutes just getting this far."

Patricia looked down at the suitcase in her hand. "Well, I'm taking mine."

Fay pushed her way through piled up furniture to the front door. It was standing open, barely hanging from its hinges. The porch was missing. In its place was a six-foot drop, a mass of broken timber, and cracked concrete. Strangely enough, she could see some daylight peeking through the trees in the distance. Not having a choice, she lowered herself down through the opening and scrambled through the rubble to the ground. "Come on, we're wasting time." Fay encouraged the others as she reached up to help Janet down. All three were on the ground when Patricia shined the flashlight to the spot where she had parked the Jeep. It wasn't there.

"I'm sure I parked it there," Patricia said. She scanned the light around. The landscape had changed substantially.

"That tree fell on it," Janet said,

pointing.

Sure enough, the large oak that had stood alone for centuries in the same spot had been uprooted. It was leaning over, blocking their view of the Jeep. Patricia had recalled Scott had considered naming their place *Lone Oak* after that tree. *Oh, my God, Scott, David, Richard?* "Do you think they are all right?"

"Who?" Janet asked.

Patricia didn't answer. She ran over to the Jeep instead and pulled small a limb off the hood. "Come on. I think it's okay."

The tree had fallen in front of the Jeep. One large branch still rested on the hood, but it was too big to move.

Patricia fumbled for the keys, she always kept them in the visor, a practice she had once admonished Scott for, telling him he was just giving a thief free access to their car. Now, she was thankful they were there. She started the engine and put the gearshift in reverse. She stepped on the gas. The wheels spun on the gravel and the car didn't budge.

"The tree branch is too big. We need to make a run for it," Janet said.

"I got this," Patricia said. She switched to 4-wheel-drive and the Jeep started to move. Suddenly, it broke free of the tree's grip and they were shooting backwards. She slammed on the brake and shifted into drive and floored it. Gravel flew from all four wheels as she raced toward higher ground. It was nearing sunrise and the darkness was fading. Fay looked back as they headed up the driveway. What she saw caused her to gasp in astonishment. She was certain they were too late. Far out to sea, there was a giant wave.

Patricia tried to follow her evacuation plan, but Highway 101 was buckled badly and when it disappeared altogether in a sheer drop-off, she turned off the highway and headed up a gravel road she had never been on before. She kept it in 4-wheel drive as she crawled along until she could go no farther. A large Douglas fir had fallen and was blocking the road. "We need to go on foot from here," she said.

The others already knew what they had to do. As their feet hit the ground, they heard the roar of the ocean sounding as if they were standing next to a jetliner ready to take off. For a moment, they froze in their tracks.

Fay grabbed Patricia. "Quick, we're not high enough."

They climbed over the tree that was blocking their path and continued up the gravel road. Behind them the sound of crashing debris, uprooted trees, and a mile of rushing water threatened to overtake them. They reached a clear-cut area and stopped. They were at the highest point on the ridge. They could go no farther.

Patricia, fearing the worst, looked at the others and started to scream. Fay and Janet were scared speechless. The giant wave had crested and continued to rush up the slope. The three stayed huddled together, Patricia screaming, Fay and Janet holding on to each other for dear life.

A few more seconds passed and the sound of the approaching destruction was too much for Janet and she burst into tears. There was a time in her past when she had learned her husband was missing in battle. The same terrifying fear gripped her now. She may never see Richard again.

Patricia started to pray, the prayer her father had taught her when she was a child. She had never been very religious, but her father had told her it would keep her safe in tumultuous times. *Only her father would use a word like tumultuous with a child,* she thought, but she had remembered the word. She thought of her father and brother, hoping they had escaped the earthquake. She looked up. *Mom, if you are watching this, please save us.* Then she said, "Lord, I am not worthy, but please have mercy and save us."

Fay wrapped her arms around the

others in a group hug. She closed her eyes. She wished she could see David one last time, but she knew that was not likely. Even in the darkest hours in the frozen solitude of the ice prison in Antarctica, she hadn't felt this much despair. *This is it*, she thought.

A crashing sound, even louder than the incoming wave, seemed to envelop them and they all opened their eyes and watched in horror as the wave rolled the Jeep up the hill toward them.

Then it stopped. The Jeep rested on its top as the water started to reverse direction. They breathed a collective sigh of relief, knowing they had escaped, but an overwhelming sadness as they watched a wasteland of broken trees, demolished houses, and dead bodies left in the wake.

Chapter 24

5:45 a.m. Aboard *Hunter*

With Danna tied up and sitting on the lower deck, Scott turned his attention to the sound of breaking timbers, splintering wood, and breaking glass as *Tranquility Bay* continued breaking apart. He went for the controls on the winch and started to bring his precious cargo back up. When the pallet of gold reached a height where he could swing the boom back on deck, he reached out with his right hand and grabbed hold, pulling it toward him. It was then he noticed the bold lettering stenciled on the gantry; **Warning 2000 lb. Max. capacity.** He stepped back and watched as the cable suspending the 2200 pounds of gold started to break, one strand at a time. It was as if time were standing still as the tiny wires, once tightly wrapped together, started to unravel and snap like guitar strings stretched beyond their limit. He had a fraction of a second before all the gold would be lost to the sea. He gave it one last effort pulling it toward him and jumped back as the pallet, still two-feet above the deck overcame the strength of the cable and crashed down hard. The cable, now free of the kinetic energy went flying like a whip catching him across an arm as he fell backwards to the deck. At that moment the pallet shattered and the net, which was supposed to contain the gold bars, popped open sending the load of ingots sliding across the deck at hockey-puck velocity. He heard a terrifying scream, turned and saw one of the ingots had hit Danna in the leg and she was bleeding profusely.

"You're going to let me die, aren't you?" She screamed.

The ship was rocking in thirty-foot seas which were too great for the auto stabilizer to manage. Scott struggled to his feet. Gold bars were sliding like blocks of ice in every direction. Dodging the obstacles, he made his way to Danna, removed a handkerchief from her pocket and stuffed it in her mouth. He quickly assessed the damage to her leg as a compound fracture. If he couldn't stop the bleeding the wound would be life threatening. He cut off a piece of the line he had used to tie Danna earlier, and made a tourniquet. He wrapped it around her leg, found a piece of the broken oar and used it to twist the tourniquet until the bleeding slowed. "Hold this," he said. "You let go of it and you'll bleed to death."

Danna stared at him through pained, narrow eyes. She was scared and hurting. She thought of her brother. The last she had seen him he had slid off the deck and disappeared. *Maybe it's better if I die*, she thought.

"What are you doing?" she gagged as Scott started sawing at the remaining rope that was keeping what was left of *Tranquility Bay* attached to his ship. The gold battering ram had destroyed the craft to the point water had flooded the engine compartment and the below-deck cabins. To keep it attached to *Hunter* would put his own ship in peril. As the rope snapped, it took only seconds for *Tranquility Bay* to be claimed by the angry, dark water.

Danna screamed between clinched teeth, "My brother was on that boat!" But Scott knew the grim reality. Her brother had already joined Don in the black water.

Scott left Danna on the lower deck and made his way to David's cabin. He found him still bound with his mouth gagged. "I thought you might be dead," Scott said, pulling the gag from David's mouth.

"What took you so long?" David asked.

"Quiet or I'll stuff this back in your mouth."

"You look pissed. What happened?" David asked.

"We haven't got time for me to explain. We need to free the others." He slashed the straps securing David's hands and legs.

They freed Richard next. "Mutiny," Richard said, as soon as the gag was out of his mouth. "You give those bastards more money than they'll ever see in their lifetime, and this is the payment you get? I hope they all get the death penalty."

"All of them? Do you know something I don't?" Scott asked. "As far as I know Don was the only one trying to take over the ship."

"I saw the three of them talking in the mess earlier and they stopped talking the second they saw me. Are you sure they aren't all in on it?"

Scott thought for a moment. "I haven't seen the rest of the crew. Let's find them and see what they have to say."

"Where's Don, I personally want to knock the shit out of him," Richard said. "He was the one who electrocuted me."

"He went over the side," Scott said.

"I would have loved to have seen that," Richard responded. Scott could not remember a time when he had seen Richard this angry.

"Follow me," Scott said. "If Bobby and Tad were in on the mutiny, Bobby is the weakest. He'll tell us what went down."

The three kept together and stopped outside Bobby's door. Scott stopped for a moment. "The moment of truth. If he's tied up, Don was in this on his own." They found Bobby tied and gagged like the others. Bobby was clearly scared. Scott could see it in his eyes. "Do you know what happened?" Scott asked.

"Don tried to take over the ship?" Bobby phrased his answer as a question.

"I'm asking you. Did you know about this?" Scott persisted.

"It was Don's idea. He wanted to take all the gold. Tad and I told him the share you offered was a fair deal. Honest. Tad and I didn't go along with it."

They found Tad still struggling with the restraints. His story matched Bobby's. At the moment, Scott didn't have any reason to doubt their story. They had been tied up with the others.

"We're bringing the ship in," Scott said. "It'll be daylight in a few minutes. Tad, you tend to the engines. Richard and I will ready the ship for sailing. David, call the Coast Guard and tell them we have an injured person on board in need of immediate medical attention; compound fracture of her right leg. Give them our location and tell them to send a medivac helicopter."

As soon as the orders were given, Scott and Richard rushed to the bridge. "Are you ready to take command of the ship?" Scott asked.

"Never been more-ready to drive a ship again." Richard hesitated and added, "You'll have to take it over the bar. I may be a little rusty."

As they set a course toward shore, David came running up to them. "Scott, I tried to reach the Coast Guard, all I get is a repeating message to turn to the emergency channel. When I tried that, I get nothing but static. Something is really wrong."

"Try to get the girls on the satellite phone." Scott's mind was racing. He knew something was wrong and tried to replay the events over the past few minutes for something he had missed. Then he realized the sudden movement of the ship, when he was fighting to take the ship back, might have been more than a freak wave.

"I tried reaching them. No response." David looked concerned. "I'm really nervous. Something terrible has happened and we're in the middle of a storm and unable to help."

Scott didn't answer. His mind was in hyper-drive and his commando instincts had kicked in. "Richard, hand me those binoculars. David, find Bobby and have him stay with Danna. He needs to take some blankets and keep her warm." He put the binoculars to his eyes and scanned the distant water. "Shit!"

"What is it?" Richard asked.

"Tsunami. I thought it was a freak wave when the ship dropped like a brick, but it must have been an underwater earthquake." He handed the binoculars to Richard. At the same moment the ship lifted abruptly.

"What was that?" David asked.

Scott turned to him. "You're still here, that girl needs attention." David wasn't about to argue. He could see this was serious.

David found Bobby, told him what to do and rushed back to the bridge. The closer they got to shore, the more floating bodies they saw scattered amongst the debris. He was beside himself with worry. "I'm going to take the chopper in and look for the girls."

"We're still in the middle of a storm. You think you can fly in this?" Scott asked.

"I sure as hell am not going to sit around and worry. I need to do something."

"If you go, take Bobby and Danna with you. She's losing a lot of blood and won't last another hour out here."

David thought about it for a moment. "I don't want the extra weight."

"She needs medical attention," Scott argued. "Richard, go help him get ready. Bobby and Danna both go, or nobody goes."

"Turn into the wind. If this kills me, I'm really going to be pissed," David said.

"Patricia has a satellite phone. Be sure and take one along," Scott said. "Keep trying."

"I've already tried the satellite phone. Their number isn't answering."

"Take it anyway, it may be the only way we can communicate with each other. You sure you want to do this? This storm is not letting up."

"It's risky, but I don't see I have a choice. If the girls are in trouble…" he didn't finish.

"Screw it, Scott said. "I'll come down and help you get ready. Richard, you take the bridge."

"Aye, aye, Sir," Richard said.

"I never thought I'd hear him say that to me," Scott said to David, as they hurried to the lower deck. "You know if I could, I'd go with you."

Scott picked up Danna and carried her to the helicopter. She was screaming at the top of her lungs in spite of the gag in her mouth. "You think this hurts?" Scott asked, unapologetically, "think about how many years you're going to be in prison once we get you to shore."

He couldn't understand the muffled sounds she made, but was certain it wasn't, "thank you for saving me".

5:45 a.m. Camas, Washington

As soon as he felt the earthquake, Dr. Jason Trask jumped out of bed and opened his laptop. He knew it was a bad one from the duration. It seemed to go on for minutes. From his computer, he could pinpoint the epicenter and the magnitude. There was no apparent damage to his home, but he was a hundred miles from the source, which was in the worst possible place it could be. It stretched the entire length of two states and was very shallow. His wife Carlene, also a geologist, was standing over his shoulder and quickly went to her own computer to help gather data.

When Jason saw the extent of it, he knew immediately it was a subduction quake. He noted the time and was thankful. He knew his son would be in bed like most of the population along the coastline. He also knew his son lived in the foothills of the Coast Range Mountains and would most likely be out of the wake of the tsunami that was certain to follow the magnitude 9-plus earthquake.

"You get dressed," Carlene said to her husband. "They're going to want you in the office. I'll monitor things from here."

On the way to his office he called his son, Gil. His call went immediately to busy, a bad sign. *The cell towers in his part of the state must be down,* Jason thought. It was still dark and there was no apparent damage along Highway 14. The highway bordered the Columbia River and he was eighty miles from the river's mouth. He wasn't concerned about a tsunami this far inland, but the quake was strong enough that damage to buildings and property in the Portland metropolitan area was probable. As he raced in a westerly direction, he considered the various scenarios that could be unfolding. He tried to anticipate the questions the press would be asking. He had numerous government officials who would want answers for their constituents. He called his office on his emergency line and the phone was immediately picked up by his assistant, Sandra Meeker, a young geologist who had graduated from the University of Idaho the prior year.

"Dr. Trask, are you on your way in?" Sandra asked.

"I'm about twenty minutes out. What do you know so far?"

She relayed information he already knew from his home computer. "Have you heard from NOAA or Homeland Security?"

"Nothing so far, but the phone has been ringing off the hook and a crowd has already gathered in the parking area."

"Are you the only one there?"

"I'm afraid so. I was on my way in from Portland when I thought I was going to be thrown off the Interstate Bridge."

"Let everyone know we'll hold a news conference in forty-five minutes. That may hold the reporters at bay until we get a statement ready."

As he continued to race toward Vancouver, the traffic became more congested, but unlike a normal workday, it was heading east, away from the city.

The David A. Johnston Cascades Volcano Observatory had been named after the young geologist, David A. Johnston, who had lost his life while observing the eruption of Mt. St. Helens, on May 18, 1980. Jason remembered that day even though he had been only six-years-old at the time. The mountain had picked his birthday to erupt and he had been visiting the temporary observatory called Mount St. Helens Volcano Observatory. Unlike the former observatory that had hastily been put together in a storefront when St. Helens showed signs of becoming active, the new observatory was state-of-the art, equipped with the latest in instruments and technology. Now, as a seasoned volcanologist, he had learned a lot about earthquakes and their ability to trigger eruptions sometimes thousands of miles away. Along the Cascade Mountain Range there were several volcanoes that could be considered active even though they hadn't erupted in centuries. Any one of them could be awakened by sudden ground movement. He hoped that wouldn't be the case with this earthquake. There was enough to worry about without having to try and evacuate the slopes of Mount St. Helens and half a dozen other mountains in the middle of a tsunami crisis. He tried calling Gil again and still could not connect. He called home to see if Carlene had heard from their son. He apologized to her for leaving without kissing her goodbye.

"You didn't even say goodbye," she said, and they both laughed.

As Jason pulled into the observatory parking lot, he saw a dozen police cruisers with their lights flashing and several news vans blocking his way. He stopped, jumped from his car and ran up to the first officer he saw.

"I'm Dr. Jason Trask, head of the observatory, I need to get in there."

"The Governor, sir. She's waiting for you. Follow me."

"Governor, which governor?"

"Oregon, sir. Sally Morris."

Jason worked for USGS, a Federal agency, but it wasn't unusual that a local politician would want a photo op with him in time of crisis. Even though the observatory was located in Washington State, it was much closer to Oregon than the state capital of Washington. It made sense the Oregon Governor would be there. "I will have a prepared statement in half-an-hour? I don't have time to talk to her right now," Jason said, brushing past the officers guarding the doors and into the building.

"What's the situation?" he asked Sandra as he came in the door.

"A few aftershocks, but no apparent activity at Saint Helens."

"That's good news. What about Three Sisters?"

Sandra Meeker had anticipated the question. "I've already notified the Mayor of Bend and the City Manager of Redmond to be ready to evacuate. There have been fifteen minor quakes on the eastern side of the South Sister. We may have magma working its way up."

"Anything else I should know?"

"The quake was a subduction quake and from its length along the zone, USGS has upgraded the magnitude to nine-point-two. There has been an evacuation notice sent out in both Washington and Oregon for a tsunami up to a mile inland. It may be too late, though. I just received a report that a seismic wave has already come ashore along the coastline of both states."

"Thanks," Jason said, "that should be enough to get the hounds off my back. You need to provide a written update every hour on the hour, understand? Only the facts. No speculation. I'm going to try and get in the air, so you're going to have to cover for me if I'm not here. Let's try to keep this disaster from turning into a media circus."

She nodded. "I can do it. Where will you be?"

"The Governor of Oregon is waiting outside."

He turned and walked back out on the steps. He was confronted by two men in dark suits.

"Just a minute," the men said, holding Jason back. "Before you make a statement, give the Governor time to get up here," one of the men said. The microphones and a podium had already been assembled in front of the building. *And now the circus begins,* Jason thought as he waited for the Governor to be assisted up the steps. He would rather be talking to his son and getting his assessment of the situation along the coast, but politics almost always took precedence. He pursed his lips and waited patiently.

Governor Sally Morris, a slender woman with thick framed glasses and dark hair, was being escorted up the steps by two very large men dressed in black. As she reached the top step there was a ruckus behind her and she turned along with the reporters.

A man was running in their direction screaming at the top of his lungs, "The Portland downtown area is flooded. The Willamette River has backed up and has gone over the sea wall."

A few seconds later another person looking at his cell phone yelled. "Downtown Vancouver is under water."

The observatory was located northeast of town and well above the Columbia River. There was no immediate danger to anyone in the lot, but it immediately caused panic and several reporters returned to their vans to be first on the scene, not knowing which story to cover.

Jason made his statement and let the Governor say a few words. "I really need to be on top of this," he said. "Send for me if you have to, but I need to go." He apologized to the Governor for being so short, and went back inside the building.

Chapter 25

Aboard *Hunter*

By the time they loaded Danna in the passenger compartment and buckled her in, the wind was buffeting them in erratic gusts. David tried to concentrate on the task at hand, but his mind kept wandering to Fay. *Why haven't they answered the phone?* He was in the pilot's seat, buckled in and ready to start the turbine engine when an unusually strong gust caused the helicopter to rock violently. The rain was coming in sheets and Bobby was soaked as he entered through a door on the co-pilot side and sat behind the instruments. He strapped himself in. David handed him a headset. "You ever flown in one of these before?"

Bobby nervously shook his head, no.

"Don't touch a thing," David said, sternly. He started flipping switches and talking to himself, as Bobby stared at the instruments in awe, not having a clue what any of them were.

The helicopter rocked again. David checked out his side window and made sure Scott was clear. He spoke to Scott through his headset. "Remember, this was your idea."

"Roger that," Scott said. "Are you ready for me to unfasten the tie-downs?"

David let out a sigh. "As good a time as any. Let me know when you're clear."

"Clear," was the next word from Scott's mouth.

"Clear," David repeated. "Starting the turbine engine."

In a few seconds the whine of the engine drowned out everything around them. Scott made certain he was well clear as the turbine spooled up and the spinning rotor turned the area into a tornado. Scott took shelter behind a bulkhead and said a short prayer to himself, before speaking into his headset. "Get the hell out of here and find the girls."

"Roger. Lifting off."

The helicopter bounced like a tethered ball in the wind for a few seconds before it hopped a few feet and disappeared off the side of the ship.

Scott swallowed hard. *What the hell happened?* In a second the helicopter rose above the ship and disappeared.

"That was interesting," David said.

"I need to change my shorts," Scott said.

"I hope the hell this weather

clears before I hit land," David said. "I'll call you soon. Stafford out."

David looked over at Bobby. He was slumped over in his seat. He reached over and slapped him lightly on the side of his face. "Wake up. I need your eyes."

"What happened?" Bobby asked, coming out of his daze.

"You went to sleep. You must have nerves of iron."

Bobby glanced over at David. "I thought we were dead."

"Cool," David said. "Did you see the light?"

"I think it was all black," Bobby said.

"Too bad. I was hoping you brought along your guardian angel for luck. Sounds like you're going to hell with the rest of us."

The sun was peeking over the horizon and glaring right into their eyes. David slipped on a pair of prescription dark glasses and flipped down the visor on his helmet. He dropped the helicopter low over the water so they could see the magnitude of the destruction. Debris was scattered and sparse at first, but as they approached land the water was a solid mass of floating carnage. Looking for something positive, David said, "At least the storm is offshore. Those poor bastards who were hit by the tsunami have enough to worry about without a storm on top of it." The closer they got to shore the better the weather was, and the worse the damage appeared. A mile from Newport the debris in the water was so thick, they couldn't see the water.

He circled the harbor at Newport and saw that the Coast Guard station had been destroyed by the tsunami. Only a few buildings remained. Most of the buildings, some that had been in place since the late 1800s had been leveled by the wave. It was no surprise. A few seconds earlier they had passed over the wreckage of the collapsed Yaquina Bay Bridge. It had stood every kind of storm for over eighty years and now was a string of twisted metal resting in the water of the bay.

"Are you sure this is Newport?" Bobby asked.

"There's the lighthouse," David said. "I'm going to see if I can find the hospital. No way is Scott going to be able to make port here. Give him a call and let him know we made it this far."

Bobby used the satellite phone to contact the ship.

Scott thanked him for the information and wished them good luck.

A few seconds later David arrived

at Peace Harbor Hospital. He saw the building was still standing, but had been heavily damaged by the earthquake. A dozen or so early responders were evacuating the building and searching for survivors. The helipad was buckled and partially missing. If he was going to get Danna help, his only choice was to continue inland.

Albany, a trip of about fifty-miles over the Coast Range Mountains, was his next best bet. He contacted the Albany City Police on his emergency channel and they promised to have an ambulance waiting at the airport. He had not been able to contact the hospital directly and the police told him that the heliport at the hospital was jammed with emergency flights from coastal areas.

"She tried to hijack our ship," David explained to the police dispatcher. "You may want to keep a guard on her."

"Should we consider her dangerous."

"Hell yeah," David said. "We have her restrained. She tried to kill the skipper and she may have killed the owners of the boat she stole." He didn't have the full story, nor did he have the time to explain the details of the attempted hijacking. He had no compassion for Danna. Right now, all he wanted to do was dump her and get back to the coast and see if he could find

Fay and her companions.

"You want to stay with her or go with me?" David asked Bobby as he was refueling at the airport. "We'll be taking off in ten minutes."

"Are you serious. I'm coming with you." For the entire helicopter ride, he had cursed himself for not letting Scott know there could be an attempt to take over the ship. Danna had contacted him threatening to tell Scott about his drug use, if he didn't go along. He had momentarily caved, when Don had promised to make them rich, but in the end, he had made the right decision. He never wanted to have another word with his ex-wife. Danna could rot in jail as far as he was concerned.

"Get back in the co-pilot seat then, I'm not your chauffeur," David said. "You need to keep your hand on that phone. It's our only link to the ship."

At that moment, Bobby couldn't remember feeling prouder of himself. He had made the right decision, yet he knew he'd have to live with the secret buried inside him forever.

Waldport, Oregon

"You think it's safe to go back?" Janet asked, "I'm getting cold." She was shivering and miserable. After the wave had subsided, a rain cloud had passed overhead and dumped on them. Looking around she answered her own question. They were stranded, even if they wanted to leave, the island they were huddled together on was no more than twenty-feet in any direction. They were surrounded on all sides by trapped water that didn't seem to be in a hurry to recede.

"I thought I was prepared," Patricia admonished herself between tears. "I did everything they told me and look at me, I bet I look a mess."

Fay laughed. "You are a mess, Patricia. All of us are a mess, but we are alive. At least you knew where to go."

"Dumb luck," Patricia said. "When I saw the highway had collapsed, I just wanted to get to higher ground."

"Can we go back?" Janet asked again.

"There is nothing to go back to," Fay said. "If the wave made it this far, there isn't anything left of the house."

Janet looked at Patricia with sad eyes. "I'm sorry, honey."

"I'm worried about Scott," Patricia said, starting to whimper again.

"They are probably having a party aboard the ship, completely unaware there even was a tsunami," Fay said.

"You were the one who told me the safest place to be during an earthquake is in an airplane or on the ocean. Chances are they didn't even notice a ripple in this storm."

"But I didn't believe it," Patricia said. "I was just trying to make you feel better." She started to cry.

Janet wrapped her arms around Patricia. "If Gil told you they would be safe if they were out on the ocean, then I'm sure it's true."

"It was Scott. He's the one who told me."

"Oh," Janet said. "I'm sure he wouldn't have said it if it wasn't true. If he said it, you have to believe him. Right now, we need to determine what we're going to do if we can make it off this godforsaken piece of ground."

"There is a shelter in Waldport at the high school," Patricia said, getting hold of her emotions. "Maybe we can make it there."

"I read someplace that there can be several tsunami waves, hours apart," Fay said. "I think we should stay right where we are."

"You're right," Patricia agreed.

Aboard *Hunter*

Scott slowly moved the ship through

miles of rubble. They were still twenty-miles from land, but the amount of debris in the water told him everything close to shore had been destroyed.

"According to David and Bobby, we aren't going to be able to bring the ship in," Scott said. "This much devastation probably wiped out the docks and everything around them. We can't even be certain the harbor channel is still there."

"I agree," Richard said. "We can weigh anchor offshore and take the lifeboat in."

"I'm not sure that's a good idea," Scott argued. "If there's another wave we could get caught up in it. Keep trying the emergency channels and see if you can raise the Coast Guard."

Richard flipped the radio over to speaker. "Listen to this, the emergency channels are all on an endless loop, warning people if they survived the first wave, to prepare for another and not return to their homes until they are told it's safe."

"Try another channel."

"All the channels are jammed with traffic. I can't raise anybody," Richard said. "It's going to be your call."

"I'm not going in until I know the ship will be safe. Can you help Tad get the gold off the deck and back in a hold?

It was scattered everywhere. We'll be lucky if it hasn't washed overboard."

"No problem. It doesn't look like we're going anywhere soon."

A few minutes later Scott took another call from David on the satellite phone.

"David, everything all right with you?"

"We're fine, but the devastation goes inland a good mile in some places and looks like it extends for miles north and south. When we were coming into Newport there wasn't much left, not even the bridge over the bay. I dropped Danna off with the police at the airport in Albany and we're heading back over the mountains to Waldport. As near as I can tell, this was the big one. The Albany police said it was a magnitude nine point two. I don't doubt it from the damage I've seen. It did more than rattle the windows in Albany. The runway at the airport had a two-foot buckle in it and I-5 is jammed with wrecked cars in several places. I'll call you when I get to Waldport. I just wanted to let you know you're not going to find a harbor, so you might as well stay out until things settle down a bit."

"Thanks for the update. I already decided to hang-tough. I'm about twenty miles offshore. The good news is the weather is a hell of a lot better this close in."

"Roger," David said. "I'll call you back in about half-an-hour, sooner if I have news."

Richard returned to the bridge. "The good news is all the gold is secure and we didn't lose a bar."

"And the bad news?" Scott asked giving him a suspicious look.

"All good," Richard said. "Bad choice of words."

"You and Tad need to be on the lookout for survivors," Scott said. "We're going to be out here for several hours more. We have a duty as sailors."

"You really think we'll find any survivors this far out?"

"Probably not, but be on the lookout just the same."

Somewhere above Waldport, Oregon

"Do you hear that?" Patricia said. "Maybe it's a plane."

"Sounds more like a train to me," Janet said.

Fay cleared her throat. She was pointing in the direction of the ocean. "I think it's another wave."

"How long has it been?" Patricia asked.

They looked at each other. None of them had a watch. They had no idea whether they had been huddled on the high ground for an hour or three. All they knew was they were wet and miserable, and another wave was coming in and they had nowhere to go. This time all they could do was wait.

At the same moment, David was circling over the Alsea Bay Bridge. It was one of the few landmarks he recognized, and he needed to get his bearings. The bridge was the newest bridge spanning a bay on the Oregon Coast, having been constructed in the late 1990's, but the highway on the north end had collapsed, leaving an impassible pit in its place.

On the south end of the bridge, there was nothing left standing in the downtown area of Waldport. Most of it was underwater. A few concrete walls and the foundations of some of the buildings remained, but that was it. The street that bordered the bay on the south was completely underwater and on the north side, the high ridge overlooking the city where Patricia, Fay, and Janet had first sought refuge from an imaginary tsunami, several buildings had collapsed and were dangling by plumbing and wiring ready to come crashing to the bay a hundred feet below. David flew north to see if he could pinpoint the spot where Scott had built his house. To his horror, the heavily populated area of Bay Shore, on the north end of the bridge, no longer existed. Not even the foundations of the hundreds of homes remained. He had heard that the south end of the development had been built on sand, and now it appeared all of it had been reclaimed by the ocean. Sandpiper Estates, a housing development to the north of Bay Shore had also been destroyed, except for a few houses on the west side of the hill stretching up to Highway 101. Along that stretch of the highway, the wave did not appear to have crested above the pavement. Farther north where Scott's house should have been, there was nothing but rubble. From the air there was no evidence a house had ever stood on the spot. Not a foundation, not even the remains of the massive fireplace that dominated the living room. At first, he thought he had mistaken the location and circled twice to be certain he was in the right spot. Even more disturbing, the gentle sloped path that once led down to the beach ended abruptly with a fifty-foot cliff that was the new coastline. North of Scott's place, a mile-long stretch of land 200 feet deep had simply vanished, leaving behind a sand cliff jutting straight down to the water.

David's heart sunk as he hovered over the spot. There was no way Fay and their friends could have survived such massive devastation.

"David," Bobby said, hitting David

on the shoulder, "do you see that?"

David snapped from his trance and looked up at the largest wave he'd ever seen. It appeared to be eye-level with them and was moving toward them fast. David shot up at full power and struggled to steady the helicopter as the tornado-like wind that was created in the wave's wake threatened to suck them into it. The wave passed only inches below them. He had never seen a wave so large and moving so fast. He let out a long nervous breath. "That was a rush."

"Too close for me," Bobby said. He saw the sadness in David's eyes. "They didn't make it, did they?"

David shook his head. "Call Scott and find out what he wants us to do next. There is no way they could have survived the first wave, let alone the second."

David would have made the call, but his voice was too shaky and he was too distraught. He had never imagined such a horrific scene as the past few hours had shown him. Fay was all he had in the world. He didn't know what he would do without her.

Aboard *Hunter*

Scott saw the wave before he felt it pass under the ship. It was the largest swell he'd ever encountered at sea, and it was dragging the ship to shore with it. Immediately he knew he was too close to shore, but it was too late. He pushed both engines to full throttle, but knew he was losing the battle. His decision to bring the ship closer to shore may have been a fatal one.

Both Richard and Tad showed up on the bridge in near panic. They had felt the ship rise fifty feet in the air like a high-rise elevator and though they didn't have landmarks to judge their speed, they knew they were drifting toward land, like a cork in a raging river, and that couldn't be good.

"Get that," Scott said, seeing the blinking light on the satellite phone. It was everything he could do to keep the ship pointed into the still rising swell. He had to keep ahead of the crest or they would be thrown to shore when the wave made landfall.

Richard gripped the satellite phone with one hand and the control panel with the other. As he listened, the color drained from his face. He turned to Scott, not wanting to relay the news, but knowing he had to. He felt like he was fighting a war in which they were constantly losing battles.

From the look on Richard's face, Scott knew it was bad news. "Take the helm, Richard," he said, grabbing the phone from him. Scott was already in full battle mode. He had been ever since he awoke, tied up on his bed. He'd dodged so many bombshells, he had hardly drawn a breath between them. He imagined this was the worst. He wanted to hear it right from the source, not relayed through a messenger. "Tell me you found them," Scott demanded.

"It's Bobby, Skipper."

"I want to speak to David," Scott said.

Bobby looked over at David who was crying so hard he could barely keep the helicopter stable."

"David's busy, but I'll relay the message," Bobby said.

"The house is gone, isn't it?"

"Everything is gone," Bobby said.

"Is the bridge still standing?" Scott asked.

"Yes," Bobby said. "Everything is so different."

"Tell David to fly along the north side of the river about a mile or so inland. That's where they would go when they felt the quake."

"But the highway is missing."

"Bobby, listen to me. Tell him to find the bridge and fly along the treetops and see if there are survivors. If they made it out in time, they will to be in that area."

Scott could hear Bobby relaying the message to David.

"Okay Skipper," Bobby said. "We're turning in that direction."

Scott was watching Richard struggle with the controls while he was on the phone.

"I have it at full power," Richard said. "I'd swear we are moving backwards."

"We are," Tad said. "I can see land coming up in the distance."

"Keep the pedal to the metal," Scott said. "If we get beached, there's no telling what will happen next."

Suddenly the ship seemed to be slowing and they began sinking, but only for a minute. As the wave reached as far inland as it could travel it had stopped, and now they were racing back out to sea. "Ride it out. We'll need to stay farther offshore to be safe," Scott said.

"You think," Richard scoffed.

"Everything is gone," Scott said, soberly. "Tad do you have family in the area?"

Tad shook his head. "My ex took the kid and moved back with her parents in Bend. At least I know they're safe."

Scott handed him the phone, "why don't you call them. I'm sure they'll want to know you're okay."

Tad made the call, but there was no answer. Disappointed, he left a message and handed the phone back to Scott.

"Too bad," Scott said, taking the phone. "Richard, could you stay at the helm. I want to be ready to take the next call from David."

Newport, Oregon

From his home in the mountains, outside the tiny town of Siletz, Gil made his way slowly toward Newport. From his house in the forest, he had a fifteen-mile drive that normally took thirty minutes or less to his office at Pacific Marine Science Center. He had fought his way around downed trees and landslides for three hours and had come to a complete impasse when he reached the highway junction at Toledo, a small mill town on the Yaquina River. He was still five miles upriver from Newport. There was no way he could continue in his all-wheel-drive Ford Edge. The stretch of Highway 20 leading into Newport was completely missing. He couldn't tell if it had just disappeared in the earthquake, or if the seismic wave came up the river far enough to wash it away, or possibly, from the amount of rubble, a huge landslide had buried it. He left his vehicle, intending to continue his trip to Newport on foot, but soon discovered that, too, was impossible. He returned to his car and saw it was low on fuel. He had dreaded the return trip home, but it seemed it was the only option he had left. As much as he wanted to help, he was stranded, unable to go anywhere or communicate with anyone along the coast. His training had never prepared him for this. He felt completely helpless.

Vancouver, Washington

Aboard an Air National Guard helicopter with Major Parker Denning at the controls, Dr. Jason Trask, Governor Sally Morris, the Governor's aide, and KPTV reporter Julie Fine surveyed the extent of the havoc from the air. They had been in the air only a few minutes when they saw the second seismic wave arrive. The extent of the damage already extended as far as they could see, from the mouth of the Columbia, north into Washington and south into Oregon. If there was a silver lining on the black cloud, it was that so much damage had already been done there was nothing left for the second wave to destroy.

Overwhelmed by the devastation, Governor Morris said, "I've seen enough. Major, take me back."

Jason didn't understand. They had barely assessed the damage. "We should

fly down the coastline south of here,"
Jason said. "There are a number of low-
lying communities along the shore." He
was aware the town of Seaside had
flooded in the wake of the Alaska
tsunami back in 1964, as well as a
number of other coastal communities, and
that wave was minor compared to the one
that had just struck. To date, the
Alaska quake had been the largest ever
recorded in North America. Based on
early reports, the quake they
experienced today could rival the Alaska
event and would certainly cause greater
havoc.

"I suppose you're right, but I
can't bear to see any more," Morris
said. "I need to get back and call
Homeland Security. We're not going to
recover from this without Federal
support."

Jason understood, but he had other
concerns. If the Governor wasn't up for
looking at more of the carnage, he'd
have to convince her that it was in her
best interest to stay in the air a bit
longer. "Ma'am, the tsunami isn't the
only problem we're facing. We've seen
increased activity along the eastern
slope of the Cascades. If you cut this
trip short, it'll be apparent to your
constituents, you're not up to the task
they elected you to do."

Sally Morris looked at him through
reddened eyes. He could see she had been

crying, but what he had mistaken for weakness had actually been an overwhelming since of grief. Telling her to buck-up for the sake of getting re-elected may not have been his best moment.

"How dare you lecture me," Sally said, vehemently. "I have family down there, and I can't get any help to them while I'm flying around up here."

"I'm sorry," Jason said. "My son is down there someplace and I haven't been able to reach him either."

Hearing Jason was just as concerned, she mellowed substantially. "You don't need to apologize. My daughter lives in Ilwaco," Morris said. "There was nothing left of the town." She wiped her eyes. "We all have a job to do. We need to do it." She leaned into her aide and he in turn relayed a message to the pilot. The helicopter swooped down and paralleled the coastline south. As each town was approached the helicopter made a wide circle. The entire trip was being filmed for later viewing. When they reached Newport, Jason felt a huge lump in his throat. If there was any way to get back to the area, he would do it. Again, he was thankful the quake had struck so early in the morning. There was nothing standing where the Pacific Marine Science Center had been located. The microbrewery where Gil and he had eaten a few days earlier was not there either. He looked off in the distance toward the hills. He saw a distinct line where the devastation from the wave stopped. Beyond it the scenery looked completely undisturbed. Hopefully Gil was somewhere out there safe.

"We don't have enough fuel to make it over the Cascades," the pilot informed those aboard. "We're returning back to the base in Portland to take on fuel, before we can continue."

Jason knew there was a USGS helicopter stationed in Portland. If it wasn't already in the air, he would hitch a ride on it. His mission was to assess the situation along the Cascade Range. There were eight other potential hazards he was concerned with. The earthquake may have awakened more of the volcanoes in his watch area. At greatest risk was the Bend/Redmond area. South Sister had threatened that area for years. *Would this be enough to push it over the edge?*

Chapter 26

Waldport, Oregon

Patricia thought she'd seen a helicopter in the distance, but it had disappeared before she could be certain, and the oncoming wave had captured all their attention. They all watched, paralyzed as the wave closed in on them. "Oh God," Patricia managed to blurt out. "I think it's larger than the first one." Shivering and speechless the three watched in anticipation at what might be their last few moments on earth. It was good they were frozen in place. To run would have meant certain death. They were standing on the highest ground around. Although the water from the earlier wave had mostly receded, the next wave would surround them again and maybe wash them away. Huge pockets of newly-formed saltwater lakes began to rise as the second wave pushed inwards. If this wave was greater than the one before, their tiny island would disappear, taking them with it. They were all looking down at their feet, wondering if the water would continue to rise. In the din of the oncoming wave, they couldn't hear the scream of the turbine from the helicopter overhead.

"I see some people," Bobby shouted.

It was the first sign of life they had seen this close to the ocean in the Waldport area. David brought the helicopter around. A man and a woman were standing on the roof of their car trying to escape the incoming water. There was no place to land and nothing he could do to help them. They watched as the water lifted the vehicle and tipped it, spilling the two into the turbulent water. They both disappeared.

"They're gone," Bobby gasped. "They escaped the first wave and are gone."

David continued to skim the tops of the Coastal pine and Douglas fir trees as the water started to recede. It looked like someone had pulled a plug in a bathtub, as higher points in the landscape started to reappear. There was little hope of finding any survivors this close to the shore. David checked his fuel and wondered if he should continue the search.

"We need to wrap this up," David said. "Is there someplace I can drop you off?"

Bobby looked at him, barely able to keep from crying. "I'm sorry we couldn't find them. I'll stay with you, if you don't mind. What are you going to do?"

"I'm going to circle one more time and return to the ship. Scott said the storm was breaking. I don't want to tell him we couldn't find them, over the phone."

"How about that ridge," Bobby said, pointing at a small area that appeared to have escaped the worst of the damage.

"They are all beginning to look the same," David said. He nosed the helicopter down and headed in the direction Bobby had pointed.

Bobby lifted a pair of binoculars to his eyes and focused in on a tiny island. "I see people there!" he said excitedly.

David circled the area and hovered for a moment. "I think it's them," Bobby said, choking back tears.

Recognizing the helicopter, Fay shouted, "It's David." Her voice was lost to the noise of the receding tsunami and the engine's whine. She hit Janet and Patricia with the frantic waving of her arms. They started waving. "It's David. We're saved!" Fay shouted.

David circled again and brought the helicopter within a hundred feet of them, but the patch of ground where they were standing on was too small for him to land. After he was certain they knew he would rescue them, he left and found a suitable landing spot a quarter mile away. He and Bobby would have to make a rescue attempt on foot.

"We need to find them," Patricia

said.

"We need to stay right where we are," Fay said, taking control. The survival training she had received when she was in Antarctica kicked in and she realized she would have to take charge, especially now that she knew they had been found. "Stay put and let them come to us. David won't abandon us."

David set the helicopter down and called Scott on the satellite phone.

Chapter 27

Cascades Volcano Observatory, Vancouver, Washington

After reviewing the seismic data, Dr. Trask issued a brief to USGS recommending the evacuation order for Bend, Oregon be rescinded. There had been a flurry of activity along the entire Cascade Range, but it had stopped. The worst threat, South Sister, which had been bulging for several years and had experienced a cluster of earthquakes immediately after the subduction zone event, had gone quiet, and appeared to return to the norm. The threat of an eruption along the Cascades had decreased significantly.

"Jason, your wife is on the phone." His assistant said, entering his office.

Jason looked at the clock. It was 3:14 p.m. and the activity inside the volcano observatory hadn't seemed to slow any. "Thanks," Jason said, picking up his phone.

"Gil called and he's fine," Carlene said, before he got out a word.

Jason breathed a sigh of relief. "How are you doing?"

"I've been watching the news. This

is bad. The worst event to hit the coastal areas in recorded history."

"I don't think I'm going to be home any time soon," he said.

"You haven't eaten, have you?"

"I'm okay. In these kinds of disasters there is always an abundance of pizza." He chuckled.

"I love you," Carlene said. "Come home as soon as you can."

"I love you, too." Jason said. He relaxed for a moment, relieved those he loved had been spared.

His assistant knocked on the door and stuck her head in. "The Governor of Washington is on the phone. He's asking about Mt. Rainier. I told him there's no evidence that they are in danger, but he insists on talking to you anyway."

"It's okay. I'll take it." He picked up his phone. "Dr. Trask, here. How can I help you, Governor Wilson?"

Waldport, Oregon

Still cold and miserable, Patricia, Fay, and Janet waited to be rescued. After seeing several snakes taking refuge on their piece of ground, Patricia climbed up on the stump of a tree which had been left from a logging operation some years back.

"How come you get the only stump?" Fay asked. "I don't like snakes any more than you do."

"What, now we're going to argue about a tree stump? How long are we going to stand here waiting for David to come?" Patricia asked. "It's been at least an hour since they flew over and we haven't heard from them. I don't think he can find his way to us."

"He is coming back," Fay insisted. "It only seems like an hour. I bet it hasn't even been thirty minutes."

"I'm getting hungry," Janet said. "I hope they bring food with them."

"I've been thinking," Patricia said. "There is only one way off this island that I can see. We should take it and meet up with them."

Fay looked at the place where Patricia was pointing. It appeared to be a log jam that bridged the end of one of the lakes. "It doesn't look stable," Fay said.

"Well, I'm tired of doing nothing," Patricia said. "We could be stranded here for days. David isn't exactly a Boy Scout. What makes you think he'll find us. He's probably lost in the woods."

The ground suddenly shook, knocking all of them to the ground. Patricia hit the hardest, unable to catch herself as her legs buckled out from under her.

Fay helped Patricia to her feet. "Aftershock. Nothing to worry about."

The sound of snapping limbs and crashing timbers caused them all to stare in one direction. The log jam burst and the lake disappeared in a flash, cutting a river through the surrounding forest.

"Well, now we have a way out," Patricia said.

Janet grabbed her arm. "We would all be dead if we would have tried walking across that."

Patricia broke down in tears. "I can't do anything right. If Scott was here, we'd all be rescued by now."

"Hey, you girls want a ride home," David called from the other side of the recently emptied lake.

Fay let out a scream. "You found us!" She turned to Patricia and Janet, "I told you he'd come."

"Thank God," Janet said, breaking down in tears.

"You want us to come to you?" Fay called out.

"That might be a good idea," Bobby called back. "David is terrible at blazing a trail."

Aboard *Hunter*

"David found the girls. They all appear to be okay," Scott announced after getting the call from David. It had been over an hour and there hadn't been another word. In that hour, they had busied themselves scouring the debris in the water, searching for any sign of life. They had taken on three passengers all from one family who had survived by clinging to the roof of a manufactured home that had managed to stay intact and was bobbing like Noah's Ark. After bringing them aboard and providing warm clothes and food, Scott and Richard had learned of the harrowing ordeal the family had suffered.

After thinking they were all safe, they had taken refuge on top of the structure hoping to be rescued from the flood, but the second wave had washed them out to sea. The *Hunter* found them twenty-two miles offshore. At the time of the earthquake, the woman and her two children had been staying at an oceanfront hotel in Depot Bay. It was only one of a hundred miracles they would hear about later, but right now, they were anxious to hear from their wives.

"I'm going to call," Richard said. "Something must have happened. It's been too long."

"David would have called," Scott said. He handed the phone to Richard.

Richard speed-dialed David and was told there was no signal. "You know what this means?" he asked Scott, showing him the phone.

"Low battery. We're going to have to wait until they can get it charged."

"What do you think he will do?" Richard asked. "With the girls, I mean?"

"I hope he drops them off at a plush hotel in an inland city," Scott said. "If the house is gone and they made it to safety, they deserve all the pampering they can stand."

"We're not going to be able to dock for a while," Richard said. "You got a plan on how we're going to get in?"

Scott shrugged. "I'm not sure. I guess we can just stay out here for a time and see if they get one of the ports cleared."

"No offense, but I can't wait to set my feet on solid ground again."

"Now I know all that time you spent in Washington has robbed the salt from your veins. Buck up; you'll have to keep your sea legs for another few days at least."

Richard grinned. "I almost forgot about the pile of gold. Maybe I'll stay with the ship."

"Skipper, there's an aircraft approaching." Tad had entered the wheelhouse unannounced. "It may be

David. He acts like he's going to land."

"Richard, hold it steady. I'm going to check it out," Scott said.

Sure enough, David's helicopter was hovering above the helipad, getting ready to set down. "What the hell, David," Scott said. "You could have contacted us before pulling this stunt."

"He can't hear you, Skipper," Tad said.

Scott realized he had switched their radio to the emergency channel. He changed channels and heard David's voice.

"Permission to land, sir?"

"You are a sight for sore eyes," Scott said, over the radio. "Get your ass down here."

The helicopter set down and as soon as the overhead blades stopped turning the door opened and Patricia stepped out.

Scott couldn't believe what he was seeing. Covered with dirt and mud from head to toe, she looked like an abandoned waif. Scott grabbed her in a bear hug and lifted her off the deck and twirled her around, kissing her hard on the lips. "You are the most pathetic thing I have ever seen." He set her down and held her face in his hands and kissed her again. "And the most beautiful."

Richard helped Janet to the deck and hugged her. She looked like she might have faired a little better than Patricia, but she, too, was smudged and covered with dirt. It was evident they had all been through an ordeal, more terrible than any of them could imagine.

Janet burst into tears. "I thought I'd never see you again."

"Me, too," Richard said. "I'll bet you could use a hot shower."

"Food," Janet said.

Bobby heard them. "I'll whip something up in the kitchen."

Fay and David had already had their reunion before taking off in the helicopter, but they both hugged each other and retired to their cabin without saying a word.

Later that evening they all gathered in the mess hall. Bobby had prepared a dinner of rib eye steak, baked potato and mixed vegetables.

Scott introduced the woman and her two children. "This is Megan Bartolomeu, her daughters, Stephanie and Ginger. They were trying to sail across the Pacific without a passport. We picked them up a few hours before you guys showed up. Since we're all here, I guess it's not too early to talk about our options."

"Options?" Fay asked.

"It's obvious we can't make port anywhere around here. Mary, you're from California, will it be okay if we drop you off somewhere closer to home?"

"I think this is the last vacation I'll ever take in Oregon." Mary said. "No offense, but I'd love to get back home."

"Why would I take offense to that?" Scott asked.

"I mean you saved us and you've been so gracious. I don't know how I can ever repay you."

"How about the rest of you?" Scott continued. "I think our best bet is to sail south until we can make port. Maybe San Francisco?"

"We still have the helicopter if someone wants to stay here," David said. "How about you Bobby, Tad?"

"Are we still going to get our bonus?" Tad asked.

David looked at Scott. "The cargo is still aboard. I don't see why not." He raised his eyebrows not wanting to let the newcomers know they had treasure aboard.

"Then I'm up for a new start in California," Tad said.

"Not me," Bobby said. "Skipper, I want to stick with you, if that's okay."

"I'm not sure where we'll be

operating from," Scott said.

"Don't we get a say in it?" Patricia asked.

"You want to go back to shore?" Scott asked.

"No, but Richard and Janet haven't said what they want to do."

"California, here we come," Richard said. "David, you promised to show me around the company headquarters. If I'm going to be working for you, I might as well see what I'm getting myself into."

"Are you sure you haven't seen enough?" David said, laughing.

"I hate to break up the party," Scott said, "but I have a ship to sail. Tad and Bobby, you want to join me on the bridge?"

"I'll come, too," Richard said.

"No. Just Bobby and Tad," Scott said. His tone was serious.

On the bridge, Scott set the ship in motion while Tad and Bobby stood by watching him, wondering why they were there.

"I saw the footage from the camera in the mess," Scott said. "Don got what was coming to him, but just because you backed out of his plan, doesn't mean you weren't at fault."

"Footage?" Tad asked.

"You think I'd run a ship without security cameras? After the attempted mutiny, I reviewed all of it. It's bad enough you were willing to go along with his plan, but in not reporting it, you two went over the line."

"I honestly thought he would drop it. After you promised to give us our bonus without waiting for the court cases to be settled, I told him, no way. I wasn't going to be a part of it, I didn't think he would do it on his own."

Scott gave Bobby a disappointed stare. He could see how devastated the man was. "I'm disappointed in both of you, especially, you Bobby. Neither of you are welcome to serve with me after we make port. Any more mutinous behavior and you'll lose your bonus. You both will be paid, as we agreed if you do your jobs until we make port. Another screw-up, no bonus.

"Skipper," Bobby pleaded, "I'm sorry. Give me another chance."

Every fiber in Scott's being wanted to believe Bobby could be trusted if he gave him another chance, but too many lives were at risk. "I gave you a second chance when I hired you the first time. I can't do it again." It was the hardest thing Scott had ever done.

Waldport, Oregon

One year later

Scott and Patricia stood outside their new home overlooking the ocean. A new cherry-red Jeep was parked in the circular drive. A small grove of oak trees had been planted where the original large oak had stood before, or as near to the spot as Scott could determine. Scott had planted a new tree for everyone he and Patricia had lost through the years and one for the closest surviving members of their combined families. Each tree represented someone they loved. All together there were eighteen trees and he could name each one of them.

Looking up at the ornately carved wooden sign over the porch, Scott said, "Someday this spot will live up to its name. Those trees will become a forest and this house a home again." The sign read, *Oak Grove, built with enduring love.*

Scott had obtained a copy of the plans for his original house from the county offices. It was fortunate they were able to retrieve them from their electronic files which had been backed up and stored in the Benton County courthouse in Albany, as the local courthouse had lost all its records in the tsunami.

They had been standing there for

nearly an hour, intently scrutinizing every hand turned log and every mitered joint in the assembly of the log structure.

"Everything looks the same," Patricia said, taking his hand and cuddling up next to him.

"Except for the landscape," Scott said. "It'll take two hundred years for those trees to get as big as the one we lost."

"But it's a new beginning," Patricia said, "and that's what the world is all about."

"Are you ready to go inside?" Scott asked. They had been inside a number of times during construction, but this was the official move-in day. All the inspections had been completed and the house was cleared for occupancy.

They walked in, but neither felt like they were home. It had been impossible to replace all the personal items they had lost. Nothing had survived the first wave of the tsunami.

"I know what you're thinking," Scott said, "but think about the first time you set foot in the house after we were married. At least you didn't have to redo my attempt at decorating this time." Scott had completed their first home and moved in before they were married.

"I'm not complaining," Patricia said. "We made that our home and we'll do the same with this one." She walked over to the wall of glass overlooking the ocean. "The view is the same."

The doorbell rang and they both turned toward the front door. It opened and Richard stuck his head in. "Janet and I thought we'd drop by and give you something for the housewarming."

Janet came in holding a vase of colorful flowers. "From my greenhouse," she said.

"Can you believe how cheap oceanfront property is around here," Richard said. It was a joke they had shared several times over the past year. The price of oceanfront property in their area had dropped significantly after the tsunami.

Scott laughed. "Leave it to you to take advantage of a depressed real estate market. If there is another tsunami in our lifetime, we'll both be in the poorhouse."

"I don't want to hear anymore talk about a tsunami," Janet said. "Richard talked me into selling our house in Virginia and building next door to you based on the assumption there will never be another tsunami."

"In our lifetimes," Richard said. "What are the odds?" He lifted a bottle of Scotch he'd been hiding behind his back. "It was a hell of an opportunity, and now that I'm a part of Stafford-Tanner Enterprises it makes sense for us to be nearby." He handed the bottle to Scott. "We should celebrate."

"I'll wait until David and Fay arrive," Scott said.

"You do have a go-bag packed?" Patricia asked Janet. "Just in case."

"Absolutely," Janet said.

They heard the whine of a helicopter outside and they all went out on the front porch to watch David bring it down in the yard. Scott had installed a large slab of concrete with a bulls-eye painted on it just for that purpose and David was the first to take advantage of it.

They all settled on the deck to watch the sunset. David opened a bottle of champagne and passed glasses around to everyone. "Fay and I have something to share," he said, filling the glasses. He skipped Fay and handed her a bottle of water. "Fay and I are pregnant."

"That's terrific," Richard said. "Janet and I are going to be grandparents again."

"That's fantastic," Patricia said. She looked at Scott and winked. They had been planning on announcing the news they were pregnant, but now it would have to wait. This was David and Fay's time.

"I have some other good news," David said. "I waited until we came up, but I think you'll find it exciting."

"When did you start becoming so dramatic?" Scott asked. "Are you running for public office?"

"All the gold we brought up was released. The subduction quake wiped out all evidence of the *Carissa* and the U-boat. Japan had no record of the gold or any proof it ever existed, and believe it or not, the submarine U-2500, was never built, according to Germany wartime records. We are the only ones with a claim on it."

"I hate to think how close we came to losing it," Richard said. "Whatever happened to those yahoos who tried to steal it?"

"Bobby contacted me a few months ago," Scott said. "He bought into a surfboard company in Malibu, got married to a 'sweet chick', his words, not mine, who likes to surf and is living the good life. He thanked me for being so hard on him. I think he really meant it."

"I'm glad to see some can learn from their mistakes," Janet said.

Scott continued. "Unfortunately, not everyone. Bobby said Tad went to Vegas and lost his bonus in a high-limit poker game. He showed up at Bobby's doorstep and asked him for a job."

Richard laughed. "That's something I'd like to have seen. That little shit was so into himself, I'll bet that was a low moment. Did Bobby hire him?"

"I don't think so," Scott said. "I saw a picture of Bobby's wife and I don't think he'd let Tad anywhere near her."

"And we all know where Danna is," David said.

"Orange is the new black," Richard said. "They should have given her the death penalty."

Scott said, "Sadly, there was no proof she ever stole *Tranquility Bay* or kidnapped the couple who owned it. My testimony was thrown out as hearsay. Believe it or not, they're going to let her walk with sixteen-months and time served."

"I can't believe we let her set foot in this house," Patricia said.

"Not this house," Janet reminded her.

Patricia nodded and gave Janet a tight smile. "I guess you're right. I could care less what happens to her."

Scott drained his glass of champagne. "With no bodies, no boat, no witnesses, and no prior record, the jury was left with my testimony. She would have gotten off completely if she'd had a compelling explanation for how she got aboard *Hunter,* but her claim to have been a stowaway, left room for reasonable doubt. I hope sixteen-months is enough to straighten her out, but I doubt it. She was pretty bitter at the trial."

Patricia was waiting for a moment to change the subject. "I finished my book," she said. "It will be out next month."

"Really!" Fay said, "I can't believe you. You build a house and still have time to write? What's the title?"

"*New Beginnings,*" Patricia said. "It was either write, or lose my publisher. I did have a lot of help, though."

Scott butted in. "Gil and Patricia were meeting so often, I thought they were having an affair."

Patricia slugged him. "Scott, that's awful, why would you say such a thing?"

"Just trying to get in on the conversation," Scott said, rubbing his arm as if she had really hurt him. "All kidding aside, I think this one will be a blockbuster and she didn't have to pay me to say that."

Patricia sighed. "It would mean so much more if he had read it."

"I want to be the first to get a

signed copy," Janet said. "After all, I am your favorite neighbor."

"Okay," Scott said, taking advantage of a break. "I'm going to grab a beer. You girls won't miss us if Richard and I show David what we've been working on?" He motioned to David. "Come into my office. Richard and I have made a discovery that will knock your socks off."

A NOTE TO THE READER

A subduction earthquake is very likely to occur along the states of Oregon and Washington at sometime in the future. Preparing for such an event is the responsibility of everyone living along the coastline and should be taken seriously. While the events depicted in this novel are fictional, they are not beyond the realm of possibility. Subduction Zone events have occurred several times in the past and it is only a matter of time before the next one strikes. The only assurance of survival is being prepared.

Other adventures with David Stafford and Scott Tanner can be found at www.larrylavoie.com.

Scott Tanner Thriller series: Crater, Sub Zero, Paradox, Ghost Flight

For more information on Larry LaVoie and his novels, please visit his blog, Scene-Stealer. http://larrylavoieauthor.blogspot.com/

ABOUT THE AUTHOR

Larry LaVoie is a lifetime resident of Oregon, and lives on the Oregon Coast with his wife Anna. He is the author of over twenty novels, most of which are placed in the Pacific Northwest. Prior to becoming an author, he worked in the development of titanium casting materials and methods which led to the introduction of titanium castings in aircraft and medical prosthetics. When he is not writing, he enjoys woodworking, bowling, and traveling.

Made in the USA
Middletown, DE
04 February 2022

59454363R00205